"I want to know your name or I won't budge," Bennett said.

"Memphis Modine." He surveyed her. "And I don't have a criminal record."

Bennett's eyes roved over the man who'd pulled her out of the Stuyvesant Club so unceremoniously. "Well, that won't be true after tonight."

"I didn't kill that woman at the club."

Bennett merely continued to stare at him, her eyes taking in his jeans and black leather jacket, his dark hair and stubbly jaw. The man looked a little rough, but not like a killer. "Back at the club, I saw you leaning over that woman's body," she managed to say.

"I didn't kill her."

Should Bennett believe this stranger? Either way, she was in trouble. If he was a killer, her own life was in danger. And if he wasn't, she didn't think she could fight her undeniable attraction to him...

Dear Reader:

We are delighted to bring you this daring series from Silhouette®.

***Intrigue*™**—*where resourceful, beautiful women flirt with danger and risk everything for irresistible, often treacherous men.*

Intrigue—*where the stories are full of heart-stopping suspense and mystery lurks around every corner.*

*You won't be able to resist **Intrigue**'s exciting mix of danger, deception...and desire.*

*Please write and let us know what you think of our selection of **Intrigue** novels. We'd like to hear from you.*

Jane Nicholls
Silhouette Books
PO Box 236
Thornton Road
Croydon
Surrey
CR9 3RU

Manhattan Heat

ALICE ORR

All the characters in this book have no existence outside the imagination of the author, and have no relation whatsoever to anyone bearing the same name or names. They are not even distantly inspired by any individual known or unknown to the author, and all the incidents are pure invention.

First published in Great Britain 1997
Silhouette Books, Eton House, 18-24 Paradise Road,
Richmond, Surrey TW9 1SR

© Alice Orr 1996

ISBN 0 373 22369 2

46-9702

Printed and bound in Great Britain
by Mackays of Chatham PLC, Chatham

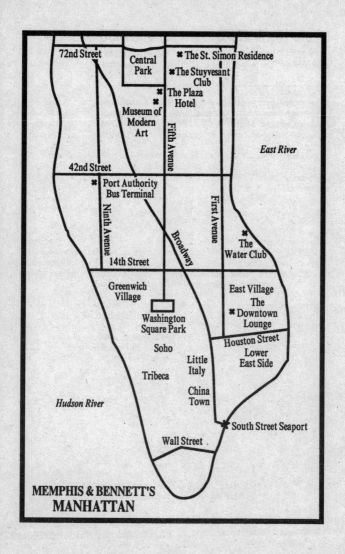

72nd Street

Central Park

✳ The St. Simon Residence

✳ The Stuyvesant Club

✳ The Plaza Hotel

✳ Museum of Modern Art

Fifth Avenue

East River

42nd Street

✳ Port Authority Bus Terminal

Ninth Avenue

Broadway

First Avenue

✳ The Water Club

14th Street

Greenwich Village

East Village

The ✳ Downtown Lounge

Washington Square Park

Soho

Little Italy

Houston Street

Lower East Side

Tribeca

China Town

Hudson River

✳ South Street Seaport

Wall Street

MEMPHIS & BENNETT'S MANHATTAN

To my husband, Jonathan—
always my romantic hero
To my editor, Julianne Moore—
a true jewel
To my agent, Rob Cohen—
who is truly in my corner

Prologue

Pearlanne Fellows kicked one very pointed toe at the carved claw foot of the billiard table and nearly fell off her stiletto heels. The fabric on the tabletop shone so fine it looked like velvet instead of the usual green felt that had been good enough for any pool shooter she'd ever known. The pockets were handwoven out of some kind of silky cord, and the wood had to be mahogany or teak or whatever.

"Expensive. That's whatever," she said out loud to the ancient paneled walls, because there was nobody human around to vent her bad attitude on at the moment. "Expensive and ugly."

She kicked a little higher at the gargoyle face a few scrolls above the claw foot. Ugly, all right, glowering at her like that in the low light from the burnished brass lamp on the leather-topped desk in the corner.

"Who cares about the phony Stuyvesant Club anyway?" she grumbled. "I'll take the DownTown Lounge any day."

But she was here, and anybody could tell she did care by the way she glanced quickly around at the door to make sure nobody had sneaked in quietly to hear her being disrespectful toward this exclusive, rich-folks place on the exclusive, rich-folks Upper East Side of Manhattan. Pearlanne was irritated to have been left alone here so long. What if one of those stiff-necked types from that party downstairs should

wander in and find her here dirtying up their precious antiques with her straight-from-Brooklyn breath? High-toners
like them probably didn't even exhale the same as other
people. They sure as hell wouldn't be jumping for joy to
have her around. She didn't expect they'd ask her to join the
club or anything half so friendly as that. Most likely she'd
end up cooling the concrete with her keester on the corner
of Fifth and Sixty-whatever.

Stitch had been gone too damn long already. Of course,
he was one of these classy-type yo-yos himself. He probably had to touch pinkies with the whole room full of 'em
before he could get out of there again. Besides, all she cared
about was the answer he brought back. She had to remember that. First things first. If it took a little longer than she
liked, she'd just have to be patient. Patience is a virtue.
She'd heard that somewhere or other.

Pearlanne sighed. Patience was a virtue she hadn't mastered yet. She wouldn't be so antsy if they had a bar in this
gold-plated pool hall. She'd already checked every pricey
antique nook and cranny. No bar in sight. Not one siphon
or a single snifter as far as the eye could see. So much for
those old English movies with butlers bustling brandy and
cocktails in and out of drawing rooms. She could sure use
some Jeeves-type action about now.

She walked to the tall, narrow window. Folds of heavy,
garnet-colored drapery were pulled back by wide sashes just
above the deep sill. She looked down onto the opposite side
of Fifth Avenue where New Yorkers and tourists strolled
along one of the prettiest sidewalks in the city. They kept
more than an arm's reach away from the stone wall that
bordered Central Park East, of course. No telling what
might be crawling around over there. Even on this side of
the wall, the occasional homeless person shuffled at the curb
or rocked back and forth on one of the backless benches,
talking out loud into the June night.

Pearlanne's watch said close to eleven o'clock, but there was plenty of traffic, both on foot and in the many cars and many more taxis that ran down Fifth Avenue. Now and then a horse-drawn hansom cab clopped by and screwed up the pace in one lane of traffic, but mostly the drivers kept the horses to the park paths that were lighted enough to be safe, or to Central Park South a few blocks away.

Pearlanne was wishing she was in one of those hansom hacks right now with Stitch and a magnum of bubbly when the door opened behind her. She spun around, half expecting that starch-collared butler she'd been thinking about to march in and drag her out by the scruff of her neck. Not that she'd stand still for it, of course. She grew up in Flatbush, and she didn't stand still for much. Luckily, what stepped through the door was definitely not a Jeeves type. She sighed again, relieved.

"It's about time," she said. "I thought I was going to be spending the night on the pool table."

"Billiards, my dear," he answered. "Billiards are played here, and maybe a spot of snooker on occasion. But never pool."

"So sorry, I'm sure," Pearlanne said in the heaviest Brooklynese she could manage. "Now, what's the word? I assume that's what you're here to talk about, not my vocabulary."

"You're one thousand percent correct about that. I have come to give you the word, all right."

"And what might that word happen to be? How big's my cut anyway?"

"Even bigger than you might have guessed, I imagine."

Pearlanne had begun to smile with pleasure at that answer when she saw something flash in the low lamplight. Her lips froze at half curve. She grabbed a handful of drapery as her too-high heels teetered under her. She had time for only one shriek before she was on the floor with the same drapery pulled down on top of her and a stain, in a shade of red far too garish for these august surroundings, spreading out from her body.

Chapter One

Bennett St. Simon attended too many functions too much like this one. They weren't her style and never would be, but she kept showing up because of the good they did and because they were part of her work. All the same, she had wanted to call her mother up earlier this evening and make some excuse or other for absenting herself, if only for this one night. Now that Bennett was here, she wished she had done exactly that. She was restless tonight, even more than usual. Most of the people here might be surprised by that, only a few would not. Those few, from her family's very prestigious crowd, were the ones who still remembered the wild streak she had exhibited in her teens. She had supposedly grown out of that wildness since. The proper people of the St. Simons' so proper set were much relieved by her reformation. Hardly anyone suspected that she sometimes felt as if she might jump straight out of her skin from restlessness. Tonight was one of those jumpy times.

Still, she *had* settled herself down, as her mother would put it, enough to feel guilty when she neglected her commitments. These days she could be depended on to finish what she started, and she had started this charity event, organized it, made it happen. Now she had to see it through so that tomorrow there would be a generous amount of money to distribute among the children's shelters she cared so much about and worked so hard for.

Bennett reminded herself of all the young, hopeful faces at the foundling home and settlement houses where she spent a good deal of her time. She didn't mind that part of tonight, which would do good for those children. They were the best part of her life right now. In fact, they mattered more to her than anything else she could imagine. They had helped her to discover how much she needed to have a cause in her life, something to work and struggle for, something to believe in. The children were all of those things to her, and she loved them for it.

In fact, she sometimes felt as if those kids were all that kept her from suffocating from everything the same, everything predictable in her life—including herself. Most of all, they provided the one exception to the safety of her existence in places like the Stuyvesant Club and her family's town house, both so out of reach behind tall iron gates. When she ventured into the parts of town where the less fortunate spent their lives, for just a little while she wasn't quite as safe and sure of everything. Being at least in proximity to the precarious edge of life made her feel more alive. Then the limo would return to carry her back to the protected, privileged world of the St. Simons once more. Of course, she had chosen this protected life for herself. It was better for her than the life of danger she had sampled several years ago, enough to get hurt and scared and come running home. Still, there were moments, like right now, when she wondered what would have become of her if she had chosen the more precarious road.

"Bennett, marvelous do," piped someone as Bennett skirted yet another gaggle of prosperous men in well-cut suits and women in smart little black dresses much like her own.

"Glad you're enjoying it," she said, and smiled on cue.

Bennett would have been welcome to join the chatter, but she had heard it all before and doubted she would have anything to add that she had not already added on numerous other occasions, to the point where the sound of her own voice repeating itself had turned to garble in her ears.

She surveyed the elegant room. As usual, the Stuyvesant Club had trotted out a fabulous buffet. The entire second floor was given over to the event. At least partly, Bennett had her mother's formidable and considerable influence to thank for that. When Dilys St. Simon wanted something, people understood that, despite the relentless graciousness of her tone, she intended to have her way, no matter what. The best course was to capitulate on the spot before she asked, or demanded, even more.

"No question about that at all," Bennett muttered to herself. Nobody knew better than she how true that was or how much she was expected to be Dilys, Jr. She loved her mother and admired her, too, but Bennett didn't want her mother's life. Yet, that was exactly where she seemed to be headed. By all indications, she was destined to become a leading light of uptown society in the best Dilys tradition. The burden of this eventuality was weighing especially heavy on Bennett's shoulders tonight.

"If you want to beg for my body, you needn't mumble. Speak right up."

Royce Boudreaux had materialized next to her, probably out of a nearby conversation he would also just as soon avoid. He and Bennett spoke regularly about how bored they were with this scene. Bennett had little choice but to attend. Society dos were the way to get society money for the institutions she helped support. Royce could make no such excuse, but he kept showing up all the same.

"I am most serious about this, my dear," he continued.

"You are a generous soul, Royce. I've always said that about you." Bennett smiled, enjoying the distraction of his banter, meaningless as it generally tended to be. At the moment, meaninglessness was preferable to her own discontented thoughts.

"You must understand I make this offer for a limited time only, on an exclusive basis, that is. At midnight, I become part of the buffet. It's 'Smorgasboard, anyone?' from then on."

Bennett laughed out loud, maybe even a bit more loudly than was appropriate for the Stuyvesant Club. "See how talented you are? I wouldn't have thought I had enough good humor left in me tonight to manage a laugh."

"And people say I'm useless. I shall expect you to speak up on my behalf to the contrary."

Bennett smiled. She took his arm, and Royce steered them out of the crowd toward the periphery of the room. She didn't look up at him. She knew he would be staring down at her as he so often did, and she wouldn't want him to detect that she was one of those people who thought of him as basically useless.

"Oh, no!" Royce exclaimed. "I didn't manage to segue us out of the fray quite fast enough after all. It's the Hesperus, and she's on her way to wreck me, I'm sure."

Bennett knew without looking that he was referring to her mother. Dilys didn't care for Royce. Even when he and Bennett and Forth were in day school together, Dilys had been biased against Royce. She didn't like the cut of his jib, she would say. Bennett's brother, Forth, who didn't like Royce much himself, would defend him anyway. "An eight-year-old doesn't have a jib, Mother," Forth would say. He had that wry way of talking even when he was a child.

"Mr. Boudreaux, how are you this evening?" Dilys St. Simon asked.

She had stepped into their path. They had no choice other than to stop and talk to her. Dilys was like that. She didn't give you alternatives, about much of anything.

"I am lovely, Mrs. St. Simon, but of course not nearly as much so as yourself," Royce said with a charming smile that might have been almost sincere.

"Mother, aren't you impressed with the turnout tonight?" Bennett asked, to divert Dilys's attention in case she had one of her anti-Royce barbs on the tip of her sometimes sharp tongue.

"I believe we discussed that earlier, dear. You needn't resort to idle conversation to protect your friend from me. I am on my best behavior this evening."

"The keepers of the Stuyvesant will appreciate your not bloodying the carpets with me, blue as the stain might be," Royce quipped. "But I was about to take my leave anyway." He lifted Bennett's fingers and touched them to his lips. "Your servant, milady." He turned and bowed slightly toward Dilys. "And yours."

Dilys nodded her head ever so slightly in something less than acknowledgment. Royce reached into his jacket and pulled a card from an inside pocket. He handed it to Bennett.

"My new private number," he said. "Call me. We'll lunch ... or whatever."

Bennett had to smile. She knew Royce had said that to get Dilys's dander up, and her right eyebrow rose to the occasion. She would hardly be expected to stand for any "whatever" between her daughter and a wastrel like Royce Boudreaux. Nothing to do with snobbishness, either. As Royce had pointed out, his blood was easily as blue as that of the St. Simon family any day. Dilys wasn't a snob anyway. Her ideas of what was and was not manly were very clear-cut. Idleness turned up decidedly on the not-manly list. The only leeway she gave anyone on this account went to her son. No matter how many schemes he might concoct or projects he might claim to have in development, Raeburn St. Simon IV, known from toddlerhood as Forth, wasn't any too productive himself. Dilys simply refused to recognize that. It was possibly her only blind spot.

Of course, the danger of men like Royce Boudreaux had other significance for Dilys. Bennett had run off with one of them back in her wild days. They made it all the way to Mexico before Dilys's bloodhounds finally tracked them down. Bennett had left a trail of credit card charges so wide, she wasn't hard to find. She had since concluded that, if she really wanted to disappear back then, she would have carried cash. Maybe she'd suspected that her traveling companion might rob her if she did. She had told herself he was harmless, like Royce, but perhaps her basic instincts had been more perceptive than that. Perhaps, she had known he would turn out to be so irresponsible he was dangerous. Or, maybe that was giving too much credit to the silly, reckless girl she had unfortunately been in those days.

Even more significant was the possibility that she hadn't really wanted to cut the umbilical cord to her family's world after all, only to stretch it for a while. Either way, Bennett understood how her misadventures might come to her mother's mind when she saw a dashing ne'er-do-well like Royce on her daughter's arm. Bennett might have offered the reassurance that she was so far from her Mexico escapades she could hardly remember what it must have felt like to be that crazy young girl instead of the predictable twenty-eight-year-old she had become. She didn't offer such reassurance because it would have meant hearing it out loud herself, and the sound of those words were likely to make her more restless than ever.

Meanwhile Royce had slipped away into the crowd. Dilys passed her small, delicate fingers over the smooth helmet of her perfectly silvering hair. If her hairdresser had anything to do with that very natural looking blend of ash and age, Dilys would never tell. Artifice of any kind was not a thing she was likely to admit.

"I saw Quinton earlier. He is looking particularly handsome this evening," she said.

"Now you are making idle conversation on behalf of *your* friend."

"Your friend, too, Bennett. You should never forget that. He may want to marry you, but he also cares about you. In our circle, the two don't always go together."

"What about love, Mother? Does that enter in, as well?"

"You really do want everything, don't you?" Dilys smiled and showed some of the few wrinkles she sported even in her late fifties.

"You and Daddy have everything, friendship and love."

"That is true." The color rose just perceptibly in Dilys's petal-pale cheeks. Little other than the subject of her beloved husband could do that.

"I want that for myself, too."

"Are you so certain you can't have it with Quint?"

"I barely know him, or that's how I feel anyway."

She and Quint had a long history of years together. Still, as far as she was concerned, they remained totally separate entities. There might be understanding and even affection between them, but nothing closer than that. Even so, Quinton Leslie did appear to be one of the nicest men she had ever known. If she wasn't in love with him, she probably should be. Her glance swept across the room in search of his serious gray gaze.

There he was, near the opposite corner, dutifully holding up his end of what was most likely an excruciating conversation with one of the dowager types who frequented events like this one. She probably had a grandniece or some other young protégé in tow and was checking Quint out for husband potential. The grandniece would be a lot better for him than I am, Bennett couldn't help thinking. Especially if she knows for sure whether she wants him or not. Especially if she doesn't think of him as a stranger in the emotional sense who was, nonetheless, one more of the entirely too predictable elements in her life. Bennett looked away just as she thought Quint might be about to catch her eye.

"I'm going to find Forth," she said.

She hoped to avoid an explanation to her mother about thinking of Quint as a distant familiarity. The subject was simply too discouraging though, to her credit, Dilys wasn't asking Bennett to explain anything right now. She was also looking for an excuse to escape from Quint's sight line. She really didn't want to talk to him tonight if she could help it. He would ask to take her home. Then there would be awkward moments outside her gate while she didn't invite him in. She preferred to avoid that if she could.

"Tell him to come and speak with me," Dilys said.

"What?"

"Your brother. You said you were going to find your brother." She gave a small, impatient sigh. Absentmindedness was not something with which Dilys had much personal experience. "I would like to speak with him when you find him. We're having a few people in for late supper at the house. I would like him to be there."

"I'll tell him, Mother," Bennett said.

She could already guess Forth's response. He would definitely not be about to spend a glorious Manhattan evening having supper with his parents and their crowd. A spring night promised too much chance of excitement for him to waste time on such sedate company. Sedate was not Forth's cup of tea. He was every bit as wild and reckless as Bennett had been in her younger days. Of course, Dilys had never sent the bloodhounds after Forth. A mild reprimand was the worst he ever got from his mother, and his father and stopped trying to reform him long ago. Bennett understood the difference between what was expected of her and what was expected of her brother. He was the son and heir. He could chart his own course and get away with it, no matter how irresponsible his choices might be. Everyone assumed he would don the St. Simon mantle when it was passed on to him. In the meantime, he was free to do what he pleased.

Tonight, as on so many other nights, what he pleased would be to ignore his mother's invitation. Ordinarily Bennett would end up doing the filial duty at her parents' gathering in Froth's absence. She wasn't sure she could handle it tonight. First of all, Quint would be there, so she wouldn't be able to avoid the awkward moments after all. Secondly, that event would be even more properly usual than this one, a carbon copy of all those she had attended before it. Bennett suddenly felt as if she might actually suffocate. She took a deep breath and set out across the crowded floor, moving perhaps a bit too fast for the Stuyvesant Club.

Maybe she should go out on the town with Forth tonight. He was always inviting her. He didn't expect her to say yes. She never did, but maybe tonight would be different. She was sicker than ever of being a good girl and doing what everybody expected. She was especially sick of representing the St. Simon offspring and making precisely the perfect impression when she did. She shone so brightly on those occasions that hardly anyone noticed Forth's perpetual absence. She didn't often bother with thoughts of how unfair that might be. This evening, however, she felt inclined toward one of those nights on the town that her brother took as his rightful due. She could club-hop with the best of them. At least, she'd been able to back in the old days. Why not set her reformed image on its ear for a few hours?

She looked around for Forth, but he wasn't in this room. She'd have found him easily if he had been. Even in the most sophisticated company, Forth stood out as more so. Bennett smiled at the thought. She loved her charming brother as much as her mother did, and though Bennett wasn't as blind to his shortcomings as their mother tended to be, she forgave him just about everything. He was too winsome to stay angry with for long. Besides, she was beginning to wonder if he might have the right attitude. Look where turning dependable had gotten her? Feeling stuck and miserable, that's where!

Forth wasn't in the wide corridor outside the reception hall, either. Divans and padded footstools filled the corners and lined the walls. Couples and groups sat talking, but Forth was not among them. It was going on midnight. He could have left already, but Bennett doubted that. The best clubs were hours away from coming to true life, especially for a fellow like Forth, who always showed up fashionably late. He would most likely stay around here as long as the bar was still open. After that, he might chat with Bennett for a while. She would mention that he should put in an obligatory appearance at the family homestead, and he would inevitably slip away at that point, like mist among the tapestries. She would often not even see him go. That's how talented an escape artist her big brother had become. She was reminded of her own years of sneaking out windows and bribing the servants not to tell. She wondered if she had any of those instincts left in her these days.

She finally found Forth in the library, a cavernous room of high ceilings and tall bookcases with leather couches redolent of generations of pipe smoke. Only in very recent years had this room, and others like it in this staid establishment, been opened up to use for events like this one. Some of the more senior members would never get over grumbling about that. Traditions tended to be as old and sacrosanct here as the label of brandy that was the house favorite.

Forth was ensconced on a couch near a bay of windows looking out onto Central Park. The shimmer of gold around the streetlights was visible through the windowpanes like a halo just beyond his blond head. Bennett smiled at the image. Much as she adored her brother, she knew that he was anything but an angel. The way he bent his head toward his companion, as if fascinated by her every word, was evidence of that. Sonia Jade was hardly likely to be fascinating. Her range of interest ran the gamut of society gossip and back again. She could, or at least would, talk about nothing else. That was not exactly Forth's cup of tea, either, but Sonia was very beautiful. As Bennett had often observed, from the male point of view, physical beauty in a woman can make up for a lack of just about everything else.

"Bennett," Forth exclaimed as he looked up to see her walking toward them. She thought she spied a plea for rescue in his eyes. Maybe Sonia's physical charms weren't enough to hold him captive after all.

"Bennett, darling."

Sonia didn't make much effort to sound sincere. She was probably about as pleased by the interruption as she would be to find every other woman in the room wearing an exact copy of her very stylish party dress. She and Bennett exchanged brief hugs. They knew each other mostly from a few years back, when that season's bout of restlessness left Bennett desperate enough to try out Sonia's circle for a while. Unfortunately, or probably fortunately, Bennett wasn't as mindless as Sonia and Royce and the like. She could have fit into their world, but she didn't want to. She'd needed an adventure, not a stultifying dose of vapidity. That was simply a junior version of the Stuyvesant Club.

"Sonia and I were just now talking about wandering by Lucille's," Forth said. "I have a marvelous idea, Bennett. Why don't you join us?"

Bennett recognized the name of the popular late-night supper spot of the moment. Ordinarily she would have responded with something about Lucille's not being her kind of place. "I might just do that," she said instead. The way she was feeling tonight, vapidity could be better than nothing.

"Don't tell me you're finally going to satisfy your curiosity about my nocturnal habits," Forth said with a twinkle in his blue eyes.

"Maybe it's time I rediscovered some nocturnal habits of my own." Maybe it's time I got back to being more like you, brother dear, she thought. Loose, irresponsible, free as the breeze.

"Come on in. The water's very interesting," Forth quipped in his usual offhand, amused manner that sometimes made Bennett suspect he was laughing at her and what he considered to be her pose as a reformed character.

"I just might do that."

Too bad Bennett wasn't actually as sure of this possibility as she sounded. Too bad Bennett wasn't sure about much of anything at the moment. Suddenly she was almost overwhelmed by the urge to get away, from the Stuyvesant crowd, from Forth. Maybe most of all from herself.

"You two enjoy yourselves," she said as she turned to leave.

"Are you coming along to Lucille's later?"

"I am giving it some serious thought," Bennett called over her shoulder only half truthfully. Lucille's didn't really feel like the solution to her personal brand of restlessness. To her, the society club scene was only another kind of sameness dressed up in glamour and sophistication. What she needed was some *real* excitement. She simply wasn't certain what that might be.

"Well, you know where to find me," Forth called after her when Bennett was at the library door. She gave a little wave without looking back.

Bennett was on her way to the elevators that would carry her downstairs to the coat booth when she saw Quinton coming out of the reception room just down the corridor. He hadn't noticed her yet, but if she continued on to the elevators or the staircase, he was bound to see her. She really didn't want that to happen. She was feeling pretty out of sorts at the moment. Being with Quint was sure to intensify that feeling. The stairs to the upper floors were to her left. She took them all the way to the top, as fast as her narrow-skirted dress would allow.

Bennett had been in the Stuyvesant Club often enough to know about the other set of stairs and the service elevator at the opposite end of the third floor. She could take either down to street level with little chance of encountering anyone she knew. She headed along the carpeted hallway with that plan in mind. Closed doors lined the corridor on both sides. She had hoped there'd be no one up here at this hour. A single door ahead on the right appeared to be ajar. A patch of soft light spilled out onto the carpet.

Bennett approached the open doorway with caution, moving to the right side wall as she came closer. She thought this might be the billiard room, but she wasn't sure. Her intention was to slip past without being seen. If she moved swiftly and quietly, she might just make it. She peeked cautiously around the edge of the door frame to find out who might be inside before making her dash. What she saw froze her to the spot where she stood. All thought of escape was forgotten amidst her shock and terror. That moment of forgetfulness would prove to be her undoing.

Chapter Two

The light was not bright in the billiard room, but Bennett had no trouble making out the scene. In fact, she would never forget it as long as she lived. The first thing she noticed, oddly enough, was the way the lamp glow picked out red highlights in the man's hair as he bent over the bundle on the floor. Bennett was aware, through the haze of her shock, that she had to remember details like this one for reporting later on. She couldn't tell how tall he was because he was down on one knee in a crouched position, but his shoulders were broad under the black leather jacket that struck her as too hot to be worn on a June evening.

She didn't want to look at the other, more disturbing, aspect of the scene, but she couldn't keep herself from doing so. Once she had looked, her gaze was glued to the spot even though she longed to turn away. What, at first glance, had appeared to be a bundle on the floor was more than that. The bare half of the tall window had led Bennett to conclude initially that the bundle itself must be made up of a drapery that had been pulled from its attachments. The man crouched over the bundle had pulled back the folds of heavy material at one end. He remained still as a statue staring down at what he had revealed. Bennett could see, past his shoulder, just enough of what he was staring at to make her gasp out loud. From beneath the folded-back drapery peered a dead-white face.

The man jerked around to stare at Bennett where she stood rooted in the doorway. For a split second, those roots held firm, as if she were in a nightmare where movement becomes maddeningly slowed or even impossible. By the time she snapped herself out of that trance, he had moved like lightning out of his crouch and across the room toward her. She was making her first step to run down the hallway when he grabbed her in a harsh and powerful grip. His fingers clamped around her upper arm so tightly she could almost feel the bruise forming there. He dragged her inside the billiard room and closed the door.

"Don't make a sound," he said in a tone that was more a growl than a voice.

Bennett knew she should have screamed the minute she saw him, but she wasn't the screaming type. She was too accustomed to taking care of things on her own to have a natural instinct to call out for help. He still had hold of her arm. When he reached around her waist from behind and pulled her to him, imprisoning her arms at her sides, she realized he wasn't carrying a weapon in either hand. She began to struggle, kicking out fiercely. She connected with one of his shins, and he grunted in pain. She took a deep breath to let out a yell that would have come from the very bottom of her lungs had he not let go of one of her arms to clap his hand over her mouth.

"Do you want to end up like her?"

He jolted Bennett around to face the bundle on the floor. The woman lying there was probably in her late twenties and very pale except for the bright red lipstick and dark eyeshadow she was wearing. Those kohl-rimmed eyes held Bennett's gaze. They were partly open and fixed, as if eternally fascinated by the old oil painting of a hunt club scene on the wall. Bennett could tell that the young woman was dead.

"She was in the wrong place at the wrong time, and she got killed for it," he said. "You're in the wrong place at the wrong time, too, lady. So, you'd better do what I say. No hassles. No arguments. Do you understand me?"

She could feel his breath on her neck. She could also hear the desperation in his voice. He was out on the edge, and she had already guessed that made him capable of following through on any threat he made, no matter how violent. Bennett definitely didn't want to end up like the woman on the floor, and if this man had killed once tonight he might be ready to kill again. Bennett had never been so terrified in her life, but she had to keep her head clear. Her life could depend on it.

She nodded her head as much as was possible with his hand clamped over her mouth. That hand was partly covering her nostrils, as well, and she was beginning to have trouble breathing. She could tell by the breadth of his chest behind her and the tension in his arms that he was strong enough to smother her or break her neck in an instant if he chose to. She had to keep him from doing either of those things, especially since she was already gasping for breath.

"If I take my hand off your mouth, are you going to scream?"

Bennett managed to move her head from side to side. She struggled to breathe while he must have been debating with himself what to do. Then he pulled his hand away from her mouth. She gulped in air and might have used it to scream, but he had moved his free hand from her mouth to her neck. His reach was long enough to circle her throat and so wide that it stretched her chin upward. She had been freed from one death grip only to be caught in another. Tears of fear and frustration rose to Bennett's eyes. She wasn't the panicky type, but she felt herself on the verge of doing exactly that. A tear broke loose from her lashes and trailed down her cheek all the way to his hand at her throat. She thought she perceived a slight loosening of his grip, just enough for her to manage a few strangled words.

"I'll do what you say," she said. "You don't need to hurt me." She hated to sound like that much of a coward with anybody, but her instincts told her it was a better approach than her natural belligerence would be right now.

He clamped his arm tighter around her waist and arms, as if to compensate for the loosened hold on her throat. "You're damned right you'll do what I tell you, lady. You haven't got much choice."

His grip around her body had pulled her dress up high on her thighs. His own thigh was thrust between hers in a manner that would have been intimate if it weren't for the circumstances. She had worn stockings and a garter belt because it was unseasonably warm tonight. Now she wished she had on panty hose instead. She was uncomfortably aware of the tops of her stockings coming close to being exposed. She hoped that he was too desperate at the moment to notice. His hard body and intruding thigh told her she wouldn't have much chance of stopping further invasion if he decided to try it.

"I haven't seen your face," she rasped. "You could lock me in here and get away."

She had already decided what she would do if he took her advice. She would run to the window and call out to the street for help. Somebody was bound to hear her. Her captor hesitated, as if thinking over her suggestion. He loosened his throat hold a bit more, just enough for Bennett to be able to look down at the body on the floor once more. She hadn't noticed the dark stain on the drapery before. Some of that stain had spread to the gold fringe trim where she could make out the scarlet color. From beneath one edge of that fringe, right next to a small, open evening purse,

protruded the long blade of a hunting knife. Its shiny surface was mottled with more crimson stain.

Bennett felt a strain behind her eyes instead of tears this
time. The man holding her so roughly and rudely, as if she
no longer possessed her own body or had any say over what
happened to it, was a brutal murderer. And she was likely
to be his next victim.

"If I left you here," he said, "you'd be yelling and hol-
lering before I was hardly out the door." She could feel him
glancing around the room. "There isn't even anything to tie
you up with. Those curtain ties wouldn't hold."

She was tempted to argue that they would hold, but she
suspected he wouldn't go for that. He might be stupid and
crazy enough to commit murder, but she sensed that he
could be pretty smart otherwise. She felt her last chances of
survival slipping away. Her only hope was to stall him till she
could make a break for it or until somebody else happened
along the corridor outside. She tried not to think that nobody would be likely to come in here even if they were on the
third floor. The hour was too late for billiards. The crowd
downstairs would be thinning out by now. Even so, she had
to do whatever she could to save herself, and stalling for
time seemed to be her only choice. Until that moment, it had
never occurred to Bennett that she would do almost anything to stay alive. She braced herself against that awareness, but she didn't deny it.

"Maybe we could work something out," she said, trying
her best to sound conciliatory with his fingers still gripping
her throat.

"What we can work out is that you're leaving here with
me," he said.

"No," she shouted, loudly enough for him to clamp his
hand over her mouth.

Being forced to leave here with him could prolong this
ordeal indefinitely. She'd be his hostage, and Bennett knew

what usually happened to hostages. They had a habit of ending up dead.

"Shut up and do what I tell you," he growled, "or you'll be sorry."

He dragged her over to the body and let go of her mouth while he stooped down and grabbed the knife from beneath the drapery. At this closer range, Bennett could see the look of surprise in the dead girl's eyes. Bennett turned her face away, but not before she saw him wipe the knife blade clean on the stained drapery. Her stomach rolled, and for a moment she thought she would be sick. The moment passed, leaving her more shaky than she wanted to be. She needed to stay alert for any chance of escape. He brought the knife blade next to her throat where his fingers had previously been.

"Make one false move, and you'll end up under that curtain with her," he said.

"Did you kill her?" Bennett couldn't help but ask. She was pretty sure he did. For some reason she wanted to hear him say it, though she would probably be more scared than ever once he had.

He wrenched her around toward the door. "Figure it out for yourself."

He hauled her across the carpet to the door then stopped for a moment to listen. She listened, too, but she heard nothing. He used his knife hand to open the door a crack. She might have screamed then, but she knew that could set him off. She would have to wait for a better opportunity, no matter how desperately she wanted to do something right now to get away from this maniac.

There was no one in the corridor. He opened the door and pulled her out of the room, then shut the door behind them. She had hoped he would leave it open. The murder scene would be discovered sooner that way. Maybe he'd thought of the same thing. He looked first up then down the corridor. She hoped he would take the direction toward the front of the building and the gathering downstairs, but he didn't. He turned right toward the back elevator and stairs. He dragged her along for a moment, then hefted her clear of the floor and carried her. Bennett was not small, five foot eight to be exact, and more rounded than her mother and lanky brother. Yet, this man carried her as if she had no substance at all. He once again lifted her dress along with her body, well above her stocking hems this time.

"Put me down," she said. "I can walk by myself."

She had only whispered that, but she could feel his tension rise at the possibility of being heard.

"I told you to shut up," he said, and touched the metal of the knife blade to the skin of her throat. He put her down anyway but kept one arm around her waist. "You walk right, or I'll kill you."

Bennett nodded and strained away from the knife. She could feel her heart pounding in her throat very near the blade. When he continued down the corridor, keeping close to the wall, she had to scurry along with him. At the end of the hallway, a narrow flight of stairs led downward at their left. The service elevator was straight ahead. That elevator went to the basement. The custodian's room was down there, Bennett knew. When she was making arrangements for tonight's event, she had spoken with the custodian about working late. He had said he would be in his basement room if she needed him. She needed him, all right. Now all she had to do was get her captor to take the elevator instead of the stairs.

"Take the stairs," she said when he hesitated. "It's safer that way."

He hesitated only an instant longer before dragging her to the elevator door and pushing the button. "Why would you want me to be safe?"

"Maybe it's myself I'm worried about. If you run into somebody, I might be in even worse danger than I am now."

"Shut up," he said.

She did as he demanded and waited with him for the elevator to arrive. She allowed herself a small sigh of temporary relief. Her strategy had worked. The elevator rattled to a stop and the door slid open. He had to pull the inside cage door back by hand. While he did that, he kept a tight grip on her body and arms. He pushed her ahead of him into the elevator cage and dragged the heavy, creaking gate closed behind them. She held her breath as he examined the control buttons next to the door opening. She let herself exhale when he pushed *B* for basement.

She didn't move or make a sound as they traveled downward. The elevator was an ancient contraption, maybe even as old as the Stuyvesant itself. The cables strained audibly. She hoped that would attract some attention but knew it would more likely be ignored. As they approached the second floor and then the first, she wished for a stop and the doors to open, but that didn't happen. The cables didn't make their final groan and clump the elevator cage to a jolting halt until they had reached the basement. Bennett suddenly remembered her earlier wish for some adventure in her life. "Be careful what you wish for," some obviously very wise person had once told her.

Bennett's wish had come true. Now she must summon her courage for what lay ahead.

Chapter Three

Bennett hadn't gotten a clear look at him yet. He was still behind her with his arm clamped around her waist and the knife point at her throat. She could tell he wasn't the Stuyvesant Club type. The rough material on the thigh he had thrust between her legs was denim not suiting. As for the jacket, some of the younger members of the Stuyvesant set might wear black leather because it was chic, but not the way this man wore it. She guessed it might be his primary uniform.

She had glimpsed his hands. They were broad and strong, with long fingers. He was a head or so taller than she was, maybe six feet or a little over. He smelled, oddly enough, very clean, like freshly washed linens in the breeze. He hadn't shaved recently. She'd felt the roughness of his whiskered cheek against her face when he leaned over to growl in her ear. His hair was dark, with those reddish highlights she had noticed when she first saw him in the billiard room. He was solidly built. She had been yanked against his body enough times to know that.

He was definitely not a regular in her crowd. She was certain of that. But why was she so certain? The answer to that was immediate and instinctive. She knew he hadn't been around her before because she would have noticed him. He would have stood out from the rest as far more virile and imposing. Even the ones who worked out and were in good shape, like Quint, didn't have the same kind of physicality as this man, the way his muscles tensed into urgent tautness ready to spring to action at any moment. The prospect of what that action might be in this situation brought Bennett back to full alertness. She tucked away the details of his description for future reference and reporting.

As they approached the basement level of the building, something other than the man behind her suddenly captured Bennett's attention. What was the custodian's name? She intended to call out to him the minute the elevator doors slid open. Her captor didn't have her mouth covered right now. His hands were otherwise occupied. She suspected he might gag her again with his knife hand once they were out of the elevator. She was bargaining on a few seconds in between when she could scream for the custodian. But what was his name? She had to remember his name!

Bennett had kept her fear at bay until now. She had flipped herself into crisis mode. Keep cool, she'd told herself. She had managed to take that advice till this moment. The blank space in her mind where the custodian's name should have been was threatening that cool control. She felt the numb grip of panic tighten her chest and reach for her throat, just as her captor's fingers had done back in the billiard room. With that panic came a more stark awareness of her circumstances than Bennett had thus far allowed herself to acknowledge. She was the all but helpless prisoner of a desperate murderer, and she had slim chance of escaping him.

Her breath caught against the constriction in her throat. She tried to swallow but couldn't. Every sinew in her body was stretched to maximum tension, as if any attempt to bend might snap her in two. But what she was most aware of and most frightened by was the sensation of her throat being clamped shut, against breath, against sound. What if her voice couldn't force itself out when she needed it? She couldn't test that terrible possibility without risking his hand over her mouth once more. On top of that, she couldn't remember the damned name. As the elevator doors creaked open, Bennett knew that all she could do was try.

She opened her mouth and willed the shout to emerge. He helped by clamping his arm more tightly around her waist. That seemed to force the sound up, pushing a rush of breath past the barrier in her throat. With it came the words her voice had found before her consciousness could realize they were there.

"Help me," she shouted more loudly than she would have thought herself capable of. "Help me, plea—"

His hand cut her off then. "Shut up."

He had hesitated outside the elevator. She could feel his head turn as he looked up and down the narrow, dimly lit hallway. He must not know which way to turn. He probably hadn't been in the basement before. Bennett gasped against the pressure of his hand. She prayed for this precious moment of hesitation to be her salvation.

"Who's out there?" From the other end of the hallway, the custodian's voice came like the answer to her prayer. "What are you doing there?"

She couldn't see him. She was being held too tightly to move her head and look in his direction, but he had obviously seen them.

"You let her go." The voice was louder but not any closer. He wasn't running after them as Bennett hoped he would. "Let her go or I'm going to call the police."

"Stay where you are, old man," Bennett's captor growled. "Or I'll use this on her right now."

The hand was suddenly off her mouth as he brandished the knife at the custodian.

"Anson, get help," she cried. The name had popped into her head like magic. "Get help now."

''Miss St. Simon, is that you?''

Her mouth was covered again before she could answer, but Anson had recognized her. He would run upstairs now for help. She couldn't expect him to attempt a rescue on his own. He was an old man, just as this brute had pointed out. Meanwhile, she was being dragged down the hall in what was unfortunately the direction of the rear door. He had no choice but to go that way with Anson blocking the other end of the hall that led to the front of the building. This was one of those strokes of dumb luck that had fallen in her captor's favor. She could only hope that the next opportunity would be hers. She forced her fear into submission. She had to keep herself under control for the moment when that opportunity might arise.

The basement's rear door opened onto a recessed area below street level with several concrete steps leading up to the pavement. The man pushed Bennett through the door and into the shadowed area just outside. She listened for the sound of Anson following but heard nothing. He would be hurrying, as fast as someone his age could manage, upstairs to tell them what was happening. Meanwhile, there were people on the street, passing less often on this side block than out on Fifth Avenue, but enough for her to attract some attention if she called out. He would have to take his hand off her mouth if he was going to get her out of here without being noticed. She would scream then, even louder than she had to alert Anson.

''If you're thinking about raising a holler, you'd better think again,'' he said, as if he might have read her thoughts. ''You took me by surprise with that old guy back there. It won't happen again. Remember this?'' He laid the cold steel of the knife blade against her cheek. ''Do you remember it?'' he repeated when she didn't answer.

Bennett nodded her head. The feel of the blade made her breath come faster again in gasps behind his hand.

"Don't think I won't use it," he said, "and not just on you."

Bennett caught her breath. What did he mean by that?

"You give me trouble, and I'll grab the first fool I can get my hands on off the street and do to them what happened to that girl back upstairs. And it will be your fault if I do. Do you want that on your head?" He pressed the blade harder against her cheek. "Do you?"

She shook her head again, more vigorously this time.

"Okay," he said. "I'm going to take my hand off your mouth and we're going to walk up there into the street. One peep out of you and I'll do some serious damage. I've got nothing to lose now. If I go down, I'm taking a few of you with me. Don't forget that."

He pulled her with him to the concrete stairs. He didn't take his hand away from her mouth until they were about to leave the shadows. Bennett gulped in the night air. She sometimes complained of exhaust fumes on the street, but she wasn't complaining now. The city air tasted country sweet, car exhaust and all.

"See her?"

He jerked Bennett around toward the street just visible above the top of the steps and their wrought iron railing. He was talking about an elderly woman who was walking slowly and laboriously along the side street toward Fifth. She had a small dog on a leash with her.

"She'd make a good target," he said. "She's not even moving very fast."

"Could you really do that?"

"You bet I could. If you don't believe me, try one false move and you'll find out I mean every word."

Bennett understood that she had better take him very seriously. When he pushed her up the rest of the stairs and onto the pavement, she didn't resist. The elderly woman looked at them for a moment then returned her attention to her dog. She'd be an easy target, just as he said. Bennett couldn't let that happen.

"We're going to walk along here real nice," he said, heading them toward the corner and the busier scene on Fifth Avenue.

"You don't really think you can get away with this, do you?"

"I think I might as well try." He walked them faster. He had his arm cinched tight around her waist, pulling her close to his side. To a passerby they might look like lovers out for a stroll. "Like I said before, I've got nothing to lose."

They were at the corner, and the light was about to change. Bennett looked back to see where the older woman might be now. Consequently Bennett's attention was distracted when he suddenly let go of her waist and grabbed her arm. He was pulling her in a very fast walk, almost a run, off the curb into the street.

"Come on," he said. "Look like you're having a good time. You're my girl and we're out on the town, running across the street here like a couple of kids."

He was moving as he spoke and pulling her along with him. She had to run to keep up or fall in the street. She stole a frantic glance at the lineup of yellow cabs on their mark to take off the minute the light turned green. All those cabbies cared about was getting down Fifth Avenue as fast as they could. They weren't even looking at her, and she knew it. She raised her free arm to wave hard at them anyway. No one seemed to notice.

"Wait," she called as they neared the other side.

"They aren't listening. They'll just think you might be a fare," her captor said as he clamped his arm back around her waist and half lifted her up onto the curb. "So, why don't you shut up while I pick out a good victim over here on this side of the street."

Bennett glanced up and down the block. Unfortunately, there were several prospects, from the ragged man on a nearby park bench to the tourist couple with a child between them, all three gawking at the elegant buildings across the avenue. A stone wall bordered this side of the street, with the dark of Central Park beyond the wall. Bennett might have called for help, but she could feel the point of the knife through the silk crepe of her dress. Besides, she had lived in New York City all of her life, and she doubted anyone would leap to her defense against a man the size of this one with a desperate glint in his eyes.

"I think it's time for a walk in the park," he said as he hustled her across the octagonal-cut asphalt of the sidewalk and onto the Belgian block border that lined the wall.

"We aren't going into the park!" Bennett resisted as they approached an unoccupied stone bench.

He yanked hard on her arm, but she held her ground. She had been frightened before, by the body on the floor of the billiard room, by the knife blade at her throat, by being dragged along against her will. But none of that terrified her more than the prospect of entering the dark beyond this wall.

"We're going in there," he growled near her ear, "and we're doing it right now."

"Help me," Bennett yelled, just as she had in the basement of the Stuyvesant Club. She didn't care what he did to her as a result.

People did turn around to look. They may even have surmised that Bennett was being held prisoner. Still no one moved forward. In fact, the couple with the child backed off. A man did call out "What's going on there?" but he didn't come any closer.

"Keep your distance if you know what's good for you," Bennett's captor said forcefully. He moved the knife into view of the people on the street.

A woman screamed, and the couple who had backed off grabbed their child and ran up the street.

"See how much help you're going to get?" he said to Bennett. He didn't sound triumphant, just matter-of-fact. He climbed onto the bench and pulled her up after him.

"Let me go," she said.

"Not on your life."

He lifted her and set her on top of the wall. In a move too quick for her to anticipate, he was on the wall next to her. Then he pushed her over to the other side. She tumbled onto the ground between the wall and a clump of bushes. She felt her stockings tear as her knee hit a rock. Her palm came down on the edge of a metal soda can, discarded there along with other trash. He grabbed her arm.

"Please, help me," she shouted.

Bennett didn't expect much response. She was on her own now. Maybe help would come from Anson's alarm at the Stuyvesant Club, but she couldn't be certain of that. Her hand closed around the soda can as her captor pulled her to her feet. She brought her arm up in an arc that carried all of her strength behind it. She was aiming at his face, hoping to startle him into loosening his grip on her so she could get away. If he hadn't turned his head just in time, she would have inflicted some real damage. Instead, her blow glanced off his shoulder. He ripped the can out of her hand and threw it into the bushes.

"You've got some fight in you, all right," he said. "Why don't I take you over there and leave you?" He pointed toward the darkness beyond the bushes. "I've got a feeling you'd need lots of fight against whatever's in there."

"No animal in here could be any worse than you," Bennett said over the knot of terror in her throat.

"I wouldn't bet on that," he said, "especially not when it comes to animals of the human kind. Now, get moving."

Bennett could hear the traffic on Fifth Avenue—hansom cabs, taxis, cars, limousines. They were only yards behind her, but they might as well have been a world away as he took off through the bushes with her in tow.

Chapter Four

How did I get myself into this one?

That question had been flashing across the back of Memphis Modine's mind, or maybe along the side of it, ever since he'd hotfooted it out of those snooty Fifth Avenue digs he'd been glad to leave behind. At least at first, he'd been glad. Now that he was out here, he wasn't so sure. He seemed to have traded the frying pan for the fire, as they say. He'd been inside places like that Stuyvesant Club before, old buildings with lots of rooms, little cubbyholes off other little cubbyholes where he might have found a spot to tuck himself away till the middle of the night when everybody was gone. Instead, he was in the open now, in this place they call the city that never sleeps because nobody ever knows enough to go home. That meant people everywhere you turned, and people everywhere was exactly what he didn't need right now.

The woman stumbled against him, and he jerked her upright again.

Speaking of things he didn't need, how had he let himself get saddled with her? If his crew could see him now, they'd laugh till their sides split. Here he was dragging some fancy lady around, worrying one minute whether she'd bring the cops down on him, the next minute whether he was hurting her or not. He'd felt bad about the way she fell off the wall, even though she came up swinging when she did. The crew liked to ride him for thinking that way, called him the Southern Gent, playing off his name and where he was supposed to have been born.

They also called him Memphis Modine the Tennessee Machine, because when he got riled up, there was no stopping him from whatever he had in mind. He'd gotten the nickname in the first place from being brought up in a Memphis orphanage. His real first name had sounded a bit too fancy for an orphan or for a boy, either. He'd been glad to lose it. As for where he came from before the orphanage, nobody seemed too hot to find out. Memphis figured his mother wished he hadn't happened in the first place. Maybe she was from some important family, which would explain why nobody pushed too hard to find out his real identity. The South was like that in those days, which was okay with him. He didn't want a mother who didn't want him, so he didn't ask questions about his name or anything else. The question of the moment, however, was not where he might have come from but where in Sam Hill he was going to go.

He pulled her along faster.

"Please, slow down," she said. "I can't keep up."

"You'd better keep up," he said menacingly.

He had to stop worrying about how rough he was with her. What he should be worrying about was having her along at all. If he didn't have her in tow, he could make some real time. Without her to think about, he might have taken a second or two at the club to stop and figure things out better. Once on the street he might have decided it was smarter to take the alleyways than to be out here in this park where he couldn't see what was ahead for the trees and the dark. Instead, he'd had to keep thinking about her and what she might get herself up to. He'd been doing that almost every minute since he first was unlucky enough to set eyes on her peeking in the door of that room she'd have been better off to keep her nose out of. Now she was holding him back, weighing him down, and doubling or tripling his troubles.

The police would be after him now for sure, and not just because of what they'd find on the floor of the Stuyvesant Club. They'd be after him sure enough for that, but now he'd given them all the more reason to hunt him down like a dog and never stop till they'd driven him to ground and under it if they could. That all-the-more-reason was this woman here. They'd say she was his hostage. Just thinking the word made his stomach twist like it was about to crawl up his backbone. They brought in all their best guys in a hostage situation, all their best guys and all their best firepower, too. They'd have SWAT out there in no time—riot gear, gas canisters, bulletproof body armor, the whole nine yards—ready to do just what the name said, swat him down like he was a flyspeck on somebody's windshield.

What did he have going for him up against NYPD's magnum force? He had this tall society type as a drag-along, and he was stuck with her. Every time she stumbled and he lost another second of getting out of this mess, he thought about letting her go. But he couldn't do that, for more reasons than he liked to admit. First of all, she'd take off and bring the law down on him before he could make himself scarce enough to have half a chance of getting away. At least, that's what she'd try to do. She might manage it, too. She'd already shown him she was smart and had nerve. She almost got him caught back there at the Stuyvesant Club. She'd been scared half out of her little black cocktail number when she saw the stiff on the floor and the knife in his hand, but she'd stood up to him anyway. She wasn't some gutless rich kid, and that made her dangerous to him. He had to keep her close, under his thumb so tight she couldn't move a muscle or make a peep. Otherwise, she'd do him no good for sure.

Much as he hated to admit it, there was another reason, too. He wasn't about to leave any female alone in this place, no matter how much of a drag on his action she might be. He looked around as they picked their way through the trees and bushes. Anybody or anything could be crawling around out here and probably was. He'd been in enough hellholes to know what one felt like, and Central Park, New York City, had that feel. On a normal night, he'd have steered clear of this place even if he was by himself, much less when he had a woman with him. But this sure wasn't a normal night, so here he was. Even she seemed to have quieted down some, maybe trying not to attract the attention of whatever might be lurking out there in the shadows. Could be she'd recognized the truth when he warned her about there being worse animals in this place than him. Could be she was nervy enough to be stupid and try to take off on her own anyway. He wasn't going to let her do that for more than just his own sake. They didn't call him the Southern Gent for nothing.

There was one other reason for hanging on to her, and that one he really didn't like to think about, because it scared even him, and he wasn't the type to scare easy. He'd been up against high seas and bad men, and he just about always knew how to handle himself. This time was different. He always made it a point to keep away from territory he didn't know. Even when he was out on the ocean, he knew exactly where he was all the time. If the instruments went out, he could dead-reckon his way to port when he had to. He wasn't the type to get lost, either, on water or dry land. Unfortunately, this place was neither. This place was concrete. Even here in the park with dirt under his feet, he could hardly be farther from anything near the natural world. He was out of his element, and he knew it. Worse than that, he hadn't a hair's width of an idea where he was. But this little lady did. That may have been the most convincing reason of all for not letting her go.

They'd come close to the edge of the wooded area. He could see streetlights through the breaks in the trees. He knew they couldn't be at the other side of the park by any means yet. He'd looked at a Manhattan street map before coming uptown from South Street Seaport. He remembered Central Park as taking up a sizable chunk of the middle of town. This had to be some kind of service road. He didn't hear traffic, so maybe it was closed off. He sidled up close enough to see there were benches between the trees and the road. That meant there could be people, too, sitting on those benches, though he couldn't think for the life of him why anybody would come in here at night if they had a choice in the matter. Unless, of course, their choice was to prey on the poor saps who happened to be in here.

He'd yanked her up under his arm and clapped his hand over her mouth while he took a peek out between the trees. She'd obviously seen the light, too, and might try to yell or something. A second later, he learned that she'd picked "or something." She lifted her foot and brought it down hard, heel jutted like a weapon, along his lower leg and ankle. If he hadn't been wearing boots, she'd have put his right side out of commission for a while for sure, that's how hard she spiked him. Even with the boot in the way, he felt it, and it didn't feel good.

"What the hell?" he cried, louder than he would have done if he'd had time to think about it.

She twisted in his grip with what he imagined was all her strength. She had more of that than he would have guessed for a woman who showed no hard muscle he could see or feel. Still, she was out of her class when it came to a wrestling match with him. He held her tighter than ever and whipped the knife out to remind her he had it.

"You're giving me a hard time," he growled into her ear. "I told you what I'd do to you if you gave me a hard time."

She didn't stop struggling right away, and he could feel her trying to work her lips open under his grasp, most likely so she could bite his hand. She might be a Stuyvesant Club purebred, but she had some street blood in her, too. He was going to have to tame her and do it fast. He pulled her head back till he knew he had to be just about to snap her neck. He could feel her wrenching for breath under his nearly suffocating hand. His stomach turned to think he was handling a woman this way, but he knew it couldn't be helped.

"I already told you the most important truth you're ever going to know," he snarled in a tone so mean he didn't like to believe it was himself speaking. "I told you I've got nothing to lose, and you'd be smart to remember that. I could break your neck right this minute and leave you here dead without missing a beat. Do you hear me?"

She stopped struggling, but her body was still rigid and ready to start plunging against his arm again any second. He clamped his grip tighter and heard her muffled exclamation of what had to be pain. He tried to make himself oblivious to how much of a dirtball that made him feel, but he loosened his grip on her a little all the same.

"I said, do you hear me?" he snarled again.

She hesitated a moment, just enough to let him know he had a truly stubborn one on his hands. Then she nodded her head, only once and only enough to let him know he'd won. He felt some of the tension go out of her body, but not all of it. She had plenty of fight left in her. Memphis would have bet a few good dollars on that. He hoped he wouldn't have to bet his life.

BENNETT WAS SCARED, but she knew she mustn't let that fear get the best of her. Instead, she concentrated on getting her bearings. She didn't spend much time in the park ordinarily, but she had been here. Thank heaven, he'd loosened his grip on her head enough to let her see where they were headed. She still could not turn much to the right or left, especially since every move she made brought the pressure from his beefy arm. She'd thought he might actually kill her there under the tree when he came desperately close to breaking her neck with his bare hands. Surprisingly enough, that had brought her to herself more than the other way around. Not that she wasn't scared, of course. She would have to be much more naive than was her nature not to know the real danger she was in. This man was strong enough to hurt her badly. Ordinarily she liked strong men and the feeling they gave her that they could jolt the world into line just by taking it in their two broad hands. He had broad hands. Unfortunately, she was the one he intended to jolt into line.

He also seemed to know where he was going as he dragged her purposefully along, parallel to the tree line that bordered one of the access roads leading into the park from the junction of Fifth Avenue and Central Park South. Access road to what? Bennett forced herself to order her thoughts out of the immediate for a moment. Access to the zoo, that was it. She had been here earlier this spring with a group of children from one of the shelters. She tried to remember details of the zoo layout—whether there was a wall blocking the zoo grounds from the avenue, if a direct route to the avenue would be easy to find. All she could recall for sure was that they were now headed directly toward the spot where the access road met the zoo entrance. Logic told her that gateway might very possibly be barricaded for the night. What did he plan? Was he going to try to make her scale a wall or climb a fence? Were there cages along this side of the zoo periphery? Could they end up dropping down into some wild animal's lair? If they did, would she in fact be any worse off than she was right now?

He dragged her behind a tree and clamped her head tight again while he looked out at the road, probably to see if there was anyone around. They had been making so much noise crashing through the underbrush that she hadn't been able to hear much else. As he held her there still for a moment, she listened. She could hear music. Actually, what she heard was something she had been hesitant to think of as musical till now. Hip-hop they called it, or whatever hip-hop had turned into as fad of the moment. She did enough work with young people to recognize what she was listening to as the hyper-rhythmic sound that came out of those huge boom boxes kids loved to carry when they walked the streets. She might not have liked that sound before tonight, but right now those strains of disjointed melody made her feel almost like dancing.

She had already concluded that their way would be blocked into the zoo, and that there would be little advantage for him in scaling the fence, so he probably wouldn't do that. He was going to try to make it across the road. That meant they would be in full view of whoever might be out there. She hoped that was where the music came from. She'd given up any thought of breaking away. He was too strong to break away from. She'd put all she'd had into her attempt a few moments ago and nearly got herself strangled in the bargain. He would, however, have to consider letting loose the gag hold he had on her in order to get across the road without attracting too much attention.

"I'm going to take my hand away from your mouth for a minute," he said, his mind apparently on the same track as hers. "Don't make a single squawk" he warned. "Do you hear me?"

She nodded.

"I might shove this knife into you if you scream. Do you believe me?"

She nodded again. She did believe that actually, but she didn't let herself dwell on it. Otherwise, she might be too paralyzed by fear to do what had to be done. Meanwhile, true to his word, he loosened his grip on her head. He didn't take his hand entirely away for a moment, as if he didn't want to trust her even though he had no other choice. He moved his fingers along her cheek and down her throat in what, under other circumstances, might have been a caress. In this case, she recognized it as a threatening gesture, letting her know he could have those long fingers around her neck in an instant. She gasped, both at the thought of him strangling her and because she was finally able to take a full breath for the first time since he'd first muffled her mouth with his hand.

He grabbed her upper arm just below the shoulder and clamped his fingers into her flesh like a vise. She couldn't help but wince and was surprised when he relaxed his hold just enough for her to notice. She might have mistaken that for a sign of tenderheartedness had it not been for the sharp prick of the knife point which his other hand kept against her side. He pulled her along next to him out from the shelter of the trees.

He held her at an angle away from the open road so that his body blocked any view of the knife from that direction. He was also blocking her view of the road. She could see the zoo entrance off to the right. That area was deserted. She could also see the line of park benches just in front of them and the walk beyond. There was a low wrought-iron fence behind the benches. He nudged her to climb over it, and she did. He followed. He had picked a spot where there was a space between the benches, and he pulled her through that space. They were on the asphalt walk now. She could feel him looking off to the left, but she had no idea what he was seeing there. The sound of the music was louder now and seemed to come from that vicinity. This vague conclusion was all she had to go on in trying to guess if there might be other people within sighting distance. This was her only hope, and she had no choice but to act on it.

Bennett took a single deep breath to focus her strength. Then she lunged. She must have caught her captor off guard for a moment because she managed to get an arm's length ahead of him. She looked left, and there they were, not as close as she would have preferred but close enough to see. Half-a-dozen kids, boys and girls of indeterminate adolescent age, all dancing to the boom box they'd set down on the curb. The music was louder than it sounded back in the woods. She doubted she'd be able to shout over it, but she tried anyway.

"Help," she yelled at the top of her lungs, and started jumping up and down and waving her one free arm. "Please, help me."

They didn't appear to hear what she was saying, and their reaction to her jumping and frantic gestures was hardly what she would have expected. The couple of kids who were paying any attention to her at all started jumping up and down and waving their arms, too. Bennett didn't want to believe her eyes. They thought she was showing them a dance step, and they were joining in. Before she could think of some other way to signal them of her real situation, she was back in the strong-arm man's clutches again, and the kids down the road had turned back to their friends. Bennett, meanwhile, was being dragged to the other side of the road. She barely missed stumbling through a clump of still-fragrant horse manure obviously left by one of the hansom cab ponies that frequented this corner of the park during zoo hours.

"Fat lot of good that did you," he rasped in her ear, so close she could feel the heat in his words.

They had reached a two-foot wall of boulders on the other side of the roadway. She could tell he intended to mount them. She fully expected him to leap onto the rocks, as he was certainly tall enough to do easily, then drag her up their rough surface behind him. Instead, he grabbed her by the waist and lifted her then jumped up beside her. She was only mildly surprised at how easily he did that and how little apparent effort it required of him. She had already witnessed ample evidence of his physical prowess. What astonished her was that he did it at all. Why not simply drag her along like a worthless bag of bones? Was he trying not to hurt her? And why hadn't he used the knife on her as he threatened? Could there be a soft spot in his steely hardness after all?

As if to dispel that notion, he locked her upper arm in a painful grip and began climbing the hillside in front of them with her in tow. She had no idea where they were going and no choice but to follow. She did her best to keep up so she wouldn't find herself being hauled along on bloodied knees over the gravelly ground. He had slowed the pace a bit on the incline. They were back among trees again. She would have liked to ask where they were headed, but she found she had just enough breath to keep up with him. All of this manhandling had knocked the wind out of her.

Suddenly he yanked her up next to him, closer than she wanted to be. She could feel the jut of his hip through her thin silk dress and the hardness of his thigh below that hip. She was about to pull away enough so her body wouldn't be touching his when she saw movement amidst a clump of shadows she had assumed to be bushes. Two partly upright forms arose, probably human, though she couldn't see well enough in the dark to know for sure. She had heard and read about the people who frequented this place at night. Some were homeless and had made the park their residence. Others were predators and had made the park their stalking ground. Bennett remembered what her captor had said about there being worse animals in this place than he was. She hadn't believed that at the time. Just now, she wasn't so sure.

She didn't pull away from him as she had started to do. She let him hold her pressed against his side as they proceeded over the hill. He didn't hurry his pace or give any sign that he might be as apprehensive as she was. Still, something about the way he was breathing and the tautness of his arm where it circled her waist told her he was fully alert to possible danger and ready to strike out against it if need be. She couldn't help but be grateful for that. She understood how confused that was. He was her enemy, not her salvation. He was the one who had forced her into this perilous place. Still, she couldn't help knowing that, given her limited alternatives at the moment, she would rather be encircled by the leather-clad arm of this imposing man than at the mercy of whoever might be lurking in those bushes.

Chapter Five

"Where are you taking me?"

"I told you to keep your mouth shut."

Bennett had dug her heels in at the top of the hill and refused to budge. "Who is going to hear me?"

"Look, lady, you'd better shut up and get going or I'll make you very sorry you didn't."

"Then go ahead and make me sorry. I'm not moving till you tell me where you intend on taking me."

Instead of answering, he clamped on to her upper arm again and dragged her partway down the hill before she could regain enough leverage to make him stop. They were just above the path that circled the park pond. There were street lamps around the periphery of the pond, old-fashioned carriage lamps that were more atmospheric than illuminating. Nevertheless, they allowed her to do what had not really been possible before—get a look at his face. What she saw surprised her.

She had expected a coarse hoodlum, but he wasn't that at all. Staring at him now, she was reminded of the impression she'd had of a clean breeze in her first scent of him. He looked clean-cut, as well, with chiseled features that were classically handsome and not the least bit brutish. She revised her earlier assessment to observe that he could have been a member of her family's set after all, only with obviously different life experience. It occurred to her that this didn't look like the face of a murderer, at least not a cold-hearted one. If she was right, maybe she could use that to her advantage.

"I don't think you're going to use that knife on me," Bennett said. "I don't think you want to carry me the rest of the way, either. That would slow you down too much."

She was stalling for time, and she suspected he knew it. She had seen the pathway ahead and knew it was the one spot around here where someone at least halfway non-threatening was likely to come along. She intended to delay him at this place for as long as she possibly could. He began to drag her once more. She crouched closer to the ground, forcing him to strain against her shoe heels dug into the soft earth. She knew that wouldn't stop him altogether, but it was sure to slow him down some.

Meanwhile, what Bennett was hoping for came to pass. She heard voices down the path and looked up to see two figures emerging from the shadows that led to the park interior. She couldn't tell if it was a man and a woman or two men, but they were moving at a brisk pace. She opened her mouth to call out and raised her arm to wave at the same moment she realized her captor had heard the strollers, too. That didn't daunt her any. She reasoned that whatever he might do to silence her would simply arouse suspicion against him and give the signal that she needed help. Unfortunately, there was one means of silencing her that she had not thought of.

Before she had time to utter a sound or get her arm into the air, he had stepped in front of her, blocking the view of her from the path. In the same swift movement, he clamped his arms around her, pressing both of her own against her sides. She gasped at the force with which this unexpected embrace pulled her to him. Even more unexpected was the pressure of his lips over hers as he bent her backward in a fierce kiss. She tried to escape, but she could barely move at all within his powerful arms. She tried to twist her mouth away from his, but her neck was angled backward too far to allow much maneuvering.

She squirmed against him, and he took advantage of that, sliding one arm down just beneath her buttocks and lifting her off the ground against him. In that position, her wriggling hips appeared to be intent upon something much different from escape. Her thinking was shocked and muddled, but not so much so that she failed to realize what he was accomplishing. From the path below, they would look like they were locked in a passionate and mutual embrace.

In the meantime, something else equally incredible was happening. He had lifted her several inches off the ground so that her body pressed against his. He had jutted his hips forward, probably to assist in keeping her captive in that position. He moved his legs apart slightly and pushed one of her thighs between them, locking it there with his own. Perhaps he was trying to control her squirming so he could hold on to her more firmly, but the result was more intimate than that. His body apparently couldn't help but respond to hers. She could feel the hard evidence of his rapidly mounting arousal through the fragile material of her dress.

Bennett doubled her efforts to escape, thrashing against him with all her might. In answer, a moan rose from his throat. Suddenly she was truly afraid. She had been ready to face being a hostage, kidnapped against her will with only her wits to depend on. She was confident enough in herself to know those wits would stand her in good stead. Right now, however, she would need more than cleverness to save her from what she dreaded was about to happen. This man was fully capable of dragging her back into the shadows, throwing her to the ground and raping her. He had the brute strength to do that. The sound of his groan told her he also had the inclination.

She had to do something. If he managed to get her down on the ground, she would feel around for a stone or a stick and bludgeon him with it. She would make whatever noise she could manage. She wouldn't let herself be— Her desperate thoughts were suddenly interrupted by something almost as unexpected as her captor's kiss. He moved his arm from beneath her and let her drop to the ground. Then he pushed her away from him. When she opened her mouth, maybe to scream, maybe only in surprise, he clamped his hand over it while he continued to hold her at arm's length.

He didn't speak right away. She could hear the raggedness of his breath and guessed that he was not yet able to talk. She was breathing hard herself, gasping against his palm. She could feel her breast rise and fall violently beneath her disarrayed dress. She saw his gaze move downward toward that heaving and felt his grip tighten on her arm. Then he looked quickly away, turning his head in the direction of the path where the two strollers had long since passed by on their way out of the park. She heard him taking deep, deliberate breaths apparently to compose himself. When he turned back to look at her, she could not see his eyes in the darkness, but she could feel their intensity burning into her.

"You are going to come with me now, and you are not going to give me any more trouble." His voice was low and rasping, almost tortured, but also very determined. "Otherwise, I will drag you back into those woods and do to you what you know I have in mind. Then, when I'm finished, I'll throw you to those trolls we saw back there so they can do the same."

Before he had let go of her a moment ago, Bennett might have believed that threat. Her instincts told her different, that if he was the type of man who took a woman against her will, he would be carrying her off to do that right now. Still there was something in his voice besides determination. That something was rage, and Bennett heard it. Her instincts also told her she had better not challenge that anger, at least not at this moment. When he turned to stalk the rest of the way down the hill, she let him pull her along with him.

WHAT IN HELL HAD HE BEEN thinking of? To grab her like that and kiss her the way he did. What had been in his mind? What possessed him? Possessed is right, Memphis thought. But it didn't have much to do with his mind.

He'd been too long on board ship, but that had happened before. He'd also been staying away from women, except for some talk maybe, for what seemed like forever. The way he lived—a few weeks in port, then off at sea again to wherever his crew captain job took him—wasn't good for what you'd call a relationship. That was a big attraction at first, being free and in the wind. Lately, all that freedom had been getting a little old, and a lot lonely.

Maybe that explained what had happened on the hill. That and the way her pale skin looked against her black dress and, even more than that, the way she stood up to him no matter how scared she had to be. He'd probably been wanting to kiss her all along. He just didn't realize it until he actually had his arms around her. The rest of it . . . well, that happened without him ever planning it. Luckily he'd gotten himself under control before any real damage was done. Now he had to make sure nothing like that happened again. He had to keep his mind, and his other organs, focused on what had to get done tonight. His survival could depend on it.

They'd made it down the path to the curve of the lake. Looking up, he could see the tops of skyscrapers dotted with window lights above the trees that bordered the park. Traffic sounds from the street beyond the trees were muffled by the shrubbery. The path ahead was both isolated and empty.

Memphis guessed they wouldn't be running into too many civic-minded citizens here, the kind who might call the cops if they saw a guy in leather hauling along a classy woman in a cocktail dress. The types who might hang out around here at night wouldn't be likely to call the cops about anything. They just might have more than a passing acquaintance with the wrong side of the law, themselves.

To their right along the meandering pathway, a tumble of rocks sloped downward to the water. In the shimmering lamp glow he could make out a bridge arching over the middle of the pond, too quaint to be in tune with this damned nightmare he'd stumbled into. The globe lights at a subway entrance were visible above the trees to his left, and they glowed red. That meant the subway was closed, just like most ways of getting out of this mess seemed to be closed to him right now.

"Can I have a drink of water?"

He had been so lost in trying to think up a way to escape that he'd almost forgotten he was still dragging her along behind him till she spoke. He responded with a blank stare.

"The fountain," she said, gesturing toward a spigot between two benches at the side of the path. "I need a drink."

"Sure," he said. For the moment, he couldn't seem to come up with a reason to say no. He held her at arm's length while she drank, just in case she tried to flip water in his eyes or some smart trick like that.

She wiped her mouth with the back of her free hand. He was thinking how ordinary a gesture that was for someone as unordinary looking as her, when he noticed that she was staring ahead of them along the path. He followed her stare to a group of three guys hanging out on one of the benches a number of yards away. Squinting through the gloom, Memphis made out a fourth flopped down on the slope between the benches. Memphis gripped her arm tighter. He told himself he probably didn't have much to worry about from these punks—unless they decided they liked the looks of what they thought was his woman and tried to take her away from him. She must have been thinking the same thing, because she suddenly stopped straining to get away from him and shrank closer to his side.

Memphis hung back for a minute, but he knew there was no turning around now. The janitor at the Stuyvesant had to have called the cops. Memphis was surprised he hadn't heard sirens shrieking after him by now. Keep on going. That was all he could do. He made himself walk at an easy pace while he gave the once-over to the troops on the bench. None of them were his size, but together they could be a problem. He felt her shiver beneath his hand even though the night was pretty warm. She was afraid of the tough guys on the bench, maybe even more afraid than she was of him. After all, he'd had plenty of chances to hurt her. The worst he'd done was kiss her a little too hard. He'd even put a stop to that himself. He was pretty sure these characters on the benches wouldn't be so considerate.

"Stick close to me," he said, speaking low and circling her with his arm. "There may be more of them in the bushes."

He felt her head nod slightly against his jacket. He could almost hear her fear in the shallow breaths she was taking.

"Don't be scared," he said. "You'll be all right." He knew how crazy that sounded coming from him, since he was the one dragging her around in the first place. He also knew he didn't mean her any real harm. He was the Southern Gent after all. On the other hand, these park crawlers weren't likely to be gents from any direction.

He could see a break in the benches and a set of wide stone steps up ahead to the left. Those steps had to lead to the street. He'd hoped to stay inside the park a while longer, but he'd have to take his chances with the street—if he could just get both of them there in one piece.

"What you got there, buddy?" The question came in a sneering tone from one of the bench punks and was followed by a low whistle from another.

Memphis pulled her closer and kept walking. These guys looked even more like trouble now than they had at a distance. They were dressed a lot like Memphis was, in jeans and leather jackets, but he knew that was as far as the similarity went. He was basically a good guy. These guys very possibly were not.

"How about sharing, pal?"

It was the same sneering tone. Memphis could pick out who it came from this time. He was at the center of the others, probably their leader. His face would have been ugly and hard even without the leer on it. He was thinking about making a challenge. Memphis could feel it. With his back to the water like this, he wouldn't be in a good defensive position if they jumped him. He needed to keep that from happening.

Memphis had spent enough time in the streets to know the importance of attitude. A tough profile could be the best defense when a situation got down to the ground like this one was doing. He pulled himself up tall, to his full six feet two inches, and squared his shoulders. He could feel the muscles tighten into bands under his jacket. He was ready to fight if he had to. His posture would make that plain to anybody who was into the body language of the street. He turned and looked directly into the sneering face of the leader. Memphis fixed his eyes on that face and made his own as hard as steel. It was a bluff, and he knew it. They'd know it, too, but they could decide to respect his nerve in facing them down. That was the way it worked on the street.

At the same time as he was putting on this tough-guy act, Memphis kept moving toward the stone steps with the woman under his arm almost out of sight behind his body. The characters on the bench made no move to stand up or follow. They just watched and made low, rumbling noises among themselves. Then the leader nodded his head slightly. Memphis put himself on alert in case that was a signal for this crew to go on the attack. Instead, they all relaxed onto the benches. The nod had been an acknowledgment of Memphis, as one tough guy to another. He nodded in return, then deliberately moved his gaze away from the benches to the path ahead.

He would have liked to keep watching them, but that wasn't the right attitude to show them. He had to be very cool. He took even strides toward the steps, forcing himself not to move as fast as he wanted to out of there. All the time, he listened for the sound of a surprise attack coming from behind. He didn't take another full breath till he was pretty much sure that attack wasn't going to happen.

They reached the stone steps and started up. He glanced back and saw the benches at the bend of the path. The punks were there watching. They would have made their move already if they had one in mind. Memphis felt relieved even though he knew how crazy that was, considering all the bad surprises he might still have to face tonight.

Chapter Six

"We're coming to the street now, and I'd better not have any trouble from you. Okay?"

Bennett could hardly believe he was asking for her cooperation. Why would she want to cooperate with him anyway? He'd been dragging her around like a piece of furniture for about as long as she could stand now. The shoes she had on were medium-heeled but not meant for jogging through the park, and her feet were starting to hurt. She could feel a huge run up the side of her stockings, and all of this dashing around had her sweaty and out of sorts in general. Being taken hostage and fending off hoodlums in the park was not what she'd had in mind as a cure for her restlessness.

"No, it is not okay," she said, suddenly not caring if the irritation in her voice was diplomatic or not in this situation. "I'm not moving one step farther until you tell me where we are headed and what's going on here."

She'd planted herself firmly on the broad step. She knew he was easily strong enough to pick her up and carry her along with him wherever he wanted to take her. Once again, she also knew that transporting her forcibly would slow him down and make him more conspicuous than he wanted to be. She might have felt a moment of gratitude toward him for getting her away from those gang boys back there, but those feelings had quickly faded once the danger was past. He was the one who had put her in danger. She wasn't going to make life easy for him because he had to save her neck along with his own.

If he understood that, he gave no sign of anything but the opposite. Even in the dim light from the pedestal lamps along the stairway wall, she could see his face darken into a more truly menacing expression than he had worn before. For one fearful moment, she wondered if she might be pushing him too hard. Yet again, maybe she was getting to be more like him. Maybe she didn't have much to lose. If he was going to kill her eventually, he might as well make his try now. In the meantime, she was gambling that murder wasn't really in his plans again tonight. He brandished the knife in front of her face, as if to let her know just how dangerous a gamble that was.

"I told you I didn't want any trouble from you," he said through clenched teeth.

"Well, you're giving me trouble, and I don't want it, either. What's your name, anyway?"

"What?"

He looked thrown off track and confused. She supposed that was the effect she wanted, though she didn't have any clear-cut strategy for dealing with him. She was simply tired of being dragged around and even more tired of feeling totally out of control of what was happening to her.

"I said I want to know your name, or I don't budge from this spot."

He hauled on her arm and managed to drag her a few inches, but only with difficulty against her concerted resistance. She had stiffened herself into something very close to dead weight to manage that resistance. She wasn't sure how much longer her strength would last for doing that.

"What the hell," he muttered, easing his attempt to force her to move. "For whatever it's worth to you, my name is

Memphis Modine. I don't have a criminal record. I don't have much of a record of anything, so it won't do you any good to memorize my name and pass it on to your cop friends if that's what you've got in mind.''

''I'd say that won't be true any longer after tonight.''

''What won't be true?''

''That you have no police record.'' Bennett wasn't sure she could believe that anyway.

''You're talking about the woman back at that Stuyvesant place, aren't you? I didn't do that.''

Something else not to believe. Yet it occurred to Bennett that she had never considered the possibility he hadn't done the murder.

''You were leaning over her dead body,'' she said.

''I found her like that, just like you found me. Just before you came in, I'd felt her pulse and found out she was dead.''

''You told me you killed her.''

''I was trying to scare you into doing what I wanted. And I never actually said I did it. Didn't you notice that the knife was still on the floor when you came in? I had to pick it up to point it at you.''

''You could have put it down beside her then picked it up again.'' All Bennett could remember was the knife in his hand. She had been too shocked before that to notice anything and too frightened afterward to recall it if she had.

''Well, I didn't put it down and pick it up again. It happened just like I told you. Besides, what do I care what you think? You're coming with me or else.''

Bennett thought about asking ''or else what?'' but decided against it. She wasn't sure how much pushing this guy could take. She did want to stall him a while longer, though she had her doubts about what that could accomplish. If anybody was on their trail to rescue her, they would have caught up by now, or so she guessed.

"Is that really your name?" she asked. "What did you say it was?"

"Memphis Modine. And, yes, it really is my name," he said, some of the growl returning to his voice.

"That's quite an unusual name," she said, still anchored firmly to the step. "Are you from Tennessee?"

"Look, lady, I don't have time to tell you my life story right now."

"Bennett," she said. "My name isn't Lady. It's Bennett."

"And you made fun of my name? Who ever heard of a woman named Bennett?"

"It's a family name." She didn't add that women in her circle often did have men's first names. Thurston, Wallace and Wendell were all girlfriends of hers from school. But she was trying to make him relax his control a little. Reminding him of the differences in their social backgrounds wasn't likely to do that.

"Is yours a family name?" she asked.

"I don't know," he said.

His tone spoke much more to her than just those words. He didn't know because he didn't know his family. She guessed that and knew it was only a guess, but she also sensed it to be true. She thought of the kids in the foundling home. Maybe having been around them so much was the reason she understood what he had meant by those three words. She didn't say anything more. She didn't intend to go all softhearted toward him by any means. He had taken her with him against her will and done his best to terrorize her.

Even so, when he tugged at her arm again to move her along with him, she no longer resisted. She was going to make a run for it when they reached the street anyway. Then she'd turn him in as soon as she could get to a phone and call the police. Let them sort out what was or wasn't true about his claims of innocence. She was surprised to feel a twinge of something close to guilt for thinking that.

He still had a tight grip on her arm as they reached the top of the stone steps, too tight a grip for her to break loose. She didn't know where the knife might be, possibly in his hand inside the pocket of his leather jacket. She couldn't tell. She looked around at the scene from the top of the steps. A tall equestrian statue loomed to her left. She was too preoccupied to remember which war hero it represented. There wasn't much pedestrian traffic on this side of the street at this hour because of the menacing prospect of being too close to the denizens of the park in their nighttime lair. Cars drove by on the roadway. She contemplated whether running out among them was more likely to get her helped or hurt.

Down the street, along Central Park South to her right, hansom cabs were parked at the curb, hoping to pick up fares for the most popular of the city's hansom rides through the park. The drivers were out of their cabs, hanging around and chatting in small groups. Bennett deduced that Memphis would head in that direction, trying to put as much distance as possible between himself and the Stuyvesant Club. When they came abreast of the drivers, she would make her move. She knew for a fact that many, even most, of the city's carriage drivers were Irish, and the Irish had a tendency toward chivalry. She would depend on that tendency to come to her rescue. She had few alternatives for hope of escape at the moment.

Memphis Modine had been making his own perusal of the street. Now he turned them to the right, just as she had anticipated. He wrapped his arm around her again, pinning both of hers to her sides. In New York City, where most people tended to mind their own business and expected others to do the same, no one was likely to take more than passing notice of an embracing couple on the street. Even if their behavior did appear a bit odd, it would probably not merit more than a glance. Odd behavior was commonplace in New York. It was the gallantry of the hack drivers or nothing, and even they didn't appear to be paying much attention as Bennett and Memphis passed by.

Maybe he had some inkling of her plans for escape, because suddenly she knew where the knife was. He had reached across with his free arm under his jacket and had the blade pointed into her side hard enough so she could feel it. She wondered if a knife like that one could cut through leather. She remembered it was a hunting knife. They were used for dressing out deer and the like, so very possibly slashing through leather would be no problem. The thought made her shudder.

"Are you cold?" he asked.

She shook her head, thinking how strange a question that was. Why would a hostage-taker be concerned about the comfort of the hostage he had taken, especially when he was the cause of the discomfort in the first place? That didn't make sense. Again, as she had been when she got her first glance at his face, she was struck by how little this guy resembled a murderer. What did a murderer look like anyway? Wasn't anybody capable of killing somebody else given the right circumstances? Wasn't this man in so much trouble that these could be considered the right circumstances for him?

Bennett glanced over her shoulder. Behind her and across the street, the spotlighted facade of the Plaza Hotel dominated the corner. The entrance to the Oak Room was only a sprint away. Bennett had been at the Plaza, in the Palm Court for brunch, just this past week. She and her mother had lunch every Christmas, and sometimes in between, in the Edwardian Room. Bennett recalled the chandeliers and lofty ceilings. She couldn't help wondering if she would ever have lunch in the Edwardian Room again, at that table she liked best, next to one of the tall windows with their lush draperies. The thought of draperies jolted her back to the present. The woman on the floor of the billiard room had been shrouded in drapery pulled down from a tall window. Bennett shuddered again at the memory. Her captor clutched her closer in response once more.

"Take it easy," he said. "You'll get out of this all right. All you have to do is be smart and listen to what I tell you."

Bennett didn't reply. She let what he had said rerun through her mind. She was sure she'd heard a softening in his voice, a hint of concern. She was wondering what that might mean and if there was some chance she could use it in her own behalf, when she heard a screech of brakes just ahead. A long, dark sports car had veered over to the curb between two hansoms. Bennett stared. There was something familiar about that car. She had been so concentrated on running and being scared for what felt like so long now, that she needed a second to orient herself.

Then she realized what she was seeing. That was Royce Boudreaux's classic Jaguar roadster. She was almost certain of it. Her heart leapt beneath her breast. Her captor dragged her painfully against him and growled under his breath. Her elation subsided. He had seen the car, too. What match could Royce possibly be to a desperate murderer with a knife in his hand? Royce was among the last men she would consider as equal to hand-to-hand combat. The passenger side door opened, and a long leg emerged. She knew instantly that this was indeed Royce's car and also that Quint was with him in it. Suddenly she was truly afraid, more so than she had been at any other moment of this ordeal.

Chapter Seven

Memphis knew there was trouble even before she gasped and stiffened. He'd heard the car screech to a stop. He could see it now, nosed in behind one of those white carriages. The car was an old-timer, one of those long sports jobs that cost so much to keep on the road only rich folks can afford them. Memphis snapped two and two together and came up with the Stuyvesant Club. That janitor had put somebody on their tail, and here they were.

Memphis knew he didn't have many choices of what do do, especially not with this Bennett woman in tow. She was supposed to be a hostage, but he wasn't using her like one. That was probably because he didn't like the idea of it. Taking a woman and using her as a human shield wasn't something an upright guy would do. Unfortunately, the spot he was in meant he couldn't be too fussy. Upright or not, he had to take any advantage that came his way.

Memphis still had Bennett clamped next to him with her arms pinned to her sides. He pulled her around so she was directly in front of him, positioned between him and the sports car. He pulled her across the pavement away from the curbside until they were backed up against the park wall. That way he only had to keep watch to the front and sides. Two guys had gotten out of the car by then, a tall, well-built one from the passenger side and a lankier type from the driver's side. They were on the sidewalk now and coming on fast.

The carriage drivers were beginning to take notice of what was going on. The bunch closest to Memphis had stopped talking among themselves and turned around to watch. He could guess which way they'd go once they'd sized up the situation. With the drivers across the way and the guys from the car coming up on his right, Memphis had no choice but to play the hostage card. He pulled the knife out from under his jacket and brought it around in front of her face where everybody could see it.

"Remember back in that club of yours when I told you I was backed into a corner and had nothing to lose?" he whispered next to her ear.

"I remember," she said. She didn't sound as scared as he would have hoped she'd be, but she was a cool one. Maybe she was scared to death and just not letting it show.

"That was nothing compared to how desperate I am right now. You keep that in mind in case you should get any ideas about making some smart move on me."

For once, she didn't talk back.

"I don't want to hurt you," he added, "but I will if I have to."

He probably shouldn't have told her he didn't want to hurt her. Real tough guys liked hurting people. Memphis figured she'd seen too much of his act by now to believe he was that tough anyway. She did still believe he'd killed that girl back at the Stuyvesant Club, but that wasn't likely to cut much ice with her if she saw a chance to give him the slip. He had more chance of controlling the other guys than of keeping her in line. With that in mind, he moved the knife blade next to her throat and glared over her shoulder at the gang lined up against him.

"Take your hands off her," the tall, well-built one yelled.

"Stop right where you are," Memphis warned in his best tough-guy voice. "You come any closer and I'll have to cut her."

That stopped them, the muscular one out front and the lanky one just behind.

"Bennett, are you all right?" the tall one asked.

"Yes, Quint," she said. "He hasn't hurt me."

"I haven't hurt her yet," Memphis added, "but I can and I will."

"Don't worry, Bennett," the one she called Quint said. "I will take care of this."

Memphis heard something in that besides just friendly interest. Maybe she was his girl. Memphis could tell by the way she'd gone rigid against him that she was too scared now to keep from letting it show. Maybe she cared something special about this guy and didn't want anything bad to happen to him. Memphis could use that.

"Tell him to back off," Memphis said low enough for only her to hear. "I'll take him on if I have to. He'd be no match for me even without this blade in my hand. I'm a street fighter, and he's not. You know that's the truth."

Memphis could almost feel her considering those words.

"Tell him," Memphis growled, and jerked her harder against him. "Or you're going to have his blood on your hands."

Memphis was just saying what he had to say to get the job done. He wasn't sure whether he could follow through on his threats or not. He was only sure that he had to get these guys out of his face while he planned what to do next.

"Don't come any closer, Quint," she said. "I don't know what he's capable of."

"I'd say he's capable of just about anything." That was the other one talking. He'd moved up next to Quint. "He's already done one murder tonight. What matter could it be to him to do another?"

So they'd found that girl's body, then snapped their own two and two together to come up with good old Memphis as the guilty party. He wanted to say it wasn't true, but that wasn't the smart thing to do right now.

"You got that on the money," Memphis said. Speaking of money, he wondered if one of these dudes was the guy who'd gotten him to come to the Stuyvesant for his pay in the first place. "I've got nothing to lose by taking her out and maybe you guys along with her." Memphis was getting sick of hearing himself say he had nothing to lose. He didn't like how true it sounded.

"Hey there, what's going on here?" one of the carriage drivers called out in a heavy brogue from the curbside.

"You guys stay out of this," Memphis said, and glowered at the driver while still keeping an eye on the two from the sports car.

"Why don't you just leave the lass be, man?" the driver coaxed as he took a step toward Memphis.

"Hold your ground," Memphis said, "or I'll have to hurt her." He brandished the knife very near her face to show he was serious.

"Okay. Okay." The driver lifted his hands in a gesture of surrender and stepped back. "Don't go doing anything rash."

"I'll do what you guys force me to do," Memphis said, making himself sound so menacing he almost believed it himself.

"You'll do what I tell you, and you will do it this instant." That came from the lanky guy, the one Memphis wouldn't have figured for being so forceful. Then he noticed what the guy had in his hand and where he had it pointed.

"Royce," Bennett cried out. "Put the gun away. You'll only make things worse."

"How much worse can things possibly be?" Royce asked, and kept the muzzle leveled straight at them.

Memphis had to sit on the impulse to pull her behind him. The only chance he had was that this guy wouldn't hurt her. Memphis had already started moving, pulling her along with him, in the direction they'd been headed before these two cowboys horned in.

"Do what Bennett says, Royce," her boyfriend chimed in. "There's too much possibility you'll hit her if you shoot."

Memphis decided to head for the car, which just might have the keys in it. If that didn't turn out to be the case, he'd have to make a run for it, maybe let her go after all and just take off as fast as his legs could carry him. But probably not fast enough to outrun a bullet.

"Trust me, Quint," the one called Royce was saying. "I'm a masterful shot."

That was exactly what Memphis didn't want to hear, and something in old Royce's tone said it was true. Still, that wasn't the thing that made Memphis stop short for a second before it flashed through his mind that he had to make that dash for it now. He was looking straight into Royce's eyes. What Memphis saw there was that this guy was going to shoot. He had Bennett in his sights just as sure as he had Memphis there, but that didn't seem to matter. The glint in Royce's eyes signaled loud and clear that he was about a hair away from pulling the trigger.

Before that hairsbreadth of time could pass, Memphis did just about the stupidest act of his life. He pulled Bennett around behind him and held her there. He kept moving up the street all the time he did that, positioning himself between her and the shooter and pushing her along. She wasn't resisting, the way Memphis would have expected her to do. Maybe she'd gotten a good look at Royce's eyes, too. She must know that Royce had a clear, clean shot straight to

Memphis's heart. He could see that himself and it nearly took his breath away. Memphis steeled himself for facing his last minute on earth.

The thing he least expected happened next. Quint grabbed Royce's arm and started wrestling him for the gun. Royce was shouting protests, but Quint kept on struggling to take the gun from Royce's grasp. Memphis knew what he had to do. He tightened his grip on Bennett's arm and started to run toward the car. He didn't like turning his back on the scramble for the gun, but he had to make the best time possible and he could move a lot faster forward than backward.

The car hadn't looked that far away, but now that he was trying to get there quickly he felt as if he had miles to go. He still held Bennett in front of him out of the line of fire. She kept trying to see past him.

"Get a move on," Memphis said. "That guy's just as likely to hit you as me no matter how good a shot he says he is."

As if to prove that true, a shot rang out, and Memphis thought he might have heard it zing by.

"Quint!" Bennett cried out. She tried to run past Memphis, but he held her tightly.

Memphis looked back to see the two men still grappling.

"You're coming with me," he said, and started running with even more speed this time.

They were almost to the car. He didn't need her to start giving him a hard time now, but that was just what she did. She pulled against his grip and made him drag her along.

Memphis stopped dead in his tracks. "Bennett," he said forcefully, calling her by her name for the first time. "If we get out of here, maybe old Royce there will stop trying to shoot your boyfriend or you or me or anybody else he gets a bead on."

She took a second to let that sink in before he could feel her resistance go slack. He pushed her the rest of the way to the car and around to the driver's side. He didn't have time to think the prayer that surely was in order. He had to bend down to open the low door of what he now recognized to be a Jaguar XKE. A light came on along the mahogany dashboard just as Memphis realized he'd been holding his breath waiting for this moment. He let it out again with a sigh when he saw that the prayer he hadn't spoken had been answered anyway. The key was in the ignition.

BENNETT LET HIM shove her across the driver's seat and over the gearshift in the center of the small car. She had to pull her skirt up to make it. She was no longer paying much attention to the fact that the tops of her stockings were showing. She was too busy trying to understand what had happened in the street. Memphis Modine was right about one thing. Royce had looked determined to shoot somebody, and Bennett couldn't be certain who that somebody might have turned out to be.

She remembered what her mother had said more times than Bennett could count. Royce Boudreaux is irresponsible. He is immature. He cannot be counted on. Bennett had always known that was at least partly true. Till tonight, however, she hadn't understood that a person as irresponsible as Royce might also be dangerous.

She had never had a gun pointed at her before. Now she knew that it didn't matter whether the one with his finger on the trigger was supposed to be friend or foe. At the moment of staring down the black hole of a gun barrel, that gunman became the enemy.

But what about Quint? "I have to go back," she said, and groped for the door handle on her side.

"No," Memphis shouted as he turned the ignition key and the car engine roared to life. He grabbed her wrist with one hand while he grasped the steering wheel with the other. "All you'll do by going back there is maybe get your boyfriend killed. Besides, I'm not letting you out of this car."

As if to prove that, he let go of her arm long enough to switch gears into reverse and gun the car backward into the street. He must have driven one of these British models before. She knew they had a different way of shifting from other cars. Yet he hadn't ground the gears at all in executing their exit from the curb. He shifted again, and they sped forward, too fast for a takeoff into city traffic. Fortunately this lane was empty ahead of them, and cars must have slowed down behind. She heard some angry honking from that direction, but Memphis didn't appear to pay it much mind. He was too busy steering and shifting and checking the rear and side mirrors, perhaps to see if Royce and Quint had taken up the pursuit.

Bennett considered the possibility of opening her door and jumping out of the car. They were moving a little too fast for that at the moment, but she might be able to manage it when he had to slow down at a corner or for a traffic light. Unless he had no intention of slowing down for anything. He wouldn't want to attract police attention. But then, the police were sure to be after them soon if they weren't already, and this car would be fairly easy to spot even in Manhattan traffic. Mr. Modine kept saying that he had nothing left to lose so he might as well take whatever risks presented themselves. That probably included taking on some of the most aggressive drivers in the world. Bennett wondered if she might not be in even more danger now than she had been during the rest of this perilous evening. Then she remembered the streetlight shining off the barrel of Royce's gun. Playing chicken with New York cabbies was certainly less risky than facing a firearm in the hands of a fool.

"Where are we going?" It seemed she was always asking him that.

"I'll be damned if I know," he said.

He doesn't know his way around the city, she thought, and I do. There had to be some advantage in that.

They were headed west on Central Park South, toward Columbus Circle. He was still moving the car fast and recklessly, though he did maneuver in and out of lanes with skill. Bennett wondered if he had really meant to let her know he was unfamiliar with the city. That seemed like a blunder to her.

"What I do know," he said, as if reading her thoughts, "is that I'm getting us out of this part of town. Your part of town. I know my way around enough to do that. I have to keep driving in this direction till we're just about ready to drop into the river. Then I head downtown."

He was right about one thing. The part of the city he was talking about, the Far West Side, was definitely not her side of town. She knew it only vaguely from having driven through it on occasion, but she didn't have much specific knowledge of those neighborhoods. Still, she would probably know her way around better than he did. She reassured herself of that as he screeched off Central Park South and launched into the crowded traffic circle around the statue of Christopher Columbus.

She noted that he drove with confidence, as if he knew these streets like the back of his hand. Maybe he wouldn't need to slow down or stop after all. Maybe he was like one of those cabbies with a natural talent for weaving through traffic without a hitch no matter how heavy the congestion. If that was the case, she wouldn't be likely to have the opportunity to jump clear of the car. She would have to look for some other means of escape. Giving up and settling passively into captivity was simply not an option for the daughter of Dilys St. Simon.

Bennett looked around the car. The glove compartment was just above her knees, but she doubted she could get it open without Memphis noticing, especially since it very possibly had a light inside. She wasn't sure what she would find inside anyway. Maybe something to stick him in the hand with and make him slow down long enough for her to get out. That seemed too harebrained a plan to work even if she could find a weapon of some kind. Speaking of which, she wondered where exactly the knife was right now. He wasn't holding it, so he must have put it back into his pocket in order to drive. Or—her heart skipped a hopeful beat—maybe he had laid it down in his lap and she could make a grab for it.

She was careful not to be obvious about shifting her glance in his direction and downward. The light from the dashboard wasn't very bright, but she could make out the front of his tight jeans below his open leather jacket. She had to stare to see in the dim light. There was nothing in his lap. She squinted to see the space between his thighs more clearly. All she could detect there was the full bulge beneath his pants, which definitely was not the hunting knife. Even making that observation silently to herself caused her to blush, and she glanced quickly away.

"If you're looking to get out of this car, you can forget about it," he said.

He had seen her jerk her head too fast away from staring at his crotch. She said nothing in reply. He was probably right that she couldn't get out of this car. She had better concentrate on some other course of action. What could that be? Leaving some kind of trail to be followed would be one possibility, but she couldn't think of any way of managing that. She had a vision of Hansel and Gretel in the woods, dropping crumbs that were immediately snapped up by birds. She understood exactly how futile their efforts had been. She was beginning to feel equally stymied herself.

She sighed and hung her head for a moment as a wave of what felt like resignation to defeat washed over her. What she saw on the car console made hope leap into her heart once more.

Chapter Eight

Bennett preferred that her automobile be a place where people couldn't get to her, so she wasn't as familiar with mobile phones as she might have been. Still, she'd used a similar model in Forth's car and was fairly certain she could manage this one. Now, if Royce had done his part by programming some numbers into the automatic dialing memory, she would be all set. She had figured out a way to send a message, a cry for help. She understood, of course, that this was the electronic equivalent of putting a note in a bottle and casting it out to sea. She could only hope that her call for help would reach landfall.

The probability of that had a lot to do with who Royce had programmed on that first memory button. Bennett assumed it had to be somebody important in his life. With Royce, that presented interesting possibilities. His woman of the moment could have that number-one spot, or his favorite aunt who was a soft touch for a loan on a fairly regular basis, or maybe his bookie. That last was probably the most likely, which meant that Bennett's SOS might fall on ears too cynical to care. She told herself not to think about the negatives. This was her one shot at alerting somebody out there to her whereabouts, and she had to take it.

Memphis was concentrating on traffic for the moment. Bennett took that moment to review what she knew about how this contraption worked. To make a call without lifting the receiver, she had to hit the call button. Then, instead of dialing, she would go to the memory button, and finally, to the send button. She knew that there was a speaker in the system that let everything from the other end of the line be heard in the car. That was a problem. She glanced down at the cellular console as inconspicuously as she could manage. She was looking for a control to adjust the volume of the monitor. She was sure there must be one. Unfortunately, its location was not obvious from her vantage point. If she was going to try this, she would have to risk Modine hearing both the dial tone and the phone being answered on the other end. To prevent that, she could create a noisy diversion of some kind or wait for that to happen naturally.

He had made a right turn into Columbus Circle, past a line of motorcycles to the left. The circle could be confusing even for seasoned New York City drivers. Traffic was feeding in from what seemed like a dozen directions. Cars cut in front of each other in an aggressive jockeying for position. He who hesitates is lost, as they say. Modine didn't hesitate in his circuit around the loop. So far so good, for him at least. Bennett was counting on his having more difficulty exiting the circle than he'd had getting around it. Sure enough. She got her wish.

She could tell that what he wanted to do was turn immediately west out of the circle. However, the first cross street ran one way to the east. When he saw that sign he was obviously stymied for a moment. He'd have to cut across traffic to make the turn. He darted a glance over his shoulder, probably looking for a way to cut in. That moment's hesitation accomplished exactly what Bennett had said a small prayer for. Manhattan drivers were not known for their patience, and tonight proved to be no exception to that rule. Horns began blaring immediately. Even cars to either side

of them chimed in. This was Bennett's chance. She might
not have another one. The instant he turned back to the
wheel, she moved her hand as surreptitiously as possible
over the phone unit. Modine was preoccupied at the moment, and that worked to her advantage. She hit the button
to activate the phone and started talking at the same instant.

"You'd better keep up with traffic," she said, speaking
loudly as if to be heard above the car horns. "They'll run
straight over the top of us if you don't."

She had heard the buzz of the dial tone very faintly
through the din, but that was because she was deliberately
listening for it. She glanced over at Modine. He didn't appear to have heard the noise. In the meantime, she had
moved her finger quickly to the top memory button, for the
first number programmed into Royce's system, and said
another prayer that he had actually done such programming. She had to look down again to locate the send button. She couldn't afford to make a mistake and give the
wrong command. An opportunity like this one might not
arise again. A second later, she heard just enough of the in-
itial ringing tone to know she had pressed the right button,
but she didn't take time for a sigh of relief. She began talking again immediately, more loudly still this time.

"They say this traffic circle is one of the worst in the
world to negotiate, almost as bad as the one in Rome around
the Colosseum."

She had actually never heard that at all. She'd made it up
for something to say and maybe also to rattle him even more
than he was already rattled if she could. She was coming up
with another whopper to follow that one when she heard the
phone being answered. She could tell at once that the faint
voice on the other end was coming from a machine. She had
hoped for a brief response, preferably a quick hello. Modine was almost bound to hear anything longer than that.

Then one of those strokes of good luck happened, the kind that made your heart sing. A sudden break in traffic left a space available in the lane beside them, and Modine yanked the steering wheel and tromped on the accelerator, making the powerful Jaguar engine roar to nearly deafening decibels. Bennett pretended to be shocked by the noise.

"You're breaking my eardrums," she shouted. "Can't you quiet this thing down?"

That loud lament had the exact effect she'd hoped for. "No, I can't," he shouted back, as he sped around the rest of the circle to Broadway and took a right toward downtown, the only direction open to him. "You'll just have to cover your pampered little ears and put up with it."

That exchange had been long enough to cover the message on whatever answering machine Bennett had managed to reach. She would have much preferred a real live person to receive her pleas for help. There was no telling how long it would be before this person picked up his or her messages. Still this was Bennett's single opportunity, at least at the present, to do something about getting out of her predicament. She had to grab at that chance no matter how slim it might be. She also had to make sure she said what needed to be said without alerting Modine to what she was doing.

"We're headed south on Broadway," she said.

"I can see that. I'm not totally lost in this town, you know."

"I'm your hostage. You can't blame me for being concerned about whether or not you know what you're doing. I'm also Dilys St. Simon's daughter, and she taught me to be careful whose judgment I trust. She especially wouldn't want me to trust you, because you're a murderer and a kidnapper."

"I haven't kidnapped you."

"You dragged me out of the Stuyvesant Club against my will. You forced me to go with you through Central Park.

Then you stole this car that belongs to Royce Boudreaux, his beautiful Jaguar XKE that he absolutely cherishes.'' She'd wanted to stick in the color of the car as well but thought that would sound too suspicious to Modine. ''Now you're driving way too fast trying to get to the west side of town where you don't know your way around any more than I do.''

''Is this were I turn?'' he asked. They reached the corner of Fifty-seventh Street, where traffic ran in both directions.

''You're asking me whether you should take Fifty-seventh Street? You actually think I would give you that information?''

Modine had turned right without waiting for her answer. ''I was talking to myself, not you,'' he said.

She longed to tweak his already irritated temper by asking if he talked to himself often, but sarcasm at this point wouldn't serve her more important purpose. It wouldn't send any significant data over the cellular line to the machine that was out there somewhere and could cut off recording at any time.

''Which avenue are you going to take downtown?'' she asked.

''What makes you think I want to go downtown?''

Bennett's heart skipped a beat. Had she said too much and made him suspicious? ''I thought you said a moment ago that you were headed downtown. We're moving in that general direction now.''

''I don't know which avenue I'll take. The first one I come to, I guess.''

He was streaking along, finding the most empty lane and roaring down it. He had already passed Eighth Avenue. Ninth Avenue, southbound, was coming up. He clicked on the turn signal. He was having good luck with traffic lights. This one was also green.

''You're taking Ninth Avenue,'' she said.

"Is that what you'd do?" he asked as he took the turn.

"It's one possible choice for getting downtown."

He glanced over at her. "Why would you want to tell me that? Unless it's a bum steer, of course."

If it weren't for the phone that was, she hoped, transmitting her every word, she would have tried to mislead him just as he suspected.

She shrugged. "I assume you would figure that out on your own anyway. It's where you're taking me from here that I wonder about."

"To a hotel."

"What?" She was so shocked to hear that, she forgot about the phone for a moment.

"We're going somewhere to hole up for a while."

"I don't want to hole up with you," she shouted so loudly they might have heard her in the surrounding cars if it hadn't been for the noise of the Jaguar's engine.

"You don't have any choice. I need some time to think things out. I also need to lose this car. It's too easy to spot. Those buddies of yours will have run to the cops by now with a description. I'd say we've got about ten more minutes on the road at best before we get pulled over."

He was making good time down the wide avenue, weaving in and out among the several lanes. Bennett remembered the phone. She wasn't sure the other end would still be recording. Some machines will continue until the tape ends as long as there's no period of silence on the line. Hers was like that. She had to keep talking as if the recording were still activated.

"We're headed out of the Fifties into the Forties," she said, referring to the cross streets they were passing. "This area isn't exactly known for its prime accommodations."

"Prime isn't what I'm looking for," he said. "Seedy will do just fine, and I know exactly where to find it."

"Where would that be?"

"Forty-second Street," he said with some satisfaction in his tone. "Even I know enough about this burg to have heard there are lots of transient digs around there."

Bennett gasped. He was actually planning to take her to a flophouse on Forty-second Street. She had, of course, never been anywhere near such a place, but she had an idea what they must be like. She was reminded of her runaway days in Mexico and the place they were staying at the time she'd hit the bottom of her barrel there. She'd survived that, but she was a lot younger and more reckless then. She had put such escapades to the underside of the world behind her long ago. Now here she was, about to take that downward slide again.

"We're coming up to Forty-second Street now," she said, hoping the sound of the car had kept the phantom phone machine going during her brief lapse into silence. "Where do you think you're going to stop around here?"

The corner of Forty-second and Ninth was not as busy at this hour as it would have been earlier, but there were still people in the street. Unfortunately, a fair number of them didn't look like they would be a much safer bet than Modine as companion for a woman in a silk cocktail dress and family heirloom pearl earrings.

"There's a hotel right over there," Modine said, pointing toward a narrow, five-story building just off the corner.

"You mean that place above the print shop next to the deli?" Again she had to keep herself from adding that it was one building over from the southeast corner. That was too specific to get away with. There was no name on the building, only a vertical sign that spelled out hotel in flickering red neon.

"That's exactly where I mean."

"I was afraid so." He'd said he was looking for seedy, and that was just what he had found.

"Now, all I have to do is ditch this car," he said.

"If you do that in this neighborhood, it's sure to get stolen."

"The quicker somebody boosts it, the better. Then the cops will be on the chase for somebody else for a while."

Bennett hit the Off button on the phone console. She couldn't take a chance that, if the tape was still running on the other end, it would switch off suddenly and start up the dial tone again. Modine was sure to hear it this time. Besides, she'd passed on all the information she was likely to have for a while. Her bottle with the message in it was out there on the electronic ocean. All she could do was hope it didn't have to travel far before somebody retrieved it. In the meantime, she knew she should probably be more concerned than she was with what would happen to Royce's beloved car. She just couldn't think about the Jaguar right now. Her own chassis was in too much jeopardy for that.

Chapter Nine

Memphis couldn't help feeling bad about bringing Bennett to a place like this. A Forty-second Street fleabag hotel was definitely not her speed. She had to be used to classier digs. He told himself it would do her good to see how the other half lived, but he didn't really believe that. Nobody gets much good out of spending time in the gutter. He'd been close to this far down before, and he'd never gained any benefit from it that he could think of. Down and out was down and out. There was nothing better than that to say about it.

She'd been cooperative enough about getting past the desk clerk without making a fuss. A fuss probably wouldn't do her much good in a dump like this one anyway. The night clerk gave her the once-over all the same. He was probably thinking she was a top-dollar hooker and wondering why she hadn't taken her john farther uptown. Memphis paid cash up front for the room and hustled Bennett into the elevator as fast as he could manage it.

The room was what he expected it to be, shabby and dimly lit. People stayed in places like this because they were down on their luck, and places like this made sure they never forgot that. There was a bare light bulb hanging in the middle of the room with an extension cord tacked up along the ceiling from the light to the wall then down the wall to an outlet. Memphis was tempted to tell her this wasn't the way he usually lived. He reminded himself that he didn't owe her any explanations and the less she knew about his personal life and history the better off he would be.

"Tell me. What is your story anyway?" she asked, as if she'd heard his thoughts and was hell-bent to challenge them.

"What do you mean by my story?"

"You say you're not guilty. Well, if you're not guilty, what are you?"

She'd taken a seat on the only chair in the room, a rickety thing that didn't look any too comfortable. It occurred to Memphis that maybe she had avoided the bed because she was worried about what his plans might be now that he had her alone in a hotel room. He should reassure her that she had nothing to fear in that sense, but he knew it was better to keep her as scared as he could. She'd be more likely to do what he told her to do that way. Still, he didn't feel good about it. Besides, under other circumstances, if he didn't have keeping himself out of jail on his mind, she might not have been safe with him at all. She was a beautiful woman, more beautiful than she realized, he would guess. The way she stood up to him, hunting knife and all, was something of a turn-on, too. He liked a woman who could hold her own with a man, even when the odds were high against her.

"My story is that I was looking to get paid for a job I did, and that's what I was doing at the Stuyvesant Club."

"Was the job you're talking about killing that girl?"

Memphis plopped down onto the bed. "No, it was not."

"Then what was it?"

He had just told himself that the less she knew about him, the better. Now he found that he wanted her to hear the truth. Most of all, he wanted her to believe him. He understood how foolish that was. She was nothing to him. He was less than nothing to her. What difference did it make what she thought of him? It did make a difference, maybe because of how she had stood up to him and the way that made him respect her. He wanted her to respect him, too.

"I run sailboat crews," he said, "mostly out of the Caribbean in the winter and around Nantucket in the summer. Sometimes I crew a boat up the East Coast from the Islands. That's what I just did for one of your buddies at the Stuyvesant."

"Why do you say it was one of my buddies?" she asked, sounding as if he'd accused her of something.

"Because all you society types are thick as thieves as far as I can see. That's been my experience anyway, and I've crewed a lot of highbrow sails in my day." That was true, all right. Enough to be getting pretty sick of it, too. That's why he'd taken this long-haul job. The pay was better than usual, and he could put by some cash to lay off for a while and think about whether maybe, at thirty-five, he was getting a little long in the tooth to be a shipboard bum. "Aren't most of the guys you know from the Stuyvesant into sailing?"

"I suppose they are," she said.

"See what I mean? That's why I assumed this guy who hired me could be somebody you know."

"What's his name?"

"He calls himself Falcone."

She looked skeptical. "I've never heard of anybody by that name at the Stuyvesant."

"That could be true. I had a feeling the guy was using an alias. He could be anybody."

"What does he look like?"

"I don't know. I never actually met him face-to-face. We did all our dealings by messenger or phone or fax. I was hoping to meet him in person for the first time tonight."

"I see."

He could tell she wasn't buying this. He could understand why. He'd already wondered himself how he'd gotten hooked up with an invisible employer. He'd guessed there might be something shady about the deal. He'd decided that if he didn't see anything underhanded going on with his own eyes, he'd let it pass. Falcone, whoever he might be, was paying good money. Memphis needed that money to manage the layoff he'd been thinking about. So he didn't ask many questions. In fact, he didn't ask any questions at all. Now he wished he had.

"I know how fishy this all sounds," he said, "but it's the truth. Every word of it. This guy owed me money. He was overdue paying it. He sent me a message that if I came to the Stuyvesant Club tonight he'd make everything square. I sneaked in the back door and up the stairs like he said to do. That's when I found that girl dead, just a few minutes before you came along."

"So, you never met the man who hired you. You still haven't seen his face. Is that right?"

"That's right."

"I see," she said again, just as skeptically.

Memphis shrugged. What's the use? he thought. She'd never believe him. He found it hard to believe himself. "You asked for my story," he said. "This is it."

"That's too bad," she said. "The only thing you've got going for you is that it's hard to believe anybody would be stupid enough to tell a story like that one unless it was true."

"Is it that bad?"

"It's that bad."

Memphis sighed and looked out the window. The flickering red neon of the hotel sign made moving patterns on the grimy glass. His goose was cooked unless he could get himself some help fast. The cops were even less likely to believe him than she was.

"It reminds me of something I've heard called 'the this-other-dude-did-it defense,'" she said. "No matter what he's being accused of, the accused says, 'This other dude did it.'"

Memphis shook his head. Unfortunately, she had a point there. He didn't even know what *his* other dude looked like or what his real name was.

"What is your plan?" she asked. "You must have a plan."

Actually he did. He debated what he might have to lose by telling her. Letting her know what he had in mind probably couldn't do any harm, as long as he left out the specific details.

"I plan on getting to some friends of mine. Then I plan on getting as far away from this town as I can, as fast as I can go."

"Where are these friends of yours, and who are they exactly?"

"I don't think it would be good for me to have you know that just yet."

"They must be here in New York because you said you were going to see them before leaving the city."

He didn't say anything. She was smart, all right. Maybe too smart.

Finally, he said, "Look, lady, I've got to go out for a while. Then I'll be back."

"I told you my name is Bennett, not Lady," she said, sounding cool. "You're going to leave me here in this place by myself?" she asked, sounding less cool.

"I won't be gone long. You'll be okay."

"Why do you have to go at all?"

So she did prefer him to the company of street punks. He didn't know why that made him feel so good. She was his ace in the hole, nothing more.

"I have to go because of you," he said. "If you're going to be trailing around with me through the parts of town I'm headed for, you have to fit into the scene. You'll stand out too much the way you look now."

"Why don't you just let me go? That way, you wouldn't have to take all this trouble. And I promise I wouldn't say anything to anybody till you had time to get away."

He almost wanted to believe that could be true. Lord knows he didn't feel right about dragging her all over town and scaring her the way he'd been doing. She'd never done anything to him to deserve that. But then he'd never done anything to deserve what was happening to him tonight, either.

"I can't let you go," he said, making himself sound determined about that, for his own sake as much as hers. "You're my bargaining chip, the only thing I've got to trade if the time comes for that to be necessary."

She opened her mouth, probably to give him another argument. She closed it again and set her lips together in a stubborn line. She was standing up to him again. She wasn't going to beg for her freedom, especially when she was easily smart enough to know he wouldn't give it to her. He wished that stubbornness didn't appeal to him as much as it did. The last thing he needed was to start thinking of this woman as anything more than what he'd just called her: a bargaining chip and a trade-off.

"Get over here on the bed," he said.

"I most certainly will not."

"I'm not going to do anything to you but tie you up so you can't get away while I'm gone."

"You're not tying me up," she said defiantly. "I won't allow it."

Memphis sighed. He should have known this wouldn't be easy. "You either come over here willingly, or I'll carry you."

"You lay a finger on me, and I'll scream these walls down."

He could tell by the look on her face that she meant it. "Listen to me, Bennett," he said, rising from the bed in the hope that his superior size might intimidate her. "This place is only a half step up from those dark spots in the park where we were earlier, maybe not even that far. The help you'd get by screaming in here could help you into bigger trouble than you've got already. I don't mean to do you any harm. If I did, I would have done it already. I'm just not holding many cards right now, and I have to use every one I've got. You go along with me awhile longer, and you'll get out of this mess just fine. You call attention to yourself with the creeps who flop in this joint, and I can't guarantee you'll get out of this mess at all."

She didn't look very intimidated. She stared at him with steel in her blue eyes for a long minute. Then she got up and walked across the room and past him to the bed, one step at a time and at her own speed. He had to hand it to her. She really was a piece of work. Once again, he wished that didn't strike him as quite so damned attractive as it did. But he couldn't think about that now. He busied himself with tearing the bed sheet into strips he could use for tying.

MEANWHILE, BENNETT'S message had been received but not in the way she would have hoped. At the very moment she was being tied to the scarred wooden headboard of a bed with squeaking springs on Forty-second Street, a late-model dark sedan was slipping through midtown traffic in her direction. The man behind the wheel was a good driver but the worried type. The hands that steered so skillfully sported fingernails bitten to the quick. His companion was quite the opposite, cool and hip when his temper wasn't riled, adjusting the impeccable cuff that extended just the right distance from his Hugo Boss sleeve.

"I don't like this," the driver said.

"Rudy, you don't like anything."

"I especially don't like this." Rudy navigated a busy intersection with ease.

"You worry too much. We do the job we been sent to do and get out fast. We do it that way, I'll get back downtown while the night's still shakin'. Then I'll be a happy man."

"That's all you think about, getting boozed up and cattin' around."

"What else is there? You know, Rude, you oughta come out with me sometime. I'd show you how to loosen up. If anybody ever needed loosening up it's you, Rudy. I'm tellin' you true on that score."

"I'm a married man with responsibilities. I've got no time for playing around all night and sleeping half the day like you do."

"Except when I'm on the job." He straightened his hand-tailored silk tie. "I don't never sleep on the job."

Rudy blasted the horn at a pair of carousers carrying bottles in brown paper bags who had backed off the curb into traffic just past the corner of Broadway.

"I hate this neighborhood," Rudy said, sounding even grouchier. "Nothing but sleaze buckets down here. I hope they get it cleaned up soon like they say they're going to."

His companion laughed, more sneering than joyful. "You kill me, Rudy. A hit man who worries about gettin' lowlifes off the streets."

"I live in this town. I got to worry about such things."

"You live in Queens."

"That's part of this town," Rudy said indignantly. "And, you're the hit man, not me. I'm just here for backup."

"Okay, Mr. Backup. You just make sure that's what you are in case there's any trouble. From what I been told, this guy could give us a jolt if we don't catch him off guard first."

"It's not the guy I'm worried about. It's the girl."

"What you talkin' about, Rudy? The girl'll be a piece of cake. She's just a dame, after all."

"I don't like doin' women."

"You got too many don't likes, pal. Just do what Falcone sent us to do, and everything will be A-okay."

"Then, let's do it quick and get it over with," Rudy said, looking around for the best place to park the car.

His companion pulled a pair of soft, black kid gloves from his pocket and smiled. "Not to worry," he said. "They don't call me Nick for nothing. I always show up in the nick of time."

Chapter Ten

Bennett could hardly believe how easily she had convinced Memphis to tie her up too loosely for the knots to be effective for very long. She'd simply flinched as if in pain when he pulled the strips of sheeting to secure them. When he slackened the material to make her more comfortable, she twisted her wrists at an angle so that when she twisted them back again later there would be room to spare between skin and bond. Her heart was pounding all the while because she was certain he'd catch her doing it, but he didn't. He seemed too intent on not hurting her to notice much else.

She was reminded of the way he'd stepped in front of her when Royce showed up with a gun in his hand. She hadn't understood that, either. Memphis was supposed to be a criminal, a murderer, yet he had shielded her from harm, even at the possible cost of his life. He had taken her hostage to prevent harm to himself. Then he put himself at risk for her sake. It didn't make sense. Tying her less than maximum tight also didn't make sense—unless maybe he was as innocent as he claimed to be.

She couldn't think about that now. Innocent or not, he had made her his prisoner and forced her into one dangerous situation after another for his own reasons. He might not, in fact, be the villain she'd believed him to be. There was some chance, though not yet proven, that she and everybody else had been wrong about him. Still, he had used her for his purposes with little thought to how she might be affected or even injured by what he did. That was the bottom line in this case. Her first priority had to be to get herself out of her present predicament. Memphis Modine would have to take care of *his* priorities himself.

Most of all, she had to keep herself from thinking about the way her heart did a bit of a flip when he looked deep into her eyes. She wasn't quite certain when that had begun to happen. Maybe it was when he was tying her up and his hand lingered on her arm a few seconds longer than was necessary, as if he could hardly bear to stop touching her. At one point, he had stroked the inside of her wrist to soothe the skin when she flinched from the supposed chafing of the bed sheet strip. She had felt the warmth of that stroke all the way down to the pit of her stomach. She had told herself to pay no attention to that then, and she did so again now, but she was too forthright a person to try to pretend it had not happened.

All the while she was considering these things, Bennett had also been worming her way out of the pieces of sheeting around her wrists. She had rubbed her skin raw and sore in the process. He hadn't tied her loosely enough to prevent that. She took only a moment to chafe the tender areas, and to remember how much more comforting his touch had been, before starting to work on the ties at her ankles. He should have hitched her to the top and bottom of the bed. That would have made it much more difficult to get free. She was amazed that he hadn't thought of that.

Unfortunately, she had little time to ponder that or anything else. She was barely free from her restraints when she heard footsteps in the hallway outside the hotel room door. Could he be back already? She had expected him to be gone longer than this. She heard voices. It sounded like two men, but she couldn't make out more than that. Had Memphis brought someone back with him? Who could that possibly be? He'd said he had to contact some people he knew in town. Maybe he'd managed to do that. Or, the men out there could be residents of the hotel. Bennett didn't even want to think about what they might be after. Whoever her visitors were, she had no desire to stick around to meet them. She had to get out of this room fast.

Bennett remembered Mexico, where she had to use her wits to survive. Nobody cared what her last name was there or if she was from uptown or down. She could recognize a similar situation now, and the challenge was almost welcome. She grabbed the strips of sheeting and tossed them under the bed. She smoothed the worn and faded bedspread and the lumpy pillows. She wanted to make the room look as if she hadn't been there, at least not in quite some time.

She hurried to the window and pushed it open as quietly as she could manage. As she had hoped, there was a fire escape outside. She remembered seeing it, zigzagging down the front of the building, when she and Memphis first arrived there. She hiked her skirt up and climbed over the window ledge onto the slatted iron floor of the fire escape. Her pumps were a hindrance here so she took them off. She needed to get out of sight of the window, but she also wanted to hear what went on inside the room. First she lowered the window to a few inches above the sill so it wouldn't be obvious that she'd climbed out this way. Then she crouched below the sill and pressed herself back against the brick wall.

She had just barely slipped out of sight when she heard the door open. She was tempted to peek over the sill but didn't. That would be taking too much of a chance. There was street noise from below, car traffic mostly, which made it difficult to hear what was going on inside the room. A minute or two passed before whoever it was actually came through the door. That led her to suspect that this most likely wasn't Memphis. He would have rushed in, especially after seeing that she was gone.

"Dammit! There ain't nobody here," she heard a man say, definitely not Memphis.

"Looks that way, Nick. So, since you're supposed to be the smart guy, tell me what's next."

"First off, don't use names."

The other one laughed, a scoffing sound. "Who do you think's going to hear me? The cockroaches?"

"No names, no matter who's gonna hear," the one called Nick growled. "You do what I say. I'm in charge of this one."

"Okay, General," the other one said. He still sounded scoffing.

"Let's look around and see what they left."

"I don't see a thing. It looks to me like, if they been here at all, they're long gone and probably not coming back. Or maybe they weren't even here, and this place was a bum steer."

"Falcone doesn't send us out on bum steers."

Bennett almost gasped out loud. She bit her lip to keep herself from making a sound. That was the name of the man Memphis said he was working for.

"I thought you said no names, Mr. Man-in-Charge."

"You better shut up if you know what's good for you," Nick snapped.

"I think we'd better get out of here if we know what's good for us. I don't like this setup. Something's fishy. I can feel it."

"You get those fishy feelings every time you turn around. I don't know how a guy as antsy as you ended up in this business," Nick said.

"Being antsy's kept me alive more than one time. You'd be smart to get a little antsy yourself."

All the while this conversation was going on, Bennett thought she could hear them moving around inside the room, opening drawers in the dresser, looking into the closet. She wondered if either of them had thought yet to look out the window. If they hadn't, she guessed they would soon.

"The only thing I worry about," Nick was saying, "is not getting right what the boss sent me to do. I got a rep for doin' the job and doin' it right, and our job on this one is to find these two and shut 'em both up permanent."

Bennett did gasp this time. She covered her mouth to keep herself silent, but she couldn't still the pounding of her heart. They were talking about Memphis and her. She was almost sure of it.

"I'll say it again. I'm not comfortable with doing that girl," the man with Nick said.

"You're never comfortable with anything."

Bennett knew somehow that they had to be talking about her. They had been sent to kill her, as well as Memphis. She pressed so hard against the wall under the sill that the rough brick scratched the skin beneath her thin dress. She was so preoccupied with shrinking herself as small as she could get that she almost missed the next exchange inside the room.

"What the hell was that?" Nick exclaimed. There was silence for a few seconds. Bennett strained to listen. "It's somebody at the door," he said, almost too low to be heard.

Bennett tensed. That would be Memphis coming back from whatever his errand had been. He wouldn't know these two men, these two killers, were in the room. She could feel her heart pounding in her throat. Memphis was in terrible danger. A dim voice somewhere off to the side of her brain told her that she shouldn't care what happened to Memphis Modine. He was her kidnapper, and he deserved whatever he got. That voice was nowhere near as loud as the one that reminded her of how Memphis had risked himself when she was in danger, and another that said he didn't deserve to be done in by two henchmen and the boss who had obviously betrayed him.

She guessed that those henchmen would be concentrating their attention on the door. She crept quietly from her hiding place and eased herself upward just enough to peer over the sill. She saw a rather pudgy man of medium height and a taller one with reddish hair. Both had on dark suits, but the pudgy one looked disheveled, while the other one was quite dapper. She deduced that the dapper one would be Nick. She couldn't be absolutely sure without hearing their voices again, but they were silent now. They had positioned themselves on either side of the door. Bennett thought her heart might stop from terror when she saw that each of them had a gun in his hand.

MEMPHIS HAD A FEELING something was wrong as soon as he put the key in the lock. He wrote that off to ragged nerves, till the door swung open and he found out his premonition had been right. The first thing he saw was the bed where she should have been. It was empty. He didn't have time to do more than register that before two hulking shapes leapt at him, one from each side of the doorway, with two guns pointed at his head. One of the hulks grabbed his arm and pulled him into the room while the other one shut the door.

"Where's your girlfriend?" the tall redhead asked.

So they didn't have her with them. Memphis breathed a sigh of relief. Wherever she might be, she was probably better off than with these characters.

"He said, where's your girlfriend?"

The shorter guy shoved Memphis up against the wall with a thud that rattled the mirror above the dresser. Ordinarily Memphis would have been on top of him in a flash, gun or not, but he was playing it cooler than usual till he was sure she'd gotten away.

"I don't have a girlfriend," Memphis answered, staring the short guy straight in the eye.

"Well, ain't that sad." This was the redhead chiming in. "I guess you think we must be playin' with you here, or you wouldn't be giving us that smart lip stuff." He pulled his arm back and struck Memphis on the cheek. "That's to show you we don't play games. And, even if we did, you wouldn't be coming up the winner. Do you hear what I'm sayin', pal?"

"I hear you," Memphis answered.

What he also heard was ringing in his ear where this clown had smacked him. Memphis was already planning what he'd do in return if he ever got to be top dog in this situation, though the chances of that happening didn't look good right now.

"Tell us where the girl is and tell us right now."

That was the short, chubby one again. Memphis couldn't decide which one he liked least. He had decided that this guy was probably the weaker link. If he lowered his guard, and his gun, even for a second, Memphis would be all over him.

"I don't know what girl you're talking about," Memphis said.

The redhead stepped forward and took the other guy by the shoulder to move him aside. "Take this," the redhead said, handing his gun over. "We're gettin' nowhere fast here. It's time I did some serious persuading."

He reached into the inside pocket of his jacket and pulled out a pair of brass knuckles. Memphis sucked in a deep breath in preparation for the beating he couldn't stop from happening. The redhead fitted the brass finger holes over his black gloves. Memphis was watching this and wondering how long he could hold up against the kind of battering brass knuckles can give, when he noticed a streak of movement over the redhead's shoulder. Memphis barely had time to react.

That streak of motion was Bennett. She'd come from the other side of the room at a run. Memphis caught a glimpse of the open window behind her and figured she must have been hiding out there all this time. In the next instant, she was on the redhead's back. She looped a long, double strip of fabric over his head and around his neck. Memphis recognized the sheeting he'd tied her up with earlier. She pulled the strips tight and twisted them at the back of the redhead's neck, then heaved with all her might as he clutched at his throat and his face began to turn the same color as his hair.

Memphis took only an instant to register all of this before launching his own offensive against the shorter guy, who had been surprised just enough by the attack on his sidekick to give Memphis the opening he needed. He dropped his shoulder and drove it into the guy's soft belly. Memphis had figured this to be his weak spot, and that turned out to be true. The gunman went down like a thud. One of his pistols clattered out of his grip to the floor. Memphis grabbed his wrist to grapple for the other one. Memphis brought the guy's hand up then slammed it down into the floor and did this two, three more times, hard as he could slam. Finally the second gun skidded across the cheap linoleum and under the bed.

Memphis was aware of the struggle still going on between Bennett and the redhead. She had the advantage of a choke knot around his neck. He had dropped to his knees and was trying to flip her off his back. She clearly had him near to strangling, but it was questionable how long she could keep that up. Memphis had to get free to help her somehow. He raised up over the chubby guy who was flailing like mad trying to get loose from the one hand Memphis had around his throat.

Memphis made a tight fist then brought it down in a fast arc from shoulder height hard across the guy's jaw. His head snapped around, and he grunted. The guy's eyes rolled up so all that showed was the whites till the lids closed over them. He flopped down, still under Memphis. Either this guy was out cold, or he was doing a very good fake of it. Memphis had to take a chance on the former, or he might be too late to keep Bennett from getting hurt.

The redhead had finally gotten her off his back, but she was still holding on to the noose she had around his neck. He was striking out at her now. All he had to do was get some leverage, and he could do her some real damage. Memphis hopped off the short guy and grabbed the pistol that had fallen nearby on the floor. It was a nine millimeter. Memphis brought it down sharply in the center of the other guy's red thatch. The man slumped to the floor.

"You can let loose of him now," Memphis said.

Bennett looked up at Memphis. Her blond hair was tousled, there were smudges on her face, and her dress looked like it had seen its last fancy party. As far as Memphis was concerned, she had never looked more beautiful.

"Give me those," he said, pointing at the strips of sheeting in her hand. "I'll use them to tie these guys up."

Her lips moved into what looked almost like a smile. "Do it like you mean it this time," she said.

Chapter Eleven

"Where did you put the car?" Bennett asked Memphis as they hurried out onto Ninth Avenue.

"Forget the car," he said. "The car's a drag. They'll spot us too easily in that thing. We're better off on foot."

That sounded sensible to Bennett, though she didn't have much experience with being on the run so she couldn't be entirely sure what was sensible and what wasn't. She *was* surely glad to be out of that hotel room and away from those two terrible men.

"What will happen to Royce's Jaguar?" she asked.

"He's probably reported it stolen by now. I put it where the cops are likely to find it. Maybe they'll get to it before the thieves do."

"I hope so. Royce loves that car."

"Serves him right for butting his nose in."

"He was only trying to help me."

"Then why'd he take a chance on shooting you?"

Bennett didn't have an answer for that. She couldn't help being more than a little confused. Royce was supposed to be her friend, yet he had put her in danger. Memphis was supposed to be her enemy, but he'd probably saved her life. She remembered him fighting two armed hoodlums and bringing them down, with some help from her, of course. She couldn't help wanting to throw her arms around his neck and hug him tight, but she knew she shouldn't do that.

"Where are we going now?" she asked instead.

They were headed toward downtown on Ninth Avenue. Traffic was busy in the street, but the sidewalks were emptier than they'd been back on Fifth. The people Bennett did see passing hardly took notice of them at all. Though Memphis had a hold on her arm, he wasn't gripping her with the same desperate intensity as he had before what had happened in the hotel room. They had been on the same side there, and that changed things between them. She could tell he knew that as well as she did.

"Where *are* we going?" he repeated, as if to himself.

Memphis stopped walking, and she stopped with him. He looked around, then up and down the avenue. He stepped back into a darkened doorway and pulled her in after him.

"I have to rethink this," he said. "I was going to have you put this stuff on back at the hotel." He gestured with the sack he was carrying. "Then we could head downtown without being quite so noticeable."

"What have you got in there?"

"Some clothes I found in a Salvation Army box a couple of blocks from the hotel. I'd been looking for a store, but I found the box first."

"I see," Bennett said. She wondered what exactly he expected her to put on.

"Why are you so helpful all of a sudden? And why did you jump on that guy at the hotel? What's going on here anyway?"

They were in the shadows, but she could see him staring down very intently into her eyes. His touch was warm as the summer night. The light from a street lamp shone almost blue through the jet darkness of his hair. What *is* going on here? she asked herself as she felt a twinge of something quite unsettling course through her when she returned his gaze. She took a deep breath to steady herself before answering his question.

"What's going on here is that I'm not sure whose side I should be on," she said, "but I'm beginning to think it might be yours."

She still couldn't see his face clearly, but she could sense his surprise. "When did you start thinking that?"

"Back in the hotel room," she said. "Those two men were there to kill me, too."

"What makes you think that?"

"I was out on the balcony listening when they first came in. I heard them say it."

Memphis was silent for a moment. "I don't get it," he said.

"I don't, either. They mentioned Falcone, too. Isn't he the man you said owed you money? The one you told me you were at the Stuyvesant Club to meet?"

"Yeah. That's right. Falcone." Memphis sounded as if he must be almost as confused as she was.

"So, if they're trying to get rid of both of us and Falcone is involved, maybe what you told me earlier could be true."

"What I told you about what?"

Bennett hesitated. Two hours ago she would have choked on what she was about to say. Now her truthful nature, along with every instinct she possessed, wouldn't let her hold back the words. "About not killing that woman in the billiard room," she said.

Memphis nodded his head slowly, then breathed a sigh. "I'm glad to see you're finally coming around."

"I didn't say I was totally convinced yet. I'm only considering the possibility that you didn't do it."

"Look at me," he said, bending closer to her in the dim light of the doorway. "Do I look like a cold-blooded killer to you?"

He had leaned so close she could smell that oddly fresh scent of him. What light there was among the shadows caught in his eyes. She could see the passion there for her to believe him. She was suddenly reminded of another kind of passion and of the way he had kissed her in the park. She had wanted only to get away then. She wished that was all she wanted now. Instead, she found herself reliving those moments when his mouth was on hers. Her lips tingled from the memory. She was tempted to pull him down to her and experience that kiss again, with her full attention this time. She resisted the impulse long enough for him to pull away.

"Never mind," he said. "I probably do look like a criminal to you."

"Actually, you don't," she said softly.

He studied her face but didn't answer. Her female radar, which had always been quite acute, detected he might be thinking the same thing that had just crossed her own mind, about kissing her again. Much as part of her might want that to happen, she knew she must not let it.

"Show me what's in the bag," she said as a distraction.

"What?"

"The bag. I want to see what you have for me to wear."

Memphis picked up the paper sack she was pointing to at his feet.

"It's not bad stuff," he said, handing her the parcel. "I know the Sally's probably not your usual shopping territory, but this one had some possibilities mixed in among the junk."

Bennett opened the bag and was surprised at what she saw. She'd half expected frumpy rags, but he hadn't done badly. She pulled out a pair of black calf-length leggings and a black tank top to go with them. The long-tailed man's shirt could be worn as a jacket with the sleeves rolled up. He'd even found a pair of black ballet-style flats that looked as if they might be close to her size.

"I thought maybe this stuff could work out for where we're going," he said, sounding a little uneasy, as if he might be eager for her approval of his choices.

"Just as you said. They're not bad," she said. "Unfortunately, they don't go far enough if we really want me to be in disguise. I think I can take care of that though. Let's go."

She was the one who took his arm to pull him with her this time, and he was the one who resisted.

"I still don't get it," he said. "Why are you going along so willingly all of a sudden?"

"I told you. They're after me, too."

"So why don't you try to make a run back to the ritzy side of town where you'll be safe? Or, why don't you try to call the cops or get some help from your friends?"

Bennett couldn't help the twinge of guilt that nagged her. He was right to suspect she had more reasons for her behavior than she was letting on. She hadn't told him about the call she'd sent out from Royce's car phone or the questions in her mind now about what that might have to do with those thugs back at the hotel knowing where to find her. She had no idea who that call had gone out to. If Royce knew them, she might know them, too. Hers was a small, tight circle of acquaintances, after all, and Royce traveled pretty much exclusively in that same circle. Bennett didn't intend to go running back to home territory until she was sure she would find safety there. As for the police, she was also not ready just yet to get her friends in possible trouble with the law. Maybe she also wasn't so certain about making trouble for Memphis, either.

"Wait a minute," Memphis said. "You don't think this is some kind of game, do you? Like one of those masquerade parties where people run around pretending they're somebody else just for kicks?"

He was offering her the excuse she needed to explain her behavior at the moment. "Maybe there's a little of that working here," she said.

"This is no game, Bennett," he said, sounding serious. "People could get hurt. You could get hurt."

She was reminded of her thoughts earlier that evening, about her life having become entirely too safe. Suddenly she was also aware of a sensation she hadn't experienced for a very long time. Her breath came more quickly than usual. She could almost feel her blood racing through her veins. She was actually excited.

"I'm willing to take that risk," she said.

Bennett tugged at his arm again to pull him out of the doorway. This time, Memphis didn't resist.

MEMPHIS WAS WORRIED. He couldn't figure out what Bennett had in her head about this situation they were in. He'd told her it wasn't a game, and she'd said she understood that. Still, he wasn't so sure. She was almost acting as if she might be enjoying herself. After they left that doorway on Ninth Avenue, she'd insisted they hunt around for an all-night drugstore. She'd run up and down the aisles, grabbing things off the shelves as if it were Christmas. Makeup, dangly earrings, plastic bauble bracelets, even scissors, hair dye, some cheap towels and a hair dryer. She was definitely getting into the disguise thing big time.

They'd come here to the Port Authority because she said there might be ladies' rooms that had changing cubicles with sinks. He'd never heard of anything like that. They didn't have those places in the men's rooms, not by a long shot. He took her word for it anyway. Now he was wondering if he should have been more suspicious. She'd been in there an awfully long time. Maybe she'd given him the slip. Maybe this ladies' room had a back door onto one of the other corridors and she was long gone already.

Memphis didn't like that the thought made him feel almost scared—and not just because without her he'd lost the advantage of holding a hostage. His hostage plan had pretty much gone out the window of that hotel room when they'd become allies instead of enemies. Standing so close to her in the doorway had changed things, too, at least for him. He could smell her soft perfume. He'd been rushing around too fast to notice it before, or how the little blond hairs around her forehead had gone all curly and wispy from her exertions.

She was the most beautiful woman he'd ever stood that close to in his life. Just remembering it made his throat tight, but he knew how stupid that was. No matter how much they might be on the same side right here and now, they wouldn't be living in the same universe once this mess got straightened out, if it ever did. She was uptown—way uptown—and he didn't have a part of town to call his own. He was what some people call a sea tramp. He had no roots. You had to stay on dry land for a while to put those down. Even if he did what he'd been thinking about for the past few months and tried shore life again, his world would be, as he said, in a different universe from hers. He had to keep that in mind every minute. Otherwise, he'd be putting his heart in line for worse damage than those two hoods with their brass knuckles had planned for his head.

Chapter Twelve

Memphis had kept watch on the ladies' room door while troubling thoughts whirled around in his head so fast they almost made him dizzy. There'd been women in and out of the rest room, but Bennett was still inside, unless she'd found that back door he was worried about. He was just about to take a sprint around the other corridor to check out that possibility when a real knockout appeared in the doorway. Being a red-blooded man of healthy inclinations, Memphis couldn't help but look.

She was something special, all right. She had short, black, spiky hair, wild looking against pale, almost white skin. Her eyes were edged with long black lashes and just enough color to make them almond shaped and exotic. Her lips were full and very red. She had a face it was hard not to stare at and a body to go with it, dressed in tight black that suited her long legs and nicely curved places to a T. Memphis made note of all that in seconds flat. The recognition that dawned afterward, and the shock to follow, took a little longer to happen.

First he recognized the man's shirt. She had it tossed sassily over her shoulder. That's why he hadn't noticed it when he first looked at her. He'd picked that shirt out himself, and taken some time doing it. Then he remembered the earrings, big silver loops fit for acrobatics in a gymnasium.

He'd been surprised when she'd chosen them in the drugstore. They certainly didn't look like something a girl from the Stuyvesant Club would wear. That was nothing compared to the surprise of realizing this was Bennett St. Simon smiling suggestively at him from the ladies' room doorway, looking like one of the hottest numbers he'd ever seen.

"What do you think?" she asked as she walked toward him.

The tight leggings made her walk different than she had before, more slinky and sexy. Or maybe that was just another part of the character she was playing. Whatever the cause, that walk was having a definite effect on Memphis. The feelings she'd started up in him in that dark doorway on Ninth Avenue were more the tender type. The reaction he was feeling now he wouldn't call tender. He had to remind himself extra hard that this was only a disguise she was wearing. She might not have any idea the kind of thoughts an outfit like this could give a man . . . or, maybe she did.

"I think you'll fit in much better where we're headed than you would have before. On the other hand, if the plan was to be less noticeable, I think you can forget it."

"What do you mean?"

"I mean that every guy from here to the waterfront is going to break his neck to stare at you."

"Oh," she said.

A hint of blush tinted her pale cheeks. Maybe she really didn't know how sexy she looked, after all.

"What do you say we get something to eat?" he asked. "We can get away with not having you recognized now."

More than his stomach felt hungry when he looked at her. He hoped a burger would help.

"Where shall we go?" she asked.

"Someplace you've never been before. I'd bet a month's wages on that."

"Good. I love new places."

There she was again, acting as though they were out looking for fresh thrills. He was going to have to set her straight.

"Let's find a diner," he said.

"The Port Authority is a huge place. They've probably got one downstairs somewhere."

"Too many lights," he said, casting a cautious glance over his shoulder as he took her arm and hurried her toward the down escalator. "And too respectable."

Out on Ninth Avenue, it was easy to find what he was looking for, an all-nighter with a small bar in front and tables at the rear. He'd been right about the attention she would attract. The guys at the bar nearly fell off their stools trying to get a better look at her. Memphis gave them his most lethal stare in return. They went back to their beers but not until they'd taken a chance on one last peek. She walked straight past all those stares as if they weren't happening. He'd seen women act like that before and wondered how they did it. Lots of things about women made him wonder. She slid into one of the vinyl booth seats in the back, and he sat down across from her with the Formica table in between.

"I really am hungry," she said, as enthusiastic as if she'd just been ushered to a number one table at the Waldorf-Astoria instead of a greasy spoon in a dingy neighborhood on the wrong side of the tracks Manhattan-style.

Two plastic-covered menus had been stuck in against the wall behind the salt and pepper shakers and the napkin dispenser. She pulled them out and handed one across the table to him. She opened hers and scanned the contents eagerly.

"I just might be hungry enough for one of each," she said.

"You should be careful what you order in a place like this," he warned.

"What harm can possibly come from a scrambled egg?"

"You'd be surprised."

The waitress had sauntered over by then and was giving Bennett the once-over in a not-too-friendly way. That was another thing Memphis had seen women do, especially when they came upon another female who looked as good as Bennett did tonight. She smiled back a little bit too sweetly for the street-savvy way she was dressed.

"I'll have a large orange juice, three eggs scrambled, ham, home fries and coffee," she said.

"Do you always eat so much?" Memphis asked.

"No, but you seem to have worked up my appetite," Bennett answered with that same sweet smile.

"I'll bet," the waitress murmured in a sarcastic tone that made her meaning all too clear.

"You just bet on how fast you can bring two of those orders." Memphis gave her a hard look that made his meaning equally clear.

"We've got to talk," he said to Bennett after the waitress had shrugged once and sauntered off. "Like I told you before, this isn't a game we're playing. The stakes are way too serious for that."

Bennett stopped smiling. "I know," she said. "I'm very aware of what is at stake here."

Of course she was. He hadn't meant to insult her intelligence. "It's just that you almost seem to be enjoying yourself, dressing up like somebody else and all."

"Didn't you ever want to get out of yourself and be another person for a while?"

Memphis sighed deeply, as if the weight on his chest were about to suffocate him. "The way things are going, I wouldn't mind doing that right now."

She reached across the table and put her hand over his. He felt her touch like an electric jolt so sharp he almost pulled away. He tried to tell himself that had happened only because he wasn't expecting her to put her hands on him.

"Everything's going to work out," she said in such a comforting tone he could almost believe her. "Together we're going to find out what's going on here and what to do about it. I promise you that."

Memphis wasn't used to having a woman reassure him this way. It occurred to him that he ought to say something macho and in control, but he was fresh out of thoughts of that type for the time being.

"In the meantime, I have to confess that you're right," she added. "I have been enjoying this experience in a way, at least the part of it since we left the hotel. In fact, maybe I enjoyed what went on there, too."

"You liked getting roughed up by thugs?"

"I liked being out on the edge for a change. When I was on that fire escape crouched under the window listening to those hoods talk about what they had in mind for us, it was the most exciting thing that's happened to me in years." The color had come up in her cheeks again, two bright spots of pink against the creamy pale of her skin. "And when we fought those two off, I felt I could do anything I had to do. I was strong and free and taking care of myself."

Memphis stared into her eyes. He could see the excitement shining there, exactly what she was talking about. That sparkle excited him, too. He wanted to take her in his arms and show her what real fireworks they could make together. He also wanted to take her by the arms and shake her.

"Listen here, Bennett. If you've got the crazy notion that taking a chance on having some creep in a fleabag hotel blow your head off is a thrill, then you need to do some serious thinking about what's wrong with your life."

"I was doing exactly that before I first met you tonight. I've even wondered if I might have conjured you up, made you happen."

"See what I mean? Crazy notions." Memphis sounded as exasperated as he felt. He was thinking that maybe he had better cut her loose, for his own good, as well as hers.

Her hand was still on top of his. She fitted her fingers through his now and squeezed. "I'm not what you think I am, Memphis," she said softly. "That side of me you met at the Stuyvesant is a surface I put on. The truth is that the real me is closer than you can imagine to what you're looking at right now."

Memphis was so thrown off course by the way she was clutching his hand that it took him a minute to register what she'd said. She went on talking.

"It's as if we each have a number of possible selves inside us, some we live sometimes, others we live at other times. Some are more comfortable, more natural than others. I tried to be my wild self once upon a time, but I was too young to handle it and I'd hooked myself up with the wrong kind of person, as well."

Memphis was surprised to hear her echoing thoughts so much like his own, and excited, too. "I've got those opposite parts inside me, too. They go at each other so hard sometimes, I think they might pull me apart. But we can't be pulled apart like that tonight, not either of us. We've got guys after us with guns, and those guys are on both sides of the law."

"I know that, and you can rest assured I also know the seriousness of our dilemma. This is definitely not a game to me, and I wouldn't stay with you if I thought my presence might bring you harm. On the contrary. I think I can help you. I hope you will let me."

She was looking so deeply into his eyes she felt she might be able to see clear down to his soul. The waitress had returned with two cups of coffee, but neither Memphis nor Bennett seemed to notice. He put his other hand on top of hers and wished that he might never have to let go.

RUDY WAS ONLY HALF SORRY for Nick and his bruises. That little lady had sure done a number on him with those pieces of bed sheet. He'd been talking hoarse, when he talked at all, ever since they left that rattrap hotel. He was also red-hot mad, so Rudy was keeping his distance and driving, that's all.

"You'd better find those two real soon, or I'll know the reason why," Nick said for about the half-dozenth time since they'd started driving up and down the mid West Side.

"I'm doing the best I can," Rudy said. "We don't exactly have much to go on here."

"We got what we got. You'd better find him anyway."

"Look, Nick. Falcone told us where they're probably headed. I say we go there and wait for them to show up."

"*You* say? What makes you think I give a damn what you say?"

Nick's forehead had turned so boiling red it was hard to tell where his face ended and his hairline began. His eyes were bugged out, too. He looked like he just might explode any minute. Otherwise, Rudy wouldn't have let a remark like that last one go by so easy. He knew how much trouble Nick could be when he got a mad on. Rudy didn't want any more trouble tonight than they already had, which was plenty. For that reason and that reason only, he kept his mouth shut, but it wasn't easy.

"I got no intention of chilling my heels waiting for nobody," Nick was saying, grumbling almost to himself as he leaned forward in the seat to peer through the windshield at the passing street scene.

Rudy had been keeping at cruise speed as much as he could manage, but that wasn't easy to do in Manhattan traffic.

"Slow it down, fool," Nick snapped. "I can't see nothing."

Rudy sighed. Maybe that's 'cause there's nothing to see, he said to himself as he slowed down and waved at the cars behind him to go past. He didn't much care for being passed by other cars. That's how come he made such a good wheel man. He was getting to like this job less every minute.

"I see him," Nick yelled out, "and he's mine."

He had the door open and was ready to jump out almost before Rudy could edge the car toward the curb. He squinted through the windshield, trying to pick out who it was Nick had seen. He spotted a guy in a leather jacket. Dark hair, burly build. It could be this Modine character. Rudy shoved the car into neutral and kept it at idle while Nick bounded out of the car and darted between two parked cars up onto the sidewalk. He pushed past a couple of people on his way to the guy in leather. They turned to look at him then moved on fast the way they'd been headed. The hate in Nick's face was likely to make anybody want to run away. Rudy wished Nick would calm down a little. It wasn't good to attract too much attention, especially when you had it in mind to take a guy out.

Nick was right behind the guy in leather now. Nick grabbed the guy by the arm. Rudy would have bet a bundle that Nick had a gun in his other hand. Rudy got ready to take off fast in case Nick did something that required a quick getaway. Normally he would have smarts enough not to try anything too drastic on a crowded street like this. The mood Nick was in right now, who could tell whether his smarts would be working or not.

Rudy watched the guy's arm go up in the air as Nick spun him around. Something about the way the guy did that put

Rudy on alert. For a minute, he wasn't sure what for. Then it struck him. This was the wrong guy. He'd flung his arm up like that in a defensive move, to hide behind it. Rudy'd seen enough of Modine in action in that hotel room to know this wouldn't be what he'd do. He wouldn't hide behind nothing. He'd come on strong. Even Falcone had said that about Modine. He had to be watched out for because he came on strong.

Sure enough. When Nick got this guy in the leather jacket turned around so he was facing the street, Rudy could tell right off it wasn't Modine. Nick looked like he was about to clobber him anyway. He still had hold of his arm and was glaring into the poor guy's face, which had turned as white as Nick's was red. Rudy was arguing with himself about whether he'd better haul himself out of the car and break things up before Nick made such a big stink in the street that the cops got called in. Rudy'd just about decided he had to do that, like it or not, when Nick finally let loose of the guy, gave him one last nasty look and headed back toward the car.

"You sure scared that poor sap out of ten years' growth," Rudy said as Nick jumped into the car and slammed the door way too hard behind him.

Usually Rudy would've had something to say about how he hated it when somebody treated his automobile that way. Since Nick really seemed to be at flash point now, Rudy buttoned his lip one more time.

"I'll scare somebody a lot worse than that before this night's finished," Nick said between gritted teeth.

You're close to scaring me, Rudy thought. He didn't say that or anything else out loud as he maneuvered the sedan into traffic as fast as he could to get away from the nosy bystanders on the street who were watching the car with too much interest.

"Get back to Ninth Avenue," Nick barked.

''We already did Ninth Avenue twice.'' Rudy was getting a little fed up with Nick acting like the drill sergeant in charge of this operation.

''I don't care if we did it a hundred times. We're doing it again.''

Nick was twisted around in the seat so that his jacket bunched around his shoulder holster and what was in it. Nick was a hothead, all right, and hotheads shouldn't be allowed to play with guns. A hothead just might shoot before he had a chance to think. Rudy, on the other hand, was a cool head. He flicked on the left-hand turn signal and headed for Ninth Avenue.

Chapter Thirteen

"Where are we going?" Bennett had lost track of how many times she'd asked him the same thing tonight. "I know you want to keep your destination to yourself, but maybe if you told me I could help us get there."

Memphis looked at her with wariness in his eyes. He obviously still didn't know if he should trust her. She wasn't sure if she should trust her, either. She wasn't being completely up-front with him after all. She hadn't told him about the car phone signal, and she wasn't sure she ever would, but she needed to know his plans. She could barely stand running around Manhattan like this with no idea whatsoever where she was headed. Dilys St. Simon's daughter had to be more on top of things than that.

"We're going to South Street Seaport," Memphis said with the suddenness and resignation of someone who has just made a risky decision.

"What's down there?"

Bennett had been to a benefit gala on one of the vintage tall ships that was docked at the seaport as part of the marine museum's permanent exhibit. She'd had a lovely time. She could still remember the sound of the harbor breeze blowing through the rigging.

"My crew mates," Modine said. "They're on the boat we docked this afternoon."

"And you think they will be able to help you."

"I think they'll try."

"I see." Bennett had the feeling that just trying wouldn't be enough to get him out of this mess, which had become her mess, as well.

"I haven't got a chance of working this thing out by myself," Memphis said.

"I'm here."

"Yeah. So you are." There was that suspicious tone and wary look again. "But for how long?"

Bennett didn't answer that. "May I make a suggestion?" she asked.

"Go ahead."

"Sit down here for a minute." She took his arm and steered him toward an empty stoop leading up to a heavy, red door. His hard muscles beneath her touch made her heart quicken. She had to remind herself to concentrate on the task at hand.

He hung back. "We need to keep moving."

"A couple of minutes won't matter." She pulled harder on his arm. "I want your full attention."

Memphis shrugged and let her lead him to the stoop. He sat down on the cement steps. When he was settled and watching her intently, she positioned herself squarely in front of him.

"I think you should try to get yourself out of this predicament instead of running away from it."

"How am I supposed to do that?"

"Well, I don't have all of it worked out yet, but I think you should try to find out who did murder that girl in the billiard room."

"Pearlanne Fellows."

"What?"

"Pearlanne Fellows. That's the name of the girl in the billiard room."

"I thought you said you didn't know her."

"I don't."

Bennett was beginning to feel confused. "Then how do you know her name?"

"I found it in her purse."

"When did you do that?" Bennett suddenly realized that he'd been keeping secrets from her, too.

"Just before you came barging in."

Bennett let that sink in for a minute. Had he been going through the dead woman's purse out of curiosity or because he'd just killed her and wanted to rob her, too?

"Is that all you found?"

"No," he said after some hesitation.

"So? What else did you find?" Bennett could tell she was going to have to pry this out of him one fact at a time.

Memphis sighed. He looked past Bennett for a moment toward the traffic moving down Ninth Avenue. He was obviously trying to decide how much he should tell her. Bennett was still standing on the sidewalk in front of him as he sat on the stoop. She leaned forward and put her hand gently on his arm.

"You can trust me," she said, though she wasn't entirely certain that was true.

He turned back toward her to study her face. She felt the blush of her own uncertain trustworthiness rise in her cheeks. Or did his scrutiny make her blush for other reasons? She was glad the streetlight wasn't bright enough to let him see her change of color. She almost wanted to tell him to keep his secrets to himself, like she was keeping hers.

"I found her address and this." He reached into his pocket and pulled out a matchbook before Bennett had a chance to be noble enough to tell him not to.

She took the matchbook from him. It was purple with large, white circles and came from someplace called the DownTown Lounge. Bennett had never heard of it. She opened the cover, hoping to find a clue inside. Apparently that kind of happy discovery only happened in mystery novels. The cardboard folder was bare.

"This is something to start with at least," she said, tapping the name of the club on the outside of the cover.

"Start what with?"

"Investigating."

Memphis shook his head. "You're really serious about this, aren't you?"

"I'm perfectly serious. If you didn't commit the murder but you are likely to be accused of it, you don't have a choice. You have to take matters into your own hands and prove your innocence. I don't know any other way to do that than to find the real murderer."

"You've been watching too much television," Memphis said, and started to get up from the step.

"No, I have not," Bennett said emphatically, looking away from him toward the street in exasperation.

What she saw there took only an instant to register. Quickly she put her hands on Memphis's shoulders to push him back onto the step. He opened his mouth in surprise and probably to protest.

"Don't say anything," she said.

What she had in mind was the reverse of what had happened in the park. There, he had kissed her to keep her from being noticed by the two people passing by. This time, she was shielding him from being seen. That was where the similarity would end. Meanwhile, all she could think of was the dark sedan she had noticed coming down the street slower than the rest of the traffic. She had needed only a single glimpse of the face peering out of the passenger's side window to recognize the man she had seen in the hotel on Forty-second Street, the one she'd hopped on and nearly strangled. He might have noticed her, also, but she didn't think he would know her if he had. She looked too radically different now for him to make the connection. She was fairly certain of that. Memphis was another matter.

He looked up at her, startled and maybe even a little defensive, as if she might be about to attack him. In a way she was, but not in the manner he probably imagined. She straddled his legs with her own and slid quickly onto his thighs. She could feel the rough denim of his jeans through the thin material of her tights. She tried not to be distracted by the heat that roughness sent coursing through her.

Her face was close to his. The apprehension in his gaze turned to bewilderment as she slipped her hands behind his neck. He opened his mouth to speak at the exact second she leaned forward to place her lips on his. Instead of the closed-mouthed kiss she had planned, something very different happened. He responded instantly to her embrace by putting his arms around her and pulling her close. He hadn't closed his mouth.

She felt his tongue between her lips and knew she should prevent it from moving farther. What she should do was lost, however, in the onslaught of sensations that suddenly overtook her. The heat that had begun in her thighs when they first touched his, exploded into flame in her loins.

She ground her body against his despite herself. All the while, their tongues moved and twined about each other with a hunger like nothing she had ever known. The only thing she could think of was how much she wanted to taste him, to smell him, to intrude herself as close as one person can be with another. He moved one hand from its urgent explorations of her back and waist to pull the front of his jacket open so he could press her more tightly against his chest.

Bennett did moan then. The whisper-thin lace bra she was wearing beneath her black tank top was no protection at all from the friction of his muscular chest across her aroused nipples. The tingling there was fast turning to an ache. Under other circumstances, she might have felt uneasy, even embarrassed to need a man so much and to be so obviously unable to hide that need. Right now, to her great surprise, she didn't care about any of that. She cared only about how much she wanted him and how wonderfully alive that made her feel. At the tantalizing moment when she thought that needing and wanting would grow too intense for her to bear, he reached up and pulled her face away from his.

"Why are you doing this?" he asked in a husky voice that was also close to breathless.

Bennett didn't comprehend his words at first. The strength of his arms held her maddening inches away from his lips. She longed to melt into those arms and never leave.

"I want to know what's going on here," he said.

I would have guessed that was fairly obvious.

That thought flashed through Bennett's brain, but she was not yet quite able to speak. Then she remembered the less obvious reason for the kiss—why she had started it in the first place.

"The car," she said. The words came out in a strangled breath.

"What car?"

She turned her head and looked toward the street. The dark sedan was nowhere to be seen. It had apparently already blended into the line of traffic headed downtown.

"I guess it worked," she said, still in a daze.

"What worked?" Memphis was beginning to sound impatient though his eyes still gazed at her with a softness that melted her heart.

Bennett cleared her throat and willed herself to concentrate on the business at hand.

"I saw that redheaded thug from the hotel," she said. "He was in a car headed straight toward us."

Memphis was silent for a second. "Did he look like he was checking out the street?"

"Yes, that's what he was doing."

"Did he see us?"

"He may have looked at me, but I don't think he would have recognized me."

"Yeah." Memphis swept his glance over her. "I don't guess he'd know you now."

"I don't think he saw you, either," Bennett added.

"So that's why you did this?" He nodded toward the way she was still sitting, straddled across his thighs. "You were keeping Red from getting a good look at me."

The way Memphis was staring straight into her eyes made Bennett suddenly ill at ease. She moved to raise herself from his lap, but he kept his hold on her arms too tight for her to get away.

"Yes. That's what I was doing," she said.

"Was that *all* you were doing?" he asked. He didn't relax his stare.

She stood up more insistently this time. He let her go, but he slid his hands down her arms and slipped his fingers through hers.

"I asked you a question," he said. "I want an answer."

The pressure of his fingers threatened to set her tingling again. She took a deep breath.

"I don't have an answer," she said, and pulled her hands away from his.

Before he could touch her again, she had bounded down the steps to the sidewalk and was beyond his reach.

Chapter Fourteen

Memphis didn't know how to figure her. Worse yet, he didn't know how to figure himself. She had his head going places he had no business being, considering the fix he was in. With most other women he'd met, right now he'd be saying, "She kissed me. So what's the big deal?" Except that, with this woman it *was* a big deal. Because what had happened to him on that stoop wasn't just a kiss. It was more in the neighborhood of an earthquake.

Even thinking about it made him tense. He clenched his muscles against the feeling of being on the edge of out of control. He hated that. He might be a drifter in a lot of ways. At least, that's what most people thought. Still, drifter or not, he kept a tight hold on himself, especially in rough waters. Even tonight, when he found that body and ended up taking Bennett hostage, he'd kept his head. He might not have known what his next move would be. He'd had to make up each step as he got to it. All the same, he'd been sure that he'd been the man in charge. Then she kissed him, and all that went out the window.

Right now, all he could be sure of was that what had happened didn't strike him as any masquerade kiss, only meant to keep him from being seen. She hadn't been able to say it was, either, probably because she was too much of a straight shooter to lie when she was asked a simple, up-front question. That was one of the things he liked about her, the way she had to say exactly what she was thinking or say nothing at all. Some people could twist the truth this way and that, but not her. Like he said, that was one of the things he liked about her—one of the too many things.

They'd been walking down the street without talking to each other for almost a block now. She had her head down as if she were afraid she would trip over something. He had a feeling it was him she didn't want to fall over. Memphis was glad she wasn't looking at him. Otherwise, she might see in his eyes just how much he didn't want to keep his hands off her. He wanted to feel her move against him again and hear those soft sounds she made and smell the sweet, wild scent of her. He was thinking he'd have to do a sprint around the block to stop himself from grabbing her right there in public. She turned toward the corner as if to cross the street.

"We should go this way," she said, still not looking at him.

"Why?" Memphis was glad of the distraction from the heated tension he was beginning to feel.

"Because they might decide to search this street again."

"I'd guess they'd figure us to be long gone from here by now."

"You could be right, but I would feel safer off Ninth Avenue all the same."

The light changed, and Memphis followed her across the wide avenue. He'd lifted the collar of his leather jacket to hide his face from view. No telling who else might be on the lookout for him. Maybe those two hoods, Nick and the other one, had some friends. Maybe the cops were in the mix now, too. Memphis hurried across the street without looking toward the cars lined up to his left waiting for the light to change. She continued along the cross street in the general direction of midtown. Memphis glanced up at the green and white street sign. It said West Thirty-sixth.

"Where are we headed?" he asked. She'd been the one to ask that before. He could see they'd traded places since then.

"Penn Station," she answered, scurrying along the walk as if rushing to get in from the cold, though it was a warm night.

"What are we going to do there?" he asked.

"That's up to you. We can catch a subway there, but you have to decide which one."

"Can we get a subway to the Seaport?"

She nodded her head, but her spiky hair didn't move out of place from where it stood up straight and cute on top of her head. Memphis figured she must have put something on it to make it do that.

"You can get a train that will take you to the Seaport with a transfer. I'm hoping you won't choose that one though."

"Why not?" he asked, stretching his stride to keep up with her. He'd noticed before how fast women in New York City walked, as if they all had someplace really important to go.

"Because I think you should do what we were talking about before and see what you can find out about that poor woman and who may have killed her. I have an idea our redheaded friend may have something to do with it."

"You could be right about that."

"He's not in charge, of course," she said. "He's obviously a hireling. Maybe Mr. Falcone hired him to kill her just as he hired him to kill us."

"But who is Mr. Falcone?"

She stopped so suddenly that Memphis walked a step beyond her and had to turn around to face her.

"That's precisely the question we need to answer," she said. "Who is Mr. Falcone? He is the key to everything."

She was animated again, looking straight at Memphis instead of marching along studying the sidewalk the way she had been doing. He longed to ask her why she was so damned interested anyway. Was it just because she thought her own hide was in danger, or did she care about what happened to him, too? Asking that might send her marching off again, so he didn't.

"I suppose you have a plan," he said, "about where we should take this subway to other than the Seaport."

"The matchbook," she said, stepping toward him close enough to start him feeling jumpy again. "Give me the matchbook you found on the body. What was her name?"

"Pearlanne Fellows." Memphis fished the matchbook out of his jacket pocket and handed it to Bennett.

"'The DownTown Lounge,'" she read off the cover. "It's on the Lower East Side," she said, pointing out the address at the bottom.

Memphis had heard enough about New York City to recognize that as one of the tougher parts of town. Bennett had to know that, too, but she didn't seem to mind as she took him by the sleeve and hurried him off toward what he guessed must be Penn Station. Right now, he didn't much mind where they were headed, either. Like the saying went, he'd follow her anywhere.

NEEDLESS TO SAY, Bennett St. Simon had never spent much time on the Lower East Side, not socially anyway. A couple of the children's shelters she worked with were down there, but closer to Chinatown. And she had never visited them after dark. It occurred to her that she probably should be scared, but she wasn't. Instead, she was excited. She knew enough about downtown nightlife to be aware that a place like the DownTown Lounge was considered very cool. She remembered enough about her young, wild days to understand exactly what cool meant.

Bennett went out to clubs herself back then. There'd be that moment when she was just about to enter a place. She'd wonder who was going to be there, what was going to happen. The excitement would charge higher as she got closer to the door, when she first heard the music. She'd check out her outfit one last time and quicken her step in anticipation. She quickened her step now and wished for a second that Forth could see her here, so far out of what everybody thought to be her element and ready to fit right in.

She could tell from the number of people spilling out the front door that this had to be a hot place. A big man with a handful of bills appeared to be the doorman. He checked everybody over before letting them in. Bennett couldn't tell what he might be looking for, because he didn't appear to be turning anybody away. Of course, they all looked like they belonged here. The crowd was young, hip—which meant they looked like they couldn't care less about being here—and almost all of them were wearing black.

Bennett had the outfit and the hairdo and the makeup to fit in. She concentrated on projecting the attitude. She lifted her chin at a slightly belligerent angle and flattened the expression on her face to no expression at all. She wished she had a piece of chewing gum to crack offensively loud and maybe a pair of extradark-lensed glasses to complete the picture. What she did have was the perfect guy on her arm. She noticed several attractive young women giving him a once-over glance. Just a flicker of an approving smile altered their impassive faces for a moment. Bennett wondered if Memphis noticed, too.

The doorman was collecting money from everybody who went inside. Memphis handed him a bill as they were nodded in. Bennett wondered how much money he had with him. She had none, and no credit cards, either. All of that was in her handbag in the car back at the Stuyvesant Club. She didn't like carrying a purse around with her most places.

Her car keys and comb and a tube of lipstick were in her coat pocket in the checkroom of the club. She had left with nothing but the clothes she was wearing. Memphis had been the one to pay for her purchases at the all-night drugstore, their meal at the diner and the subway ride downtown. He'd even bought her a shoulder bag at one of those late-night variety stores to hold what was left of her cocktail dress and shoes and other odds and ends she'd picked up along the way tonight.

Memphis said he'd been after Falcone to pay the money Memphis was owed. That could mean he'd needed that money, which, in turn, could mean he was close to penniless now. Bennett had her pearl heirloom earrings in the shoulder bag. They were wrapped in a piece of tissue paper and stuffed into the toe of one of her pumps. She could always sell those earrings if need be. Any number of jewelry stores uptown would be happy to have the sale. This part of the city would probably have pawnshops, as well. She wasn't sure exactly how a pawnshop worked, but she could figure it out if she had to. They were valuable pearls, but not worth as much to her right now as getting through tonight. Besides, they weren't the only pair of heirloom earrings in her jewel case, and jewelry didn't matter much to her anyway.

The music was even louder inside than it had been in the street. It sounded like a live band, but Bennett couldn't see far enough down the long room to tell. The lighting had not been designed for seeing at much of a distance. The light was, in fact, a deep and shadowy shade of purple that seemed to puddle in the air like pockets of gloom. Punctuating this purple haze were bright spots of white beaming down from round, recessed fixtures in the black ceiling. The bright beams shone like polka dots on the otherwise purple crowd. In order to be noticed, all anybody had to do was step into one of those spotlights. Several club types had done just that, striking attitudes that were most advantageous to show off their tuned-in outfits and their tuned-out looks.

Memphis and Bennett avoided the spotlights. As her eyes adjusted to the purple gloom, Bennett saw that the front of the room nearest the door was lined with couches along the walls. The couches were full. The coffee tables were covered with glasses and snack bowls. The conversation level was high as everybody shouted over the band. Despite their vacant facades, Bennett could tell that these people were having a good time. They might look bored, but they really weren't, not the way she had been bored back at the Stuyvesant. Many of them were her age, but she had felt much older than this crowd for some time now. She didn't feel old right now. She must not look it, either, judging from the number of male stares directed her way, easily as much attention as the women were giving Memphis.

"Let's check out the back," he shouted over the noise.

"Okay," Bennett shouted back. When he took her hand to lead her through the crowd, she couldn't help feeling a surge of happiness at being here with him no matter what the circumstances.

The back of the room was even more packed with partygoers than the front. The band was dimly lit. Bennett guessed that might be some kind of anti-stardom thing. These downtown places prided themselves on being anti this or that, especially anti-fashion, while ending up to be as much into trend as anybody else, maybe more. The crowd stood in front of the bandstand, sometimes swaying a little, but mostly listening. Conversation wasn't much of a possibility here. Bennett had hoped to question somebody about Pearlanne Fellows. That wasn't going to be feasible back here. Bennett pulled on Memphis's hand and gestured in the direction they had come from. He followed as she threaded her way toward the bar.

"Nobody's dancing," Memphis shouted just as the final crash of the song ended, leaving his final word to be yelled out. Several people turned to glance his way. "How come nobody dances?" he asked more quietly.

"My guess is that it isn't considered hip to dance, at least not in this place."

Memphis nodded and smiled. "I guess I'd better not ask you to dance then," he said. "We wouldn't want to be unhip."

"We also wouldn't want to be conspicuous."

"You're right about that," he said as his smile faded, as if he had just been unpleasantly reminded of what was really going on with them tonight.

A long-legged woman in faded jeans vacated one of the bar stools. Bennett beat two other contenders to the space. The bartender working this end was a woman. Bennett recognized that as a lucky break and gestured for her to come over.

"I'm looking for a girlfriend of mine," Bennett said when the bartender finally made her way past the three people she'd been serving when Bennett sat down. "Her name is Pearlanne Fellows."

"Pearlanne. Yeah, I know her." The bartender's long earrings swung and danced as she talked. "Where are you a friend of hers from?"

"We used to hang together." Bennett did her best to duplicate the loose, laid-back speech she'd heard from the shelter kids.

"I don't remember seeing you around," the bartender said, looking skeptical.

"I been away for a while. I owe Pearlanne some money. I want to pay her back if I can find her."

"Really?" The bartender looked more receptive. Bennett had hoped the mention of money would do that. "See that woman with the blond buzz? The one on her way into the john.''

Bennett looked where the bartender was pointing just in time to see a woman with a platinum brushcut disappear through the door marked Ladies.

''That's Liddy,'' the bartender said. ''She and Pearlanne are pretty tight. She could tell you more than I can.''

''Thanks,'' Bennett said, being careful not to smile too widely and look out of it. ''Wait for me here,'' she said to Memphis.

She could tell by the way the bartender was looking him over that he wouldn't be lonely on his own. Bennett was tempted to drag him along with her. She knew how much men seemed to like dangling earrings, as if their movement put them into some kind of trance. She glanced back at the bar. The bartender was talking to Memphis. Bennett turned reluctantly toward her destination. She had a mission to accomplish. She couldn't be worrying about who was hitting on Memphis. That shouldn't be a concern of hers anyway. She pushed through the ladies' room door knowing that, somehow, what Memphis Modine did and with whom he did it had become a concern of hers whether she wanted it to be or not.

Chapter Fifteen

Bennett had never seen a ladies' room like this one. The purple-and-white theme continued here with wall surfaces alternating those two colors like a huge checkered table-cloth blanketing the room. The light was low, too low in fact to allow for any serious makeup repair in the wide mirrors, which were also tinted smoky purple. A video screen set into one wall played the scene from *Singing in the Rain* where Gene Kelly ruins his shiny dance shoes tromping in and out of puddles.

She checked herself over in the mirror while she waited for the blonde to come out of the stall area in the back. For a couple of seconds, Bennett wondered who belonged to that dark-haired image in the mirror. The connection to herself came with a sudden jolt. This is what everybody was seeing when they looked at her. First of all, that one bottle of hair dye and those crude scissors had made her appear about ten years younger. She'd gotten her body back, as well. She didn't exactly dress in frumpy clothes ordinarily, but she didn't let her figure show much, either. The tights and tank top she had on now left very little to the imagination. She might have been self-conscious had this not been a disguise that made her into somebody other than herself, at least for a while.

"I like your do." The blonde had come up next to Bennett and was admiring her reflection in the mirror. "Where'd you have it done?"

"My hair?" Bennett asked, thrown off balance for a moment. "A place uptown," she said. "It's called the Bus Terminal."

"Really? I've never heard of it. I'll have to check it out. Very chic." She pronounced it "chick."

"You're Liddy, aren't you?" Bennett asked.

"How'd you know that? Have I run into you before?" The blonde turned to look directly at Bennett. "I don't remember, if I did."

"The bartender told me about you. She said you know an old friend of mine. Pearlanne Fellows." Bennett did her best to sound offhand. "I been on the road for awhile, and I was hoping to hook up with her again."

"You're on the wrong end of town for doing that," Liddy said. She'd pulled a small wide-toothed comb out of her small purse that hung from a long, thin strap over her shoulder and had an appliqué of Betty Boop on the front of it. "Pearlanne's been catching some classy scenes lately. I don't even see her much anymore."

"Do you know where she's been hanging out exactly? I'd like to look her up."

Liddy waved her comb in a generally upward direction. "Way north of Fourteenth Street from what I hear. That's all the way uptown to us downtown types. She's supposed to be trailing with some guy who's turning her on to the better things in life, if you know what I mean."

"Have you ever seen this guy she's been with?"

Bennett knew the minute she said it that she sounded too eager for somebody who was only casually checking out an old acquaintance. Liddy had been poking at what hair she had with the small comb. The way her eyes narrowed a little in the mirror suggested she'd picked up on Bennett's eagerness.

"What did you say your name was?" Liddy asked.

Bennett almost gave her real name, then stopped. Whoever heard of anybody named Bennett barhopping on the Lower East Side?

"Vangie," she said. That had been her nickname when she was a very little girl, short for Evangeline, the middle name she had inherited from her maternal grandmother. "I just need to find Pearlanne because I owe her some money and I want to pay her back."

"Well, that's a rare one. Somebody going out of their way to clean up a debt."

Oh, no Bennett thought. She doesn't believe that, either.

"You look like the kind who'd do that," Liddy continued. "I can see it in your eyes." She leaned closer to the mirror. "Check it out for yourself. See how your eyes round up on top. That means you're a truth teller for sure. I've been studying up on it. The art of eye reading, it's called. Goes back to the Tibetan monks, or maybe it's the Native Americans. I don't remember which."

"So, can you tell me anything about Pearlanne?" Bennett hoped her truth-telling eyes might be worth some information.

"I can tell you I never saw her boyfriend. This place must be too heavy on the slum side for him, if you know what I mean. Though I heard they met each other at a Rave, if you can imagine that."

Bennett tried not to let on that she really didn't know what that meant. She seemed to remember something from a magazine about raves being wild parties that moved from place to place.

"Usually only young kids make those gigs," Liddy was saying. "I can't bear that techno stuff myself, too far off the planet for me. Pearlanne's another story. Sort of can't get where she fits in, if you know what I mean. Slippin' around uptown, jumping into a mosh pit in some warehouse. Like she's looking for a place to be.''

Bennett nodded, feeling suddenly sad that Pearlanne's search had ended so tragically on the floor of the Stuyvesant Club. Maybe it was that tragedy and wanting somebody to pay for it that made Bennett take a chance with her next question.

''This guy Pearlanne's been hanging with, would his name happen to be Falcone?

Liddy tapped her comb against the black marble veneer of the vanity and stared into the mirror for a moment. ''You know, I did hear his name once, but it wasn't a last name like that one you said. I remember. It was Stitch. She called him Stitch.''

''An unusual name,'' Bennett said, feeling she'd just headed up another blind alley.

''Yeah, almost as weird as how he got it. Pearlanne said they called him Stitch because he used to smuggle stuff inside clothes being shipped from other countries.''

''He was a smuggler?''

''That's what Pearlanne said. Of course, Pearlanne talks a lot, sometimes too much. Who knows if everything's the God's honest or not.''

Bennett wondered if talking too much might have been what brought Pearlanne to her bloody end on the billiard room floor.

''You know, now that your mention it, I think Pearlanne might have told me his last name once, and it just could have been what you said.''

''Falcone?''

''Yeah, that sounds about right. Well, good luck finding her,'' Liddy said, jamming her comb into the tiny bag and pulling out a silver-cased lipstick. ''What she told me last time I saw her makes me guess we won't be catching her act down this way soon."

"What was that?" Bennett managed to sound casual this time. "What did she tell you?"

Liddy couldn't answer at the moment. She was too busy bearing down hard with her lipstick so that the color came out very red. She worked her lips together to even out the tone, then surveyed the result in the smoky glass, where the purple tint turned the red almost black. Liddy smiled, as if pleased with what she saw, and returned the lipstick to her purse. She pulled her short, tight dress straight over her thin hips and settled the purse strap onto one narrow shoulder. She was obviously about to leave. Bennett was tempted to repeat her question but knew that sounding too pushy would be an unwise move. Liddy was at the ladies' room door before she turned back to Bennett, who was following close behind.

"She said she was coming into a load of dough. I almost fell out when she told me. Pearlanne never has two pennies to rub together." Liddy had pushed the door partway open. Now she stopped in her tracks. "Come to think of it, I'm surprised she had any to loan you."

She pouted her red mouth in puzzlement for a moment while Bennett held her breath. "Oh, well," Liddy said at last, pushing the door farther open and exiting against a group of women on their way in. "You never know what to expect from some people and Pearlanne's one of those, if you know what I mean."

"Maybe her smuggler friend was coming through for her after all."

"Maybe," Liddy shouted back. "Oh, do you want to hear the wildest part of all? Pearlanne said this guy was doing his smuggling thing on sailboats. Can you imagine that?"

Liddy didn't wait for an answer to that as she shoved her way out into the crowd that looked even more dense now in the bar area. She lifted one hand and flicked her very red tipped fingers in a wave without turning around toward Bennett. Then she was gone as if drawn into the press of bodies by a magnet of excitement and music in the back room.

Bennett allowed herself to be prodded and elbowed the rest of the way out of the ladies' room. Once outside, she leaned against the wall for a moment, trying to sort things out in her mind. Had Pearlanne been at the Stuyvesant for the same reason Memphis said he was there? To get a pay-off from Falcone? Could that be the windfall she told Liddy about? Did that money have something to do with Pearlanne's murder? Most important, who was Falcone anyway?

The part she didn't want to think about had to do with the smuggling Liddy had mentioned. She'd said that Stitch and Falcone might be the same person, and that he was involved in illegal smuggling aboard sailboats. Memphis crewed just such a craft. Bennett didn't believe in coincidences, certainly not enough to avoid the possibility that there could be a connection between Falcone's illegal activities and Memphis. Maybe he hadn't murdered Pearlanne Fellows, but maybe his hands weren't perfectly clean, either. Bennett could hardly believe how desperately she wished that wouldn't turn out to be true.

She pressed back against the wall. The confusion of so many unanswered questions, the music, the noisy crowd seemed as if they were about to smother her. She took a deep breath and assured herself she wasn't going to suffocate no matter how scarce the air seemed to have become. Suddenly she had the urge to get to Memphis as fast as she could. With him next to her, maybe this panic would pass. She would feel safe again. At the edge of what remained unconfused in her consciousness, she knew how crazy it was to equate safety with her kidnapper. She also knew that Memphis was more than that to her now.

She scanned the room, slightly disoriented for the moment as to which direction the bar was from here. All that was truly visible through the purple haze was the beams of white light from the ceiling. What Bennett glimpsed in the bright pool from one of those beams made her heart stop dead still in her chest.

His face was turned away from her for the moment. The cocky way he held his head was familiar, but it was the flash of his unmistakably red hair that stopped her heart. Nick was here in the DownTown Lounge, and he was headed straight in what she now remembered to be the direction of the bar—and Memphis.

Bennett threw aside any thought of caution. Whatever confusion she'd been feeling was left behind at the ladies' room door as she shoved her way through the crowd. Bodies got in her way. She used her own to bulldoze past. She had to get across this room before Nick, and she didn't care how she did it. A spray of beer wet her arm from a tilted glass as she barreled on.

"Keep on slammin', girl," a male voice called out after her.

She guessed, again from her magazine reading, that he was referring to another dance craze that had something to do with the mosh pits Liddy had mentioned. Right now, Bennett knew she was capable of slamming and moshing with the best of them.

She looked around for Nick and caught a glimpse of his red head still in the same spotlight. He'd stopped to talk to somebody. Bennett felt a surge of relief and hope. It also occurred to her that, if he knew people here, this might be proof he also knew Pearlanne and could possibly be connected to her death. She forced that thought, however interesting it might be, out of her mind and pushed harder than ever toward the bar. She saw Memphis and grabbed his hand almost in the same instant.

"Come with me and don't look back," she said tersely.

Memphis took one look at her face and followed her at once without a word, into the crowd and in search of the rear exit. Before this moment, Bennett would never have thought of a back alley on the Lower East Side as sanctuary. That's exactly what she was thinking now.

NICK LOVED BEING in the spotlight. Everybody could see him then, and that was just how it should be. They see him, and they know he's nobody to be messed around with. The babes could see him, too, how he stood out from the rest of these creeps. They liked the cut of his threads, and the cut of the rest of him, too. Like this one who'd stopped to ask where he'd been and held on to his arm till he had to shake her off.

"Later, baby," he said.

He couldn't remember her name or where he'd run into her before. He hardly ever knew one dame from the other. Maybe that was because while he was chatting up the first, he was almost always looking over her shoulder for the next. That's how it was with him and babes.

There was another one of them waving at him now. The bartender. Nick couldn't remember her name, either. Maybe he'd never known it. He'd go over there and give her a thrill anyway. That was why he'd ditched Rudy for a while. The action made Rudy jumpy, got him talkin' that happily-married-man crap. What a drag. He was better off out there trolling for Modine and the chick. Needle and haystack. That's how much of a shot there was at finding them two tonight. In case anything did turn out to be shakin', Rudy could give a jingle on the cellular. For now, it was long past midnight, burnin' toward daylight with no time to lose. Nick waved back at the bartender and gave her a look that said *I know what you want, babe, and I've got it.*

"Have you seen Pearlanne?" the bartender asked before he hardly had time to elbow his way through the crowd that was three-deep at the rail.

"Not tonight." That wasn't true, but Nick didn't worry much about telling the truth.

"An old friend was in here asking for her. Something about owing her some cash."

"You don't say." That got his attention. Maybe the cops were nosing around already. How'd they figure her so soon for a regular at this dive? He didn't like it. "So what'd you tell this friend?"

"I told her to talk to Liddy."

"This friend was a chick."

"Definitely. Maybe even your type, hotshot." The bartender smiled as if she might be trying to come on to him, at least that's how it appeared to Nick.

"Maybe. Give me the details."

"On the tall side. Black hair shagged out on top. Dressed kind of street easy. Cool looking, but you can forget it if you're thinking about trying to score. The dude she was with is one hundred percent stud. If she hadn't come back for him, I'd have glommed onto him myself."

"Did either of these two glamour girls have a name?" Nick didn't like being compared to some Bowery bum rocker, but he had to put up with it till he got what he needed here.

"He was named after some city in the South," she said while drawing a beer for a customer. "I don't remember what her name was. I don't think it was mentioned."

Had to be the St. Simon woman. She might have changed her look the way chicks can do, but she wasn't putting nothing over on him.

"I know what her name was."

Nick caught the flash of platinum out of the corner of his eye. He'd known Liddy for about as long as he'd known Pearlanne. He'd even thought about making it with Liddy before she went and damn near snatched herself bald-headed. He liked his women with a little more hair.

"You into eavesdropping now?" he asked.

"I wouldn't think you'd have anything to say I'd be that interested in. I just happened to catch the drift of what you two were going on about."

"So how'd you find out this chick's name, and what is it, anyway?"

"We got to swapping stories in the ladies' room," Liddy said.

Nick could tell she was angling for him to buy her a drink. He didn't think he'd bother.

"What's her name then?" he asked.

"How come you're so interested?"

Nick was having a hard time holding on to his temper. He didn't like getting the runaround from anybody, especially not from some nowhere, nobody, bald-headed blonde. He had to keep the clamps on, though, or she might decide to keep quiet about what he needed to know.

"She's asking about Pearlanne, and I'm wondering why," he said.

"According to her, she owes Pearlanne some money and wants to look her up and pay her back."

"Believe that and I got a bridge to sell you," he scoffed. "So, what's this nosy broad's name anyway?"

"Vangie's what she said it was."

That threw Nick off a little. Falcone had told him the mark's name was Bennett St. Simon. Where'd you get Vangie out of that? But Nick was sure it had to be her, and the guy with the name like a city down in yahooland had to be Memphis Modine.

"How long ago was she here?" he asked.

He saw the look exchanged between Liddy and the bartender. Liddy was passing the signal to be cool. He'd never trusted her anyway.

"I'm not sure. A while ago," the bartender said. "They were here one minute, then they were gone. Maybe they're out in the back catching the tunes. It's too busy in here for me to be keeping track of the customers, even the hunky ones."

She must've wanted to make that last clear because, after she said it, she took off down the bar to wait on a couple of guys who were waving to get her attention. Liddy had taken off, too. He could see her working her way through the crowd toward the back room. Maybe she was intending to warn Modine and this St. Simon chick.

Then it hit him. The description the bartender gave. Short black hair. Real hip looking. He remembered something he'd seen out of the car window when he and Rudy were cruising Ninth Avenue. Some girl kissing a guy on a doorstep. The reason Nick remembered it was because of the way she was all over the dude. Almost turned Nick on to look at it. He'd been so busy checking her out, he almost didn't notice the guy she was with. Except for the black leather jacket. Nick was real good with picking out details like that.

Nick put all of it together now. It could add up to the two he'd been after for sure. He remembered her face well enough to guess it could be St. Simon after some make-over work. That would be a smart move, doing her up so nobody'd recognize her. He touched the place on his neck that was still sore from the way she'd come close to throttling him back at that fleabag hotel. He'd recognize her all right, but when he got done with her maybe nobody else would.

Chapter Sixteen

The quiet of the street was as much a shock as the havoc of the club had been. Bennett needed a minute or two to regain her bearings and remind herself that she didn't have to shout anymore. What she did have to do was think. She had told Memphis the reason for their hasty exit. They'd shouldered their way to the rear door with him in the lead since he was far better equipped for shouldering. The alley was dark except for one hooded light over the exit. They nearly fell over a phalanx of trash cans as they ran toward the street.

"I imagine you want to go to the Seaport now," Bennett said breathlessly, answering the destination question instead of asking it this time.

"That's right," Memphis said. "Are we headed that way?"

"Actually, we're not." Apparently he hadn't managed to get his bearings as quickly as she had.

He stopped and turned around as if to head in the other direction.

"I don't think you want to do that," she said. "We would have to go past the DownTown Lounge or closer to it than I care to be with Mr. Nick in the area."

"That's true." Memphis didn't sound the least bit winded, though Bennett could feel her heart hammering in her chest.

"I also don't think it's a good idea for you to go back to your ship."

"Boat," he said. "It's not large enough to be a ship."

"It's large enough to hold a great deal of trouble for you if you get caught anywhere near it." Bennett had spotted a pay phone on the next corner and headed toward it. "May I borrow a quarter?" she asked.

Memphis reached into a pocket of his jeans as he reluctantly followed her. "I get the feeling you have a plan," he said. "What is it?"

"I don't know if I'd call it a plan quite yet. It's more an approach to a plan at this point."

Bennett took the quarter he offered her and hurried up the curb to the aluminum phone carrel. She said a silent prayer that this would be a working phone rather than a vandalized one. When she lifted the receiver, the dial tone was music to her ears.

"Then tell me your approach to a plan," Memphis said when he caught up to her.

"In a moment," she said as she punched in the number she was so pleased to remember. "What corner are we on?" she asked.

Memphis checked the street signs. "First Avenue and East Fourth," he said.

Bennett nodded. "This is Bennett St. Simon," she said when the car service answered. "I need a car at First Avenue and East Fourth Street." There was a hesitation on the other end of the line. They weren't accustomed to having her call from anywhere near this neighborhood, though they certainly must have picked Forth up in worse parts of town on any number of occasions. Her family had been using this service for as long as she could remember. "I'll be going to the Plaza Hotel," she added.

"Yes, Ms. St. Simon" was the rapid and very polite answer. They were talking familiar territory again.

"Can you make that a rush pickup?" she asked. "I would rather not spend very long on this particular corner."

"Of course, Ms. St. Simon. We will be there right away."

"Did I hear you say you're headed for the Plaza Hotel?" Memphis watched her with a curious expression on his face as he waited for an answer.

"*We* are headed for the Plaza Hotel."

"Oh, no, we're not." He raised his hands as if to ward off the possibility. "I think this has to be where we say goodbye."

Bennett grabbed his hands in hers. "No, it is not," she said so emphatically she even surprised herself. "You are coming with me. You have to."

"Why do I have to?"

Memphis took a step toward her. He was gazing directly down into her face. She continued to clasp his hands.

"Because the solution to the mystery of Pearlanne Fellows's death is on my end of town not yours," Bennett said, returning his gaze just as directly, even though the chaos that gaze created inside her tempted her to look away.

"How do you figure that?"

"What I learned at the DownTown Lounge is that Pearlanne had been spending a lot of time uptown lately. She apparently had a gentleman friend there, a gentleman who is probably named Stitch Falcone."

Memphis sighed and nodded his head slowly. She'd gotten his attention this time.

"That's probably why she was at the Stuyvesant Club, to meet Falcone just like you were." She was about to repeat what she had learned about smuggling and sailboats, but something made her hesitate. What if she should not be trusting Memphis after all? What if having too much information and talking about it was the cause of Pearlanne's death, as Liddy had suggested? Bennett wasn't going to make the same mistake.

"I would guess that Falcone either *is* the murderer or he *knows* the murderer," she said. "Apparently he spends his time uptown rather than downtown. If that is true, I think I can help you find him."

Bennett wasn't certain she should be doing even that. All the same, though she might have doubts about Memphis, she still wanted to help him. She had committed herself to that, and she wasn't ready to give up yet. Meanwhile, Memphis continued to stare into her eyes.

"You could be right," he said at last. "Besides, my choices seem to be pretty limited right now."

"Exactly."

Bennett scanned the avenue for the car service vehicle. It occurred to her that the driver might not recognize her in her outfit. She turned to walk toward the curb, but Memphis gripped her hands tighter and wouldn't let her go.

"There's one more thing I need to know," he said, capturing her with his gaze once again. "Is solving this mystery the only reason you don't want us to split up and go our separate ways?"

She felt the smile rising from her heart to her lips. The warmth of his eyes flushed through her, like a candle's rosy glow, melting any doubts or questions in its path. She squeezed his hands and said, "No, that is not the only reason. We can talk about the rest of it later."

The glow grew rosier and warmer as she considered the fact that "later" they would be in a hotel room—just the two of them—and nowhere near Forty-second Street this time.

MEMPHIS COULD HARDLY believe his eyes when a long, black limousine pulled up at the corner.

"I take it this is for us," he said.

"I thought they would send something less ostentatious." Bennett sounded embarrassed.

"That last name of yours seems to bring out the first-class in people."

First-class or not, the limo driver looked as if he had his doubts about her, too. He lowered the window no more than an inch when Bennett walked up and rapped on it.

"Don't worry, Kevin," she said. "It's really me. I've been at a costume party."

Memphis couldn't help but admire the way she spieled that lie off so smoothly, without batting a pretty blue eye, and followed it up with a smile dazzling enough to roll any man's window down.

"Sure thing, Ms. St. Simon," Kevin said.

Memphis heard the door locks click open. Then Kevin was out of the car like a shot, hopping to grab the rear door handle. He even bowed a little at the waist as Bennett ducked her head to climb inside the car. Memphis nodded his head as thanks for the courtesy, but Kevin wasn't having any of it. He gave Memphis the fish eye as he slid onto the plush seat next to Bennett. Kevin was obviously an old hand at this limo business. There was no use trying to fool him about who belonged in one and who didn't.

Kevin climbed back into the front seat, on the other side of the sliding panel of black glass, and the car purred away from the curb. He picked up speed, moving north along the almost deserted avenue. Memphis couldn't blame him for wanting to make tracks out of this part of town. There were plenty of hard cases on these mean streets. Any one of them would love to get his hands on a rig like this one, and whoever had the bad luck to be inside it, too.

"So much for being inconspicuous," Bennett said.

"I was just thinking something like that. About sticking out like a neon sign in the woods."

Bennett laughed, and he realized this was the first time he'd heard her do that. There hadn't been much to laugh at tonight up till now. Maybe she had a point about getting away from the rough side of things for a while. He would have liked to reach over and take her hand and tell her that, along with how much he loved the way she laughed, but something stopped him. This whole situation was too weird to be believed. First, he'd found the murdered girl on the billiard room floor. Next, he'd taken a beautiful woman for a hostage. Now here he was, in a black stretch limo headed for a place too fancy for him to even think about going before tonight.

None of this felt real. None of it felt as if it could be happening to him. He was starting to wonder if *he* even felt real. He should probably tell himself to relax and enjoy it, go with the flow like they used to say. His nerve endings were screwed up so tight, from everything that had been going on these past few hours, he might never be able to relax again. On the other hand, if and when he could find enough free space in his head to let himself kick back, this was the kind of place to do it in.

The interior of the car was black as the outside—leather-lined doors and ceiling trimmed in polished chrome—except for the seats, which were a color that reminded him of old wine or maybe even brandy. He'd never sat on a car seat that felt like this one. Hell. He'd hardly ever sat on a sofa like this. The cushions were deep and wide. He tried to keep himself from thinking about how it would be to lay Bennett down right here and make love to her. Kevin would probably be over the seat in a flash if he thought anything that out of line was going on back here anyway. The partition might be made of black glass, but Memphis would bet money

Kevin had his ways of knowing exactly what was going on in his ride. Memphis smiled at the thought.

"Are you enjoying yourself?" Bennett slid closer to him.

"Now I am," he said.

His hand was fairly itching to take hold of hers. All the same, he couldn't bring himself to touch her. The only way he could explain it was that he was feeling shy, and Memphis Modine had never been shy so much as a New York minute in his entire life.

"This is my first limo ride," he said, hoping to get his mind off the track it had been running on.

"Since you work with yachting types, I would have thought you had ridden in lots of these things."

"I work *for* yachting types, not with them," he said with a laugh. "There's a big difference. For one thing, they don't take the hired help out for a cruise around town."

There'd been kind of a sharp edge in the way he said that, but she didn't let on that she noticed. She was too classy for that. Like when she didn't ask if this was his first time in a limo. She'd waited for him to say it, and even then she didn't make a big deal out of it. That was classy, too.

"Well, they should," Bennett said with a smile as dazzling as the one she'd given Kevin earlier.

"Should what?" That smile had his thoughts much more fuddled up than he liked them to be.

"Your employers should have taken you out driving with them," she said. "I'm sure they would have enjoyed your company."

"Does that mean you enjoy my company?"

Memphis almost groaned. He'd made that sound so much like a line he could hardly believe his own ears. He also had trouble believing how rattled she made him feel just by sitting next to him. That wasn't because he felt out of place in this high-toned car, either.

Bennett had looked up at him instead of answering. When she did speak, her voice was so low he could barely make out what she was saying. "I enjoy your company," she said, and he was ninety-five percent sure he heard a throb in her tone.

Memphis leaned toward her. He was in so much trouble tonight, the last thing he should be thinking about was this woman's lips, but that seemed to be all he *could* think about. His face was almost to hers. Up this close, her eyes looked big as planets and bright as stars in the night sky. He was about to lose himself among those heavenly bodies when the car made a sudden lurch and they were thrown apart, almost to opposite ends of the wide seat.

"I think Kevin just might have done that on purpose," Memphis said after he straightened himself.

"You could be right about that. He may have the St. Simon family agenda in mind."

"I'd say it's a fair guess my name isn't on that agenda anywhere."

"You could be right about that, too," she said. "But I haven't always toed the family line."

He would have loved to ask her how exactly she had strayed from the straight and narrow, but he didn't want to waste time talking about her family ties. He knew these minutes with her were precious because they would most likely be few. He wanted to treasure every one.

They didn't move close to each other again for the rest of the ride, yet there was a heavy feeling in the air that something was going to happen between them and it was going to happen soon.

Chapter Seventeen

Bennett had never brought a lover to the Plaza Hotel. It occurred to her that she had never been this eager to bring any man anywhere. She had the limo drive straight up to the main entrance, where the Plaza flag flew next to the Stars and Stripes as if this great hotel were a country all its own. She had long been a respected citizen of that country, but she had never come here looking as she did tonight. On another occasion, Kevin might have volunteered to go in ahead and smooth the way. He made no such offer, probably to show her how little he approved of whatever shenanigans she was up to.

Bennett took Memphis's hand as they climbed the red carpetted steps under the medieval-style canopied marquee toward the brass revolving doors. She looked up to find him gazing down at her as if all of the gilt and glamour of the place were nothing compared to her in his eyes. She clasped his hand tighter before she had to let go to enter the door.

In the foyer a vast crystal chandelier held court over a pedestal table topped by an immense vase of fresh flowers in a towering arrangement. The blue-blazered security guard watched Memphis and Bennett with special interest. She flashed him a brilliant smile as she towed Memphis past, onto more red carpet with more gilt in a heraldic design. If Memphis was awed by this place that had awed so many, he kept those feelings to himself and strolled along as if he made this trek every day. He didn't even appear to be impressed by the tall mahogany cases along the walls, displaying the crown jewels of Plazaland, which actually came from some of the most exclusive shops in the city.

The registration desk was off another grand foyer with a white mosaic tile floor and yet another vast chandelier and floral arrangement. Bennett could have brought them in directly through this entrance. She wasn't quite certain why she hadn't. Either she wanted to show off the Plaza to Memphis, or Memphis to the Plaza. She couldn't decide which. Another blue-blazered security man looked as if he might be equally curious about her motives. He was carrying a walkie-talkie. She wondered if his counterpart at the main entrance had signaled ahead about the arrival of two very unexclusive-looking types upon this so exclusive scene.

Bennett wasn't the least bit fazed by this. She had been born and bred to the art of always belonging absolutely anywhere she went. She marched straight up to the registration desk and announced who she was and that she was staying in the St. Simon suite for the night. Even so, there was a delay while the night manager was summoned. Bennett remained patient. Patience was a grace, and this was an occasion for employing grace under fire. When the manager came, she put her masquerade party line to good use again, along with the brilliant smile that made her look just like her mother. The ploy was as effective as Bennett had planned it to be. Within minutes she and Memphis were on their way up the Plaza tower to the family suite. The manager being the soul of typical Plaza discretion, no mention had been made of their lack of luggage.

The suite was actually leased to her father's firm. Business guests and occasionally family visitors were housed here when they came to the city. Bennett had assisted in hostessing small receptions in the elegant receiving room. She had even stayed overnight here herself on the occasion of one debutante ball, charity affair or another. She also knew for a fact that Forth had held more than one impromptu party here for his carousing friends. However, as she had already noted, this was the first time she had brought a lover to the Plaza Hotel. The thought made her heart race even faster than the express elevator they were in.

MEMPHIS HAD NEVER FELT so much like a fish out of water in his life. He'd wanted to turn tail and take off the minute he first set foot on that red carpet outside. If he hadn't been with Bennett he probably would have. On the other hand, she was beautiful and the kind of wonder of a woman he had always wanted to meet but never seemed to. She was taking him into a hotel with her, maybe even to the same room together. He wasn't going to let feeling a little outclassed interfere with that. He wasn't so sure any of this was really happening anyway. He could fully imagine being jolted awake out of this fantasy at any moment.

All the same, they'd made it past the bruiser guards with the crests on their jacket pockets. They'd even made it past the woman at the registration desk who'd glared holes straight through his leather jacket, just about the same way the limo driver had done. Now they were up on one of the high floors of this palace of a place, headed for the St. Simon family suite, no less. He couldn't help chuckling at the thought of Memphis Modine, the motherless child with a foundling basket blanket for a pedigree, on the arm of a woman whose family kept digs in the Plaza Hotel.

"You seem to be having fun," Bennett said. She must have heard him chuckling.

"Why not?" he said, managing to sound cool.

If truth were known, he could hardly have felt less cool, and not just because of where he was. He had a strong case of the jitters just about to break surface, and she was the reason. He couldn't think of anything in creation he'd rather do than take her in his arms and carry on where they left off back on that stoop on Ninth Avenue. Even the memory of that kiss made his lips burn to touch hers again. He thought she might have been giving him some signals that she wanted the same thing.

It was hard to tell about women and signals. Maybe he'd read her wrong. He'd sure enough done that before in his life. Usually he wouldn't have cared much about that. He'd go ahead and take his shot and see what happened. Tonight was different because she was different. He cared about not doing anything she wouldn't want. He cared a lot about that, maybe more than he'd ever thought he could.

The opening of the door into the suite pushed all of that out of his head for the moment. He was glad Bennett had insisted they could make it up here on their own. The woman in the lobby had been set on sending a bellman along, even though there were no bags to carry. Then Bennett put that firm tone in her voice that he imagined got her just about anything she wanted most of the time. Lucky for him, it had worked tonight like a charm. He wouldn't have wanted to have some bellhop here to see him right now, almost too intimidated to step across the threshold into what had to be the most elegant room Memphis had ever seen outside the pages of a magazine.

He'd never seen so much gold in one place in his life. There was some of it woven into the rug, more into the drapes and across the windows, tall windows like the ones at the Stuyvesant Club. He didn't like being reminded of that place or what happened to the draperies there, so he turned away to take in the rest of the room.

There were chairs like those he'd seen in museums. The seats were striped and satiny and, sure enough, some of the those stripes were gold. Fresh flowers stood in vases on the tables, as if someone had known ahead of time that these rooms would be used tonight. Maybe the management kept it this way all the time, just in case one of the St. Simons decided to drop in.

Memphis not only chuckled this time, he shook his head, too. He'd have to think about whether all of this was too much or not. He'd known too many folks having hard times in his life not to think there was such a thing as some people having too much when others had so little. Sometimes, he thought that about the yacht owners he worked for, but he'd never had it shout in his ear quite as loudly as it was shouting right now.

"What do you think?" Bennett asked as she closed the double doors behind them.

"They tell me the rich are different," he said. "I guess it's true."

"Maybe not as true as you think."

Memphis heard her voice go deeper than usual at the same moment he heard her turn the key in the lock. He felt his heart trip into his throat, telling him not to move or the fantasy might end. He wanted it not to so much he was holding his breath like a kid making a wish. He turned around anyway, slowly enough not to break the spell. She was standing very still, looking up at him. There was waiting in her eyes—and expectation. He'd seen that look before, but it had never made his heart leap in his chest before, as if he were being pulled toward her and it wouldn't do any good to resist.

Resisting wasn't what he had in mind. He lifted his hands, and his arms seemed to float upward. He touched her shoulders with the lightest touch, as if she might disappear in a puff like a cloud of mist if he grabbed too hard. She stepped toward him as if to let him know it was okay to keep going. That would be the last signal Memphis needed. He could take charge from here on.

He drew her to him, close and up onto her toes. She was tall and narrow, but soft, too. She even smelled soft. He was thinking about how much he loved the smell of her when his lips touched hers. After that, he wasn't thinking much at all. He was only feeling. He wrapped his arms around her tightly and kissed her deeply, as though he would have liked to swallow her whole. He did want that if it was a way to get her under his skin, make her part of him and keep her there. He didn't let himself think about what would happen when it came time for her to leave him.

His tongue was in her mouth. He could hardly believe how warm and good it felt there. He wanted to stay there forever. She pushed her tongue past his and into his mouth, too, the small point touching every part of him there was to touch. The feel of that shot straight as an arrow to his groin. He groaned and held her tighter.

She was still on her toes and pressed so close again him that one of her legs was between his. She started to move, back and forth and closer still. She slid her hand down his back to his waist, then below, over his buttocks. Her hands on him made him want to cry out with hunger for her to touch him everywhere, against his skin, not through his clothes.

Bennett eased herself lower so she could reach to move her hand under his thigh. She pulled that thigh upward between her legs till it was pressed against the cleft of her. He vaguely remembered how thin the material of her leggings had been and wished his jeans were made of the same flimsy stuff. Even so, he was sure he could feel the heat of her through the denim, especially when she began to slide back and forth along the hardness of his thigh. She moaned, over and over as she rubbed her body against him.

Their mouths devoured each other still. They couldn't get enough of each other. He could tell that was as true for her as it was for him. He slipped both hands down her back, into the curve of her waist, out over the swell of her hips until he was gripping the roundness of her buttocks in both hands. He shoved her against him, even closer than she was already, and maybe harder than he had meant to. She cried out amidst her moans, but he knew it wasn't from pain, because she didn't want him to stop. He knew that by the way she pulled his thigh tighter to her and tortured her body against it.

He probably couldn't have stopped anyway. The way she was moving tortured him, too, the most delicious suffering he had ever known. All he could think of was wanting more and more, harder and harder. He was so aroused now he thought he might burst through his jeans. He let go of one wonderfully round cheek of hers to reach between their moving bodies for his fly button and zipper so he could free himself before the pressure became too much to bear.

She pulled her mouth back from his then and said, "Wait."

Memphis only partly heard that she had spoken and didn't take in her meaning for a moment. All he knew was that she had suddenly stopped moving against him. She was even drawing her body away from his. He didn't quite understand what was happening, and he wasn't sure he cared. He was about to sweep her into his arms and lay her down on the floor when she raised her hands against his chest and pushed gently. That wouldn't have been enough to stop him if she hadn't spoken.

"Let's slow down," she said in a voice so gravelly it barely sounded like it could be her. "I want this to last a very long time."

He eased slowly away from her then. He would have thought his mind had turned completely off by now. Still, he couldn't help thinking that even though she might want him now, to her he was just a one-time thing. The pain of that possibility was almost as sharp as the urgency throbbing in his jeans. He told his mind to shut up. If all they had was one time, then that was the way it had to be. They would make it the one time neither of them could ever forget as long as they lived.

She slipped her hand into his and twined their fingers together. "Come with me," she said.

He followed her across the gold carpet with red and green square designs woven into it. She opened a door out of the living room part of the suite and into the bedroom. There was a marble fireplace with a mirror above it, more window drapes, but not anywhere near as much gold. A crystal chandelier hung from the center of the ceiling, but the most amazing thing about the room was the four-poster between the two windows, complete with white brocade canopy above the extra king-sized width of the biggest bed he'd ever seen. He was headed toward it, already imagining what they could do with all that room, when she steered him away.

"In here," she said, and pulled him toward a door near the fireplace.

Memphis didn't mind her taking charge. He didn't always care for that in women, but with her he felt different about it. With her, he felt different about lots of things. There was a whole part of life she opened up for him, the same way she was opening the door near the fireplace.

If the rest of the suite was elegant, then the bathroom could only be described as out of this world. Out of any world he had ever lived in, anyway. He was reminded of a movie he must have seen as a kid, about ancient Rome or Greece. The tub was what he clapped his eyes on first and couldn't seem to look away from. It was white marble and very big, set back into an alcove between sets of double pillars, cream colored with gold trim. The faucet for filling the tub was also gold and shaped like a swan. Cut crystal jars lined the shelf along the side of the alcove.

Bennett let go of his hand and walked to the tub. She turned on the water and picked up one of the jars. Then she pulled out the crystal stopper and poured a slow stream of thick, shimmering liquid into the water. Almost immediately, mounds of foam began to form. She bent down to touch the water then adjusted the handles near the faucet and touched the water again. Memphis watched her as if he might be looking at a dream. She moved like a dream woman. For him, she *was* a dream woman.

She touched the water one more time and said, "Just right."

"Yes," he replied so low he wasn't sure she'd hear. "Just right."

He might not have thought the dream could get any lovelier until she stepped away from the tub and shrugged the oversize man's shirt off her shoulders. Memphis watched it drift to the floor as she slipped her feet out of her shoes. She wasn't looking at him, but she would know he was looking at her. She moved smoothly as silk, as if in a dance, a dance she was performing for him. He could hardly catch his breath from watching her and knowing he would see her like this in his mind till his dying day.

Chapter Eighteen

Bennett lifted her arms slowly and pulled her top up with them, inch by inch, baring her white skin and then the lace of her bra with the dark rounds of her nipples showing through. Memphis felt the urgency in his groin again. He had to clench his hands into fists to keep from grabbing her. She had said to make it last, and he wanted that, too.

The top was off and tossed away now. She hooked her thumbs beneath the waistband of her leggings and pushed down. They peeled off her like a second skin. She had on lace panties to match the bra, with another pattern of darkness showing through. Memphis groaned low in his throat. He knew she heard him because the glimmer of a smile curved her lips.

He could see the skin of her thighs now, creamy and gleaming smooth. His palms itched to stroke her there. He would soon. She rolled the leggings down over one slender foot and then the other. She stood up straight, turning fully toward him. Till now, she hadn't looked at him, had moved as if she were in her own private world. She looked at him now, right into his eyes, even as she reached down and turned off the water just as the bubbles were about to spill over into the room.

Bennett held her gaze on his face as her hands moved behind her back and opened the catch on her bra. She pushed the straps forward. The delicate lace clung to the swells of her breasts until she lifted it with her fingertips and pulled the bra slowly, a very little at a time, free from her skin.

"Ohh," he breathed as the wisp of lace fell to the floor. "You are so beautiful."

So beautiful and surprising, too. She had seemed very slender with her clothes on. The naked flesh of her was more voluptuous than he had expected. Her breasts were full and round and perfect, with dark pink nipples taut now and thrusting forward. He couldn't stand the waiting any longer. He stepped forward and reached out for her.

His fingers closed over her breasts. She eased them away only long enough to peel his jacket from his shoulders and get his T-shirt over his head. She fumbled a little opening his fly to push his jeans down over his hips. He would have helped her, but he couldn't bear the thought of taking his hands away from the tantalizing softness of her breasts like ripe, round fruit beneath his kneading fingers.

She stepped backward to the tub and led him with her. He wanted to touch her all over, but he wasn't finished ravaging her breasts, emblazoning his palms with the feel of them, he knew he would never forget. She stepped up into the tub, and he stepped in after her. The water on his legs was a shock at first, especially since his nerves were keyed so tight and his senses so extra keen at the moment. He even noticed the whispery sound the foam made as they lowered themselves into it.

Memphis had never been in a bubble bath before. He wouldn't have guessed how sleek and smooth it would feel, water and foam sliding warm and softly scented along his skin. He wouldn't have guessed he'd like it so much. But then, he might just possibly like anything at all as long as he was doing it with Bennett St. Simon. The thought of her name, so much a part of that other world she would have to go back to soon, might have put him off for a moment, but her movements distracted Memphis.

She picked up a gauzy yellow sponge made out of plastic lace, and poured some oil onto it from another of the crystal jars along the side of the alcove. She worked the oil through the sponge and was about to begin rubbing his chest with it when he gently took it from her.

"My turn," he said. "You've been doing all of the work."

"I love my job," she said in a purr as silky as the foam that surrounded them and framed her glistening breasts.

"I can tell," he said.

That was also a surprise, how this cool pale goddess from an ivory tower world was turning out to be the sexiest, most fully alive and hot-blooded woman he had ever known.

"Now let me show you what I like," he said.

Memphis scooped his arm around her and lifted her onto his lap in the spacious tub. Water spilled over the sides onto the floor, but he didn't care. He ran the sponge upward between her breasts, covering first one, then the other, dragging the rough-soft texture over and around her nipples, pressing harder with each circle, watching the flesh there grow tighter and darker by the second.

Bennett let her head fall back against his shoulder. Her eyes were hooded nearly closed, and her lips were parted in a sigh. He bent over her with a long, probing kiss, as he moved the sponge downward beneath the surface of the water, over her belly through the wet tendrils below. He trailed the edges of the lacy surface through those tendrils and along the silken cleft just above the opening of her thighs. She stiffened in his arms, arching against his hand, and cried out beneath his mouth.

He dropped the sponge then, unwilling to share the feel of her with anything. He rubbed the cleft gently, for it was sleek and slippery from the bath oil. He used that lubrication to help his fingers slide around and around then farther down, between her thighs and into the open mouth of her. She was warm there, warmer even than the bathwater, and smooth in a way that needed no oils or lotions other than its own.

She had moved her hands beneath the water, too, and stroked the hardness of him there. At the same time, she had begun to move against his hand, helping his fingers do their maddening magic inside her. He was moving, also, in rhythm with her stroking. They moaned together and spoke wordless sounds, full of longing and desire, against each other's lips. More water splashed over the marble onto the elegant tile floor. They neither heard nor cared.

Then she was apart from his body for a moment, still holding on to him beneath the water as she straddled him. She fitted herself over him and pushed herself down until he was deep inside her. Her head fell back again as it had before, her lips parted as she murmured words only barely intelligible about how much she needed him, how she had needed him for so very long.

He gripped her slender waist in both hands and lunged upward into her, once and then again and again and again. They moaned and called out and rocked together until one last long cry and the deepest thrust of all carried them to a place of pulsating bliss and then brought them slowly back again into the most exquisite peace they had ever known.

BENNETT HAD NEVER BEEN able to sleep in someone else's arms. She couldn't do so tonight, but not for the usual reasons. With other men, she had always been uncomfortably aware of their touch invading her rest. She had none of those feelings with Memphis. His touch on her skin seemed so familiar, his arms around her so comforting that she might have drifted off into dreams as he had, if it weren't for the questions troubling her heart. She cared too much for him already, and that frightened her. She had known him only a short time and under terrible circumstances. The tenderness she felt for him now was anything but wise.

She should have thought about that before she brought him here, before she seduced him and herself into what had happened between them. Remembering their lovemaking turned her nearly to jelly inside. She had never experienced anything like it before. She suspected nothing and no one would ever make her feel so much again, not unless it was Memphis. She had been more free and open with him than she had ever felt safe enough to be with any man. Yet, he was her captor, or at least he had been. He was wanted for murder. And he could hardly have been a less suitable man for a St. Simon woman to find herself on the verge of falling in love with. She didn't want to think that mattered, but in her heart of hearts she knew it might, if there was ever to be a long-term future between them.

But how could there be?

The frustration of being assaulted by so many unanswerables, when all she wanted to do was luxuriate with her lover, caused Bennett to stir restlessly. That must have disturbed Memphis, because he stretched beneath her for a moment. His magnificent body arched into hers, and her arms went out to him.

"Can't you sleep?" he asked sleepily.

"No, I can't."

"Grab my jeans and I'll give you a penny for your thoughts."

The night curtains had been left open on either side of the bed, and morning shone in. It struck Bennett that this was the first time she had seen him in the daylight. He looked as gorgeous and as perfect to her as he had at night. His body was lean and muscular, tanned from his days at sea. The dark hair on his chest glistened in the morning sun, and in the bright light she could see the calluses on his palms from long hours of hauling lines. She recalled those hands as smooth on her body, but she could see now that they were rough from hard work. She couldn't help wondering if other things about last night had also been an illusion.

"What's bothering you, Bennett?" He was obviously much more awake now, propping himself up on one elbow while still holding her loosely but close. "You can tell me anything."

Bennett wished she believed that as sincerely as she was almost certain he meant it. Meanwhile, she had to come up with an answer. There was no sense in trying to convince him she wasn't troubled. He was too perceptive for that.

"I've been thinking about what I found out last night at the DownTown Lounge," she said.

"What about it?"

Memphis was watching her curiously and with great attentiveness. She could easily understand why. After the way they had made love just hours ago, she should have been nestled in his arms instead of rolling around filled with restless thoughts. She'd have to make this cover story a good one.

"That woman, Liddy, said something that made me think you might be involved in something illegal," she said, "whether you know it or not."

"What did she tell you?"

His tone had lost some of its softness toward her. The harder edge to his words cut her like a knife.

"She said Pearlanne had intimated there could be some smuggling going on aboard that boat you've been crewing."

"She did, did she."

The sudden chill in his voice blew across Bennett like an arctic wind, making her wish she had never started this conversation in the first place.

"Pearlanne claimed she was about to come into some money, apparently from this smuggling deal her friend

Stitch was a part of,'' Bennett stumbled on. "At least that was Liddy's impression.''

"Well, if I had a cut of that kind of action it just might give me a motive for bumping off old Pearlanne.''

He had pulled completely away from her now so that they were no longer touching at all.

"I'm not accusing you,'' she said. She didn't know why she'd gotten into this, except that it had seemed a much less painful topic than what was truly bothering her—whether she had any business being involved with him at all. "I only wondered if you had noticed anything suspicious about these voyages you've been making.''

Memphis was sitting up now, propped against the headboard of the four-poster and looking down at her as if from a great height. "Not a thing,'' he said. "Maybe something could be going on, but I doubt it. It's none of my business anyway. My job's to get the *Fiddlehead* to her port of call, that's all.''

"What did you say?'' Bennett could hardly believe her ears. ·

"I said I run the *Fiddlehead* crew, and that's the end of it.''

Bennett didn't answer. Her thoughts were whirling about too fast for her to come up with anything to say.

"Do you have a problem believing that?'' he asked.

"A problem?'' Bennett couldn't help sounding bewildered. "No. No problem.'' Suddenly that couldn't have been further from the truth.

She slid off the bed.

"Time for you to leave?'' he asked coldly.

"I'm just going into the bathroom,'' she said, though she knew that wasn't entirely true.

He nodded but said nothing. She could feel his eyes on her as she walked naked to the bathroom door. If her over-size shirt had been nearby, she would have covered herself with it. She hadn't felt at all self-conscious about being naked with him before. Right now, however, she was too shaken to feel very much at ease about anything. She had all she could manage to stop herself from running out of the room.

Bennett would have liked to plunge herself into a cold shower, but there was only a marble tub. She couldn't do that now. He would hear her and maybe come in to join her. That must not happen. She had to be alone. She turned on the water in the sink. She needed the noise of the splashing in case she should burst into the tears that pressed so close and hot behind her eyes. He must not hear that, either. He especially must not hear that.

She swallowed hard to keep the sobs from rising and wondered at herself for being so far out of control. She never let herself get this way. But then, there had been lots of "nevers" violated since she first met Memphis Modine not yet twenty-four hours ago. Most significantly, she had never been so sexually abandoned with a man before.

"Abandoned" was the way to describe it, too. She had abandoned reason, abandoned modesty, abandoned caution. That last was the never she really never allowed herself to commit. Bennett was nothing if not cautious. Her Mexico escapade in her teenage years was the one exception to that rule of her careful life, and look how that had turned out. She had every reason to believe she was now on a collision course with personal disaster yet again.

When she had begun seducing Memphis the night before, she had thought of it as a fantasy rendezvous with a near stranger. Despite all they had been through in their few hours together, that is what they were—near strangers to each other. The distance between them had seemed like a safety zone to her. She had not anticipated how quickly that distance would evaporate in the heat of their extraordinary encounter.

Thinking herself safe, she had opened up like never before. She had told herself she was free to be as exotic and erotic as was possible for her. She had long wondered what the limits of that possibility might be. Now she knew. There were no limits, at least not when she was with the right man. Against all odds, regardless of differences in background and situation, Memphis had turned out to be that right man for her. Under other circumstances, that discovery might have made her ecstatic. Instead, she was miserable. The name of his sailboat had made certain of that.

She grabbed the white telephone on the bathroom wall. She left the sink tap running to cover the sound of her voice. She didn't know the number of the New York Yacht Club by heart so she had to dial 411 for Information. When she had the club on the line, mention of the St. Simon name got her directly to someone who could tell her about yacht registry.

"No," the commodore said. "There are not two vessels named *Fiddlehead* registered."

"Then, the boat called *Fiddlehead,* which has been docked at South Street Seaport is the same one that is registered out of your club?"

"That is right, Ms. St. Simon. But wait one moment."

The sudden silence on the other end of the line sounded like a reprieve to Bennett. He was going to come back on the phone and tell her there had been a mistake after all. The *Fiddlehead* Memphis crewed on was not the same yacht she knew.

"Yes, Ms. St. Simon," the commodore said. "I thought I saw a message about the *Fiddlehead* this morning. That vessel has been moved from the Seaport to Twenty-third Street Marina."

Bennett's hoped-for relief was gone. She had probably known there would be no reprieve all along, only a momentary delusion of it. She might as well ask the question she most dreaded to have answered.

"Do you know if Quinton Leslie is aboard the *Fiddlehead?*"

"I am sorry, Ms. St. Simon. I have no way of determining that."

"But you are sure this is definitely the same *Fiddlehead* that Mr. Leslie partly owns?" She was still grabbing for straws, and she knew it.

"One and the same."

"I see," she said. She was so confused she almost forgot to thank the commodore before hanging up.

"Anytime I may be of help, Ms. St. Simon, please do not hesitate to contact me," he said.

She wished, with more desperation than she had ever experienced in her life, that the commodore could provide the kind of help she needed now.

Chapter Nineteen

Bennett did take a shower in the marble cabinet in the corner of the spacious bathroom. She turned the pulsing massage jets up high, hoping they would pound some sense into this situation or throb her to alertness. Maybe then she could come up with some solutions to the problems that plagued her. No such answers came, but she did wash a good deal of the inexpensive dye from her hair. The resulting color was a shade of darkish auburn that she actually liked, especially after she had blown it into soft fullness with the dryer the hotel provided.

That was the wonderful thing about the Plaza. They anticipated your needs and did their best to satisfy them in advance. You could lose yourself in this rarefied world if you wanted. Bennett would have liked to do that now, but she knew she mustn't. Something had to be done, and she had to do it. She only wished she knew for sure what that something should be.

First of all, she had to get some clothes. Neither her thrift box outfit nor what was left of last night's cocktail dress would do for a trip to Twenty-third Street Marina. She had already planned to call Bergdorf's, which was just across the corner from the hotel. She had shopped there often enough that they had her sizes on file. They could quickly put together a simple day ensemble with a few instructions from

her. Then someone could bring the parcels to her hotel
room. Again the St. Simon name would get her the service
she required in a time of need. She seemed to be depending
on her name to do that for her a lot lately. She didn't like
having to do it, but she was grateful that she could.

Memphis hadn't joined her in the shower. Part of her
couldn't help regretting that, no matter how unwise it would
have been to repeat their passion of the night before. She
guessed that he must be sleeping. She was glad he could rest
from his ordeal of chasing all over Manhattan last evening.
She should try to rest herself, but she knew she wouldn't be
able to settle down enough for sleep. The secrets she was
hiding from Memphis would be enough to keep her awake
on her own, and she had a good deal more to worry about,
as well.

Bennett didn't want to think about those secrets, because
she knew that when she walked out into the bedroom and
saw his chiseled profile against the pillow, his magnificent
body outlined beneath the sheet, she would want to tell him
everything. She couldn't do that, not yet anyway, perhaps
not ever—if, in fact, there even could be an ever after for
them. That possibility seemed to grow slimmer by the hour.

She heaved a glum sigh as she pulled on the plush terry-
cloth robe with the Plaza emblem on it. At least she would
have these next few moments with him. She was thinking
about how he would look when he first awakened, how
beautiful his eyes would be, the disarray of his thick dark
hair. She pushed open the bathroom door, almost allowing
herself to feel hopeful if only for the moment. As soon as
she stepped into the bedroom, all beautiful images and even
that glimmer of hope disappeared. The bed was empty.
Memphis was gone.

Bennett walked to the four-poster in a daze. She touched
the rumpled sheets. They were cold. He had been gone from
them for some time. Then she noticed the bedside table. The

phone had been moved. She was sure of it. The phone had been on the other side of the lamp. Now it was pulled over next to the bed, as if Memphis had made a call on it—or as if he had listened in on a call being made from the bathroom.

Bennett was suddenly certain this was exactly what had happened. She went over her call to the yacht club in her mind. If Memphis heard that conversation, then he knew she was hiding things from him. One thing, at least—the fact that Quint could be involved in whatever might have been going on aboard the *Fiddlehead*. He might know this man named Stitch Falcone, too. It was even possible that Quint could be using the Falcone alias himself.

Any of these scenarios would have the potential to clear Memphis's name, and Bennett had kept them from him. Had she done it to protect her own kind? Had she done it because she still didn't trust Memphis even though she had given herself so totally to him last night? Both of these were possible. Memphis would have known that if he overheard her conversation with the commodore. Once again, Bennett was convinced Memphis had done exactly that.

RUDY HAD PARKED the sedan in a garage. He hated doing that. He considered it a challenge to find a place on the street in Manhattan and save the extra garage charge.

"It's like eight bucks," Nick complained. "You're such a cheap freak."

Nick always complained about walking the added distance, even when it was only a couple of blocks. Parking spaces near midtown hardly ever turned out to be in a handy location. Today he was complaining because the garage attendant was taking more than two minutes to get the car.

"I could drive that boat out of here myself," Nick grumbled. "I don't need some snot-nosed kid doing it for me."

"You'd probably wipe out a couple of rows of parked cars in the process," Rudy said. He wasn't in too good a mood himself.

"Come on. Come on," Nick shouted. "Let's get this show on the road."

"You've just got a mad on because Falcone called your number for once."

"What are you talking about?"

Nick's voice had a dangerous edge to it. Any other time, Rudy would have let the subject drop, but not today. Like he said, he wasn't in any too good a mood himself.

"You know exactly what I'm talking about. You were five, ten minutes behind those two down in that hellhole on the Lower East Side, and you missed the train anyway."

"I didn't miss no train." The veins in Nick's forehead stood out angrily beneath his reddening skin. "And you got nothin' to talk about, Rudy boy. Suppose I was to tell Falcone you wasn't even down there with me like you should have been. What would happen then, wise guy?"

Rudy was quiet for a minute. Nick had a point, but Rudy wasn't about to tell him so.

"See what I mean?" Nick sneered. "That shut your face for you, didn't it?"

"You're a great one to call anybody a wise guy." Rudy had meant to keep his mouth shut, but he couldn't stand it when Nick used that smart-assed tone on him. "Somebody ought to tell Falcone the real reason you were in that dive in the first place. It sure wasn't because you were doing business."

"I was taking care of business, all right. I'm always taking care of business."

Nick was talking so loudly that people walking by looked over at him where he and Rudy were standing just off the street at the top of the garage ramp. For once, Rudy didn't give a damn whether they made a scene or not.

"Yeah, I know what kind of business you're always taking care of," he said, "and it hasn't got anything to do with Falcone."

"What are you talking about?" Nick asked again.

"Chasing women. That's the business you're in, fella, and it's a twenty-four-hour-a-day job the way you work it."

"There ain't nothin' wrong with that. I'd rather be a skirt chaser than an uptight jerk like you any day."

Rudy felt his own face getting red. He might have said something really harsh to Nick, but the dark sedan had just turned the corner at the bottom of the ramp and was climbing toward them. The attendant must have hit the gas hard, the way garage guys love to do, because the big car leapt forward and was at the top of the ramp in seconds flat.

"It's about time," Nick growled.

"How's that, mister?" the garage attendant asked. He looked as though he might be almost as foul-tempered as Nick.

"I said, where'd you park the damned thing? In Jersey?"

The garage attendant curled his lip to reveal a gleaming gold tooth.

Rudy stepped forward, between Nick and the garage guy. He'd just as soon see the big palooka clean Nick's clock for him, but not today. Falcone had given the two of them an assignment, and it was clear that there'd be big trouble if they screwed up again.

"We don't want any hassles here," Rudy said to the attendant and pressed two twenties into his hand. "This is for you."

The brawny attendant looked down at the bills in his hand then up at Nick. "Check you later," the attendant said in a menacing tone and turned to hike back down the ramp.

"I don't need you taking care of things for me," Nick said, and moved to follow the guy into the garage. Rudy grabbed his arm.

"We've still got a job to do," Rudy said. "We'd better get to it."

Nick shook the hand off his arm and shrugged his shoulders hard inside his Italian suit jacket. The red of his face was a shade less bright now. He still seemed to be spoiling for a fight with anybody unlucky enough to come along, but he climbed into the passenger side of the car all the same. Rudy got behind the wheel and shoved the car into gear before easing out into traffic and heading in the direction of the Plaza Hotel.

MEMPHIS WAS MAD AT himself, even madder than he'd been at himself for being fool enough to end up at that fancy club last night holding the bag for deep-sixing a woman he'd never before seen in his life. And that was nothing compared to how big a jackass he'd made of himself with Bennett St. Simon. Just thinking the name made him feel stupid. How could he ever have been dumb enough to think a Memphis Modine and a Bennett St. Simon could make a match?

Truth was, he hadn't been thinking much about matches last night. He didn't have anything permanent in mind then. His mind didn't have much to do with what happened to him when she started taking off her clothes the way she did in the bathroom. Just thinking about it now had him getting worked up all over again. He didn't like that much, either. He never had trouble keeping the lid on what he felt about a woman. If he wanted to let himself go, he'd do that, but only when he gave the okay and had his reactions strictly under control.

With this woman, control didn't seem to be in the mix. He looked at her, he heard her voice, he let her into his head, and he was off and running whether he wanted to be or not. He'd never known anybody who could turn him on the way she did. Well, now it was time to get a grip and turn himself off. What he'd heard on the phone this morning told him there was no other choice in the matter.

Maybe it was her he should be mad at anyway. For some reason, that didn't feel like something he wanted to do. He didn't know where that came from, either. He'd started out just thinking about making love. He had to admit he'd been thinking about that a long time before it made sense to. Even when he was dragging her around the park, he couldn't help noticing how soft her skin felt and the way her body looked in that little dress. If he hadn't been running for his fool life at the time, he might have thrown her down on the grass right there.

Memphis walked faster along the crowded street. He knew that wasn't true the minute he thought it. He wouldn't throw Bennett anywhere. She made him feel something that put that aggressive part of himself straight out of commission. She made him feel respect. She wasn't the kind of woman he could push or force into anything. She was the kind of woman he wanted by his side, step by step, right there with him all the way. He wanted her for a partner, in lovemaking and maybe in everything else, too. He thought they'd made a start last night. He'd been wrong.

He hesitated at the corner of Fifth Avenue. There was a subway pole with a green ball on top of it on the next block up. He'd be best off to try that. He could figure out which trains to take from the map on the wall down there. He'd feel more at ease underground right now anyway. Up here, he got the suspicion that everybody was looking at him funny, everybody knew his face and what he was supposed to be guilty of. It could be splattered all over the papers by now for all he knew. He glanced around for a newsstand but didn't see one.

In the meantime, he didn't head for the subway entrance. He continued on the way he'd been going, across town to the east. He needed to keep moving. He had to walk off what he was feeling. Maybe if he hiked fast enough, he could walk right out of himself and what was going on with him this morning. He wasn't a guy who ran away from anything, but that seemed to be all he'd been doing since he met her—running from the cops, running from the thugs. Now he was even trying to run from himself. Of course, she could only be to blame for that last one, but he felt like blaming her for the whole mess anyway.

It was the phone call that did it. Up till then, he'd been going along like a crazy fool, letting himself believe in fairy tales. He hadn't even believed in those things when he was a kid. Growing up in an orphanage knocked that fantasy stuff out of your head real fast. He'd figured out what was and wasn't going to happen to a kid like him a long time before he was even old enough to go to school. For one thing, he knew he wasn't going to be taken home by some beautiful lady to her big, sunny house on a hill where she'd care for him and love him forever. He thought he'd chucked that delusion in the garbage years ago. Maybe he hadn't, because that's just what had popped into the back of his mind sometime last night, beautiful lady, sunny digs and all.

Memphis felt the tightness rise up from his chest into his throat. He could hardly believe it. Tough-as-nails, salt-of-the-sea Memphis Modine was all but running down the street just about half a step away from letting himself break down and cry. He swallowed the tightness and warned it not to come back. There had been lots of times in his life when he wanted to cry, most of them when he was a kid. He'd taught himself way back then that breaking down never got you anything but beaten up in this world. Let them see you've got a soft spot somewhere, and the vultures head straight for it. He wasn't going to forget that lesson now, not for anything, especially not for a woman.

Memphis squared his shoulders and looked around for another subway entrance and the means to get himself the fastest way possible to Twenty-third Street and the East River.

Chapter Twenty

Bennett needed information, the inside scoop you might call it. She'd never paid much attention to all of that—the rumors and innuendo, the latest gossip circulating among the people she knew. In fact, she had always done her best to avoid that sort of thing. Private lives should be kept private was what she thought. Back in the days of her Mexico escapade, she had been on the receiving end of a lot of that unwelcome interest herself. She could still remember how it hurt to know that everybody was talking about her. She had wished she could run away again to some place where the only person scrutinizing herself would be herself.

Today was different. There were things Bennett needed to find out, and she had to find them out fast. Luckily she had a very good idea what the best source of that information might be. She also suspected Sonia Jade would jump at the chance to get closer to Bennett, who could be the avenue to all kinds of social opportunities. Social opportunities were Sonia's number-one interest, next to gossip. Bennett turned out to be right about Sonia's eagerness to get together. She was at the Plaza Palm Court almost before Bennett had time to change into the clothes Bergdorf's had sent over for her— beige silk crepe day pants that nipped in a bit at the ankle over high-vamped taupe shoe boots; a simple cotton-knit sweater and linen-silk blend jacket in the same shade as the boots finished off the outfit. They had even included a bag with a shoulder strap.

Bennett marveled at the change a few well chosen garments could make. Last night she had transformed herself into a downtown hoyden with a few thrift box finds. She had looked the part so much that not a single person had questioned her legitimacy in that role. She had mingled with the hip club crowd and fit right in. Now she was business as usual again. Bennett St. Simon, impeccable to a fault in her oh-so-appropriate stylish uptown ensemble. Surveying the effect in the mirror, she felt a twinge of desire to be Vangie once more, hanging out in fun places, running through the late-night streets, kissing her lover on a stoop on Ninth Avenue.

That last memory plunged to her belly with such a heavy jolt of longing she thought for a moment she might sink to the floor from the weight of it. She steadied herself against the French Provincial desk that stood so graciously in front of the mirror. A wave of uncertainty washed over her. Her mother always said, remember who you are and what you represent. Right now, Bennett was not at all sure what either of those might be. She understood that Memphis Modine and what had happened between them, so very much in so very little time, was at the heart of her uncertainty. The thought of him made her question whether she wanted to fit into a world where he might not fit, as well. Even if he never came back to her, she wondered if her privileged life was what she wanted for herself any longer.

"Even if he never came back to her." The reality of that possibility thudded through her even more heavily than her sense of longing had done. She teetered perilously close to tears and had to swallow hard to keep from giving herself up to them. There was no time for any of that now. No time for regrets. She grabbed her perfectly coordinated, fine leather shoulderbag and headed, fast as she could hurry without stumbling over one of the perfectly coordinated fine antiques, for the door. She wished desperately that she felt half as well pulled together as her outfit and her surroundings.

Sonia Jade was already waiting when Bennett got downstairs to the Palm Court. As usual, Sonia was easy to spot among the generally sedate early lunch crowd. She was more colorfully attired than Bennett. Sonia's turquoise raw silk suit had obviously been chosen to set off the eyes that matched her last name. Bennett could just imagine how every man's attention had turned for a moment when Sonia walked into this room. Bennett didn't have that effect on a crowd, and she knew it. She was much too low-keyed in both look and manner to cause much of a stir when she made an entrance. Last night had been an exception. She had not failed to notice a number of admiring male glances in her direction, both on the street and in the club. Vangie, of course, hadn't been what you would call low-keyed at all.

"Thanks so much for coming," Bennett said as she sat down across from Sonia at a small, round table in the exact center of the Court.

Bennett wished Sonia had picked a less conspicuous location. The Palm Court was open to the corridor from the Plaza's main entrance and along the walkway that led to the shops and other restaurants in the hotel. Guests, lunchers, shoppers and just plain gawkers strolled along this carpeted promenade in droves. Bennett would have much preferred a corner table shielded by the fronds of the palms that gave the court its name. Sonia, however, was definitely not a corner table kind of woman. Seeing and being seen were her stock in trade. She had made certain that even the wide marble columns were too far away to provide any cover. At least, Bennett was able to position herself facing away from the more public side of the court. Sonia was obviously happy with that arrangement. She would want to be as visible as Bennett wished to remain the opposite.

"It was lovely to hear from you," Sonia said in the tight-jawed drawl she'd learned at school. "Of course, I had to juggle appointments like mad to manage this on such short notice."

"Thank you for taking the trouble to do that."

"Not to worry. I considered the effort a worthwhile one, especially for a special friend like you."

Bennett and Sonia had never been friends, much less special friends, though Sonia had certainly wanted them to be. Sonia's ambition to climb to the heady heights of the circle surrounding Bennett's mother, Dilys St. Simon, had long been very apparent. Bennett couldn't help feeling a flash of guilt for exploiting that ambition, which she had regarded with disdain in the past. She was not a person who believed that the ends justified the means. At least, she hadn't been that kind of person before last night. Since then, she would have been hard-pressed to define just what kind of person she had suddenly become.

"It is because we are such special friends that I've invited you here today," Bennett said in the tone she had to affect to get what she needed now. "I must ask a favor of you."

"A favor?" Sonia sounded a bit more distant than she had before.

"And I would be very much in your debt if you were good enough to grant it," Bennett added hastily.

"I see." Of course, Sonia did see exactly what kind of tit-for-tat arrangement Bennett was suggesting. "I would certainly be glad to be of help in any way I can. You have always been a particular favorite among my acquaintance. What was it you had in mind?"

Bennett was relieved to have the waiter interrupt at that point. The atmosphere of insincerity surrounding the small, linen-draped table was becoming so thick she thought she might choke on it at any moment. She reminded herself of what she was doing here and why it was so important. By the time the waiter had taken their orders, bowed ever so slightly then slipped away, she was ready to pursue her objective with almost no qualms about doing so.

"I need information," she said. "I wanted it to be accurate," she added, remembering that this particular wheel would be best greased by flattery, "so I naturally have come to you."

"What kind of information would that be?" The spark of interest in Sonia's green eyes was unmistakable. She obviously detected there must be something of potential interest afoot.

"I need to know if there are any men in our crowd who have been spending time recently with..." Bennett hesitated, searching for the right words. "With a woman the rest of us wouldn't necessarily know."

"You mean a townie?"

Bennett had always hated that term, which was such a snobbish carryover from school days, when certain students would use it to show how much they looked down on their less privileged, off-campus neighbors.

"A downtownie to be exact." Bennett hated resorting to such a haughty attitude. It made her ashamed to be what she was and and what she represented, as her mother put it. Even telling herself that the circumstances called for just what she was doing didn't wash the bad taste from Bennett's mouth.

"Oh, yes. The downtown-chippy syndrome," Sonia was saying. "The scourge of the low-life side. The fellows can't seem to resist the impulse to dabble in a bit of street grit every now and again, can they? But then, boys will be boys, and they hardly ever forget to come scurrying back where they belong after they've had their tawdry little taste of that sort of thing."

Bennett had to clench her teeth to keep from proclaiming that she had been on those selfsame low-life streets only hours ago and she hadn't felt the impulse to look down her nose even once during the entire experience. She reminded herself that this would not be a wise revelation to make at this particular moment when she had much more crucial fish to fry.

"Do you know of any boys who have been dabbling lately?" she asked.

"Is there anyone of specific interest to you?" Sonia asked, leaning closer over the table and making no attempt to disguise her curiosity. Subtleness was not an art that Sonia had mastered.

"Specifically, any of the fellows who would have been at the Stuyvesant reception last night."

"Oh, yes. *Those* fellows. You do know what happened there last night, don't you?" Sonia's green eyes narrowed slightly, as if she might be in the process of putting two and two together.

"I heard about it." Bennett wasn't about to be more forthcoming than that until she found out how much Sonia already knew.

"Ghastly business. Imagine it. A woman like that found dead at the Stuyvesant Club no less. Of course, every effort is being made to keep it out of the tabloids. The police are being most discreet at the moment, but who knows how long they'll be able to manage that."

"Do they have any idea what happened?" Bennett asked, allowing herself to be diverted from her primary agenda for a moment.

"Apparently she was killed by one of her own. Somebody she'd come into the club with, heaven knows by what access. We really do need to tighten security."

"Do they know who that person with her might have been?" Bennett's heart tripped faster. She composed her face, which her years as her mother's daughter had taught her so well. She must not let on how agitated this conversation was making her.

"I called absolutely everybody this morning, but I couldn't find out a thing. Except that they were both outsiders, and they had obviously come there to rob us all blind. How fortunate we were that they decided to turn on each other instead."

"Yes. How fortunate," Bennett managed to say over the expanding lump in her throat. "So, the man who killed this woman got away without a trace?"

"Did I say it was a man?" Sonia's green eyes, which didn't miss a trick, were openly probing again.

"No, I guess you didn't. I assumed it must be."

"Just so, and of course it was a man. Some kind of hoodlum lovers' quarrel would be my guess. It is all too grimy to be believed. We don't expect this sort of thing in our part of town."

Suddenly it dawned on Bennett that Sonia hadn't mentioned the kidnapping, or hostage taking or whatever they would have decided to call Bennett's being dragged off by Memphis against her will. That part of the story had been kept quiet for now. She sensed the long arm of St. Simon influence at work, preventing scandal and public scrutiny at all costs. She wondered if that cost would go so far as to include sacrificing one of their own, namely herself, to the family obsession with privacy. Surely it would have been wise to raise a general alarm, put her picture in the papers, even on television in case somebody might have seen her and be able to help in the search. Or maybe that wasn't true after all. Perhaps it was better to work quietly behind the scenes for fear the kidnapper might do something rash if frightened by a general alarm. Or, her parents could have been waiting for a ransom demand. That was so far from

what Bennett would expect of Memphis it had never occurred to her as a possibility.

"Speaking of other parts of town," Sonia was saying, "I
can tell you what I've heard, if it will be of any help. Are you
particularly interested in the fellows you know person-
ally?"

Bennett could tell she was being pumped for grist for the
gossip mill, but she didn't care.

"Yes, I am," she said.

"I see."

The waiter was back with the tea and finger sandwiches
they had ordered. Sonia took a moment to sweeten her cup
and sip from it. Bennett gripped the edge of her cherry wood
chair to keep her impatience from showing.

"Well, there's your darling brother, of course," Sonia
said finally, touching the corners of her perfectly made-up
mouth with the hem of her snow-white napkin. "He has
been known to be less than discreet in his acquaintance from
time to time."

"Have you heard that he's had a girlfriend from downtown? Recently, I mean?"

Sonia let her lovely head fall backward in a precisely
choreographed laugh. "My dear, your brother, however
totally charming he may be, never lights in one spot long
enough to have what you would call a girlfriend, whatever
part of town she might hail from."

That rang entirely true for Bennett. Much as it made her
feel disloyal to admit so, even to herself, Forth was simply
too much of a lightweight to be mixed up in anything as involved as the kind of scheme that most likely led to Pearlanne Fellows's death. Bennett was coming to suspect a
crafty and meticulous mind at work here. Much as she
adored her brother, she would never realistically credit him
with either of those qualities of thought.

"What about Royce?" she asked, suddenly remembering the gun in his hand last night and his obvious willingness to use it.

"Royce Boudreaux?" Sonia pursed her lips in a rather mocking expression that, nonetheless, allowed her dimples to show to their best advantage. "That rascal has friends all over town. Some of them are women. Some are not, if you know what I mean."

"I see" it was now Bennett's turn to say.

She did know what Sonia meant, but that didn't make it any less of a surprise. Had all that flirting Royce had done with her over the years been nothing but an act? She was beginning to wonder if she was really aware of the truth about any of the people she had thought she knew so well for so long. Could it be that many of them were wearing disguises as convincing as the one she'd put on last night?

"There is one more person in your particular acquaintance whom I have heard spoken of lately." Sonia had taken ever so tiny a bite of a crustless triangle filled with a thin layer of smoked salmon. Her napkin touched her lips daintily once more. "I do hesitate to mention him however."

"Please, tell me." Bennett could hear her own eagerness, so out of place in her nonchalant circle. She didn't care about that now. It occurred to her that she might not ever care about that again. "I need to know."

"I can see that," Sonia said, the green gleam of curiosity shining brighter than ever in her unrelenting gaze. "Still, I wouldn't want to hurt you."

A spark of insight came to Bennett in a flash. "Are you referring to Quint?" she asked.

"Actually, I was," Sonia said, more quietly than was usual for someone who enjoyed attracting attention as much as she did.

In contradiction with her usual haughtiness, there was what looked like sincere compassion in her eyes. Bennett was grateful for that. She did feel a pang of something very close to the sharpness of betrayal in anticipation of what she was about to hear. However, it was more the sadness of learning that a friend had lied than the devastation of discovering the infidelity of a true and cherished lover. Bennett had long known, in her heart of hearts, that Quint could never be more than the former to her.

"Tell me what you know," she said, so decisively she knew that Sonia would have to comply. She did.

"It has been rumored for some time now that Quint has been seeing someone, other than yourself, of course. No one seems to know who she is, so we can assume she is from outside our crowd. She could be a downtown type at that. Frankly, I hadn't considered that possibility, Quint being so, shall we say, precise about things as he is. But then, who knows what is percolating beneath even the most reserved surface, especially these days, especially with men."

"Yes. Who knows?" Bennett echoed. Her mind was running in so many directions she couldn't help but sound distracted.

Sonia reached across the table and placed her expertly manicured fingers over Bennett's hand. "I truly dislike being the one to tell you this," she said.

Something in Sonia's voice focused Bennett's scattered attention on those remarkable green eyes. "Yes, I believe you do."

There was more to Sonia than Bennett had previously realized. Suddenly she knew she wouldn't mind giving Sonia the entrée to one of the prestigious social affair committees she craved to be associated with. Maybe she could even take Bennett's place, now that she suspected she might be giving her interest to other things, though she wasn't at all certain what those other things might be.

Still there was some shock in learning that Quint had very possibly been deceiving her. A lifetime of St. Simon upbringing prompted Bennett to look away for a moment while that shock might be too visible in her eyes. That was when her attention was suddenly captured by a glimpse of red hair through the palm fronds. Nick, the tough guy who had accosted her and Memphis last night and been after them ever since, was just now walking past the Palm Court at a rapid clip. Bennett thought she might have seen his sidekick in tow, but she had to look away before she could make certain of that.

Most fortuitously, the waiter had chosen that moment to stop by their table and inquire if there was anything further he could do for them. In a move so uncharacteristic that Bennett could hardly believe she was doing it herself, she grabbed the waiter's sleeve and literally pulled him in front of her so that he was blocking the view of her from the promenade. Sonia's eyebrows shot up so high they looked as if they might become permanently implanted at her hairline.

"Is something wrong, Ms. St. Simon?" the waiter asked, looking and sounding totally bewildered, a state almost unheard of in any of the Plaza's deliberately unflappable staff.

Bennett peeked around his white-jacketed arm. The streak of red hair was nowhere to be seen, but she maintained her grip on the waiter's sleeve a few seconds longer to be sure. When she let go, he backed away a step, probably to prevent being latched onto again. Sonia's lovely mouth remained open in undisguised astonishment. Bennett understood that an explanation was in order, but there was no time for that now.

"Put this on the family account," she said to the waiter, indicating the barely sampled food and drink on the table. "I apologize for having to dash off like this," she said to Sonia. "I will be in touch with you very soon. And thank you for everything."

Bennett didn't stay long enough to hear either response. She was already headed out of the Palm Court in the opposite direction from that Nick had taken. If her mind had not been set so firmly on other things, she might have heard the gears of the gossip mill grinding into fast forward behind her.

Chapter Twenty-One

The *Fiddlehead* was a ninety-foot motor yacht with a crew of five. Ten passengers could fit comfortably on board in the four staterooms, twelve if you put a couple in the saloon. This was traveling first-class with all of what a sales brochure might call the amenities. Memphis called them toys. The *Fiddlehead* had navigated the seas from the Caribbean to the Mediterranean, but she still wasn't his idea of seafaring. He preferred the power of the sail, filling with wind, streaking along with a sleek vessel in tow. He loved the feel of it, the taste of it, the silence and freedom of it. But the *Fiddlehead* paid well and let him keep five good men in a job.

Unfortunately, she had brought him to a port of call that turned out to be a port of trouble. He couldn't wait to leave, and not just because the cops were after him. The song might say, "I left my heart in San Francisco," but when he finally blew out of this bad-luck town, he'd be leaving his heart in New York City. He knew that if he could just quit thinking about Bennett, he'd be okay. He also knew it was going to take some time and a lot of distance to make that happen. He'd been thinking about leaving the sea life behind, but today all he cared about was getting back to it quickly with no stops in between, especially no stops in jail.

The boat life was a world a guy could escape into and get lost in. Maybe a berth on a ride as classy as the *Fiddlehead* wouldn't be possible for a man with forged papers, but there were captains not so choosy who'd be happy to have a man on crew who understood the water like Memphis did. Greece was always a way to go. They didn't ask so many questions there. Sea bums had found their perfect refuge in Greece as far back as the classical days. Too bad that when Memphis thought about sailing the bright blue waters of the Aegean, the image always had Bennett at his side, on deck with the breeze in her hair and the sun warming her fair skin to a golden glow.

He could hardly believe how, in the next second after that fantasy made him feel so good, the loss of it made him feel so bad. There never was going to be any shipboard romance with this woman. There never was going to be anything with this woman. When push came to shove, she'd stuck up for her own kind. He'd been a fool not to know that would happen. Maybe he did know it and took the chance anyway, even if all he got out of it was a one-night stand and a couple of memories. Why worry about the afterward? How could he have guessed he was sticking his feelings into a meat grinder so they could be mangled and tossed out the other end. He never would have thought that could happen in a matter of a few hours, but it had. He was going to need many times that long to get back to normal, if he could ever get back there again.

Right now, though, what he had to do was keep an eye on the *Fiddlehead*. She was docked at Twenty-third Street Marina, just like he'd heard she would be when he was listening in on the phone. He'd come here to the marina straight from the hotel. He wasn't quite sure what to do next, but this was the only place he could make a connection. He knew the crew. His stuff was in his quarters on board. Besides, he was curious about this smuggling thing. A search of the boat might turn up something of interest. He wasn't sure where to start looking on such a big vessel, but he felt like giving it a try anyway. He didn't let himself think too much about the possibility that what he was really doing was looking for ways to get his mind off Bennett and just spinning his wheels in the bargain.

He'd been hanging around under the FDR Drive while he watched the *Fiddlehead*. Nobody paid much attention to guys just hanging around in this town, especially in the areas along the edges of the city like this one was. People driving by would figure he was homeless or out of work or a loiterer, if they took notice of him at all. This was a good place to be invisible, and that was what he had to be right now. He was thinking about moving in closer to the marina. He'd guess that the crew would be off checking out the city. They had spent more than enough time on shipboard already. When the chance came to go ashore, they took it. One person might have stayed behind to check on things, but Memphis doubted it. They wouldn't think twice about him being gone, either. They'd figure he got lucky with one of the shoreside girls. Memphis didn't even think to put Bennett in that category.

In the meantime, the harbormaster for the marina would keep track of the vessel. That meant Memphis couldn't get on board from the land side without going through the proper channels. Memphis had ID that showed he was heading up the *Fiddlehead* crew, but he didn't know if he dared use it. If the cops were after him, they would have been here to check him out already, unless they didn't know who he was yet. He should have grabbed the local newspapers on his way over here to find out what they had to say about last night. He would have done that if he had his head on straight this morning. Thanks to Bennett, he didn't. Anyway, he was taking a big risk to try an up-front approach here.

The only other possibility was to come in from the water side. Memphis could do that if he had to. He'd need to scout out a place to stash his leather jacket and boots. Then he'd find a place to slip into the water and swim for it. The East River currents were strong and treacherous, but if he kept close to the shore along the dockside he could make it. He started walking south along the roadway parallel to the waterfront, looking for a place to get into the water without being too conspicuous about it. He'd have to swim in from below the marina, out of sight of the dock house on the pier, then keep close in to the hulls of the other boats till he got to the *Fiddlehead* and could ease himself up over the side. The harbor man would be paying most attention to the shoreside when it came to looking out for possible intruders. He wouldn't be expecting anybody to swim in, and that would work to Memphis's advantage.

Not to his advantage was the fact that, the farther he walked the more obvious it became that he would have to make a lot longer swim to get to the marina than he would have hoped. First of all, he had to get past this fancy-looking place coming up. The two-story, long white building with lots of glass out front and pinlights in the trees looked like a restaurant, an upscale kind of place from what he could see of it. That most likely meant lots more glass on the river side of the building so the customers could get the best view. He would have to just about crawl along the shore wall to be low enough to keep out of sight. It was near lunchtime, too. The river side would probably be crowded with people, as were the outdoor tables on the deck atop the building. He'd have to do that stretch underwater for sure.

A chain along one end of the car lot had a sign in the middle of it that said Parking For Water Club Customers Only. So this was the Water Club. He'd heard of it from somebody or other on board the *Fiddlehead*. It was a restaurant, just as he'd thought, and definitely upscale. He was thinking about how he wouldn't like to end up being the luncheon theater act for the high-tone patrons of this place when something drew his attention to the parking lot. There were lots of expensive rides in there, but only one of them caught his eye. About the middle of the second row he'd spotted a long, low sports car with a slight bend in the aerial off the back. He was almost certain this had to be the same Jaguar XKE he'd been roaring around town in last night. Before he could give himself time to think about whether or not this was a smart move to make, he was on a beeline for that parking lot and the XKE.

Memphis did have his wits enough about him to check out what was happening with the doorman-attendant at the front of the restaurant. He was helping a couple of very well dressed folks out of a Town Car at the moment. At least that was one small stroke of luck in Memphis's favor on this otherwise downside-of-the-odds day. He moved quickly and got under the parking lot chain. He was at the XKE before the hairs on the back of the neck told him he'd been spotted.

"Hey, man," the attendant called out. "What ya doin' there?"

Memphis was pretty sure the guy figured he was trying to steal this car or at best rob whatever was inside it. They probably didn't get too many dudes in leather and denim coming to this place to do lunch. There was a good chance the guy would go for the cops straight off. Still Memphis had to find out if what he suspected was true. He bent down to look through the Jaguar's side window. This was the very car. He had a great memory for details. He could have picked this car out of a hundred other Jags if he had to.

"Listen up, buddy," the attendant was saying. He was louder and closer now. "I asked you what you're doing, and you'd better answer me."

Memphis was wondering which approach he should take. He could try a bluff, some kind of cover story off the top of his head. Or he could take off at a dead run. Both of these possibilities had their pitfalls, some of them deep enough to fall into and never be seen again. He was wavering between the big lie and the fast getaway when he heard a voice that blew every thought he'd ever had clean out of his head.

"That's all right, Max," the voice crooned, smooth as syrup and twice as sweet. "Mr. Sinclair is with me."

Memphis got the message right off that she'd called him that in case he needed a cover for his real name. Maybe she'd seen the papers, and he was splashed all over the front page so she had to be careful about giving him away. He should have cared about all of that more than he did. All he could care about was that she was here. He looked up to see the attendant already on his way back to the front door of the restaurant and Bennett St. Simon walking toward the Jaguar, looking like either an angel from heaven or the devil that wouldn't quit haunting Memphis's soul.

Chapter Twenty-Two

Bennett busied herself with bending down and looking into Royce's car so she wouldn't have to look Memphis in the face or see him glaring back at her. There could be no question now that he had heard her on the phone in their room at the Plaza. That was what had brought him to this part of town.

"What are you doing here?" he asked. Apparently he was not willing to let her avoid him for long.

"I came to see this car," she said, preferring to give him only partial answers at the moment.

"Were you feeling nostalgic for our little tour of the city last night?"

So he was going to be like that—sarcastic and difficult. She was reminded of when they'd first met the evening before. She could feel the same tension between them now. He was the aggressor and she was the enemy, the annoying stranger who had to be kept in line.

"I'm not nostalgic about anything," she said.

That was altogether untrue. She was already remembering last night at the hotel as from the distance of years of regret for its loss. She wanted to tell him that, and of how she didn't want that loss to be inevitable. On the other hand, she didn't want to get her heart broken, smashed apart right here on this too-public spot by the harsh words he might very well speak to her. She must have succeeded in silencing those possibly hurtful words because he did not answer. He made a harrumphing noise instead, obviously to show his disgust with her in general. She busied herself with pushing the side window vent. Luck was with her, at least in this. Royce had neglected to lock the vent, and it creaked open. She strained to reach inside far enough to grab the door handle.

"What are you doing?" he asked, sounding more annoyed than ever.

"I am breaking into Royce Boudreaux's car."

She pulled up on the handle, and the door swung open.

"I can see that," he said.

She ducked down to climb onto the driver's seat on one knee, just far enough to get to the car phone on the console between the seats.

"I asked what you're doing," he insisted. "Don't give me any half-baked answer. Just tell me straight out."

"What will you do if I don't?" His belligerence seemed to be contagious.

"This is what I'll do," he said.

He turned sharply and walked away. Bennett needed a second to comprehend that he was leaving. He was headed at a determined pace down the street in the direction of the marina. He had been coming from that direction when she first saw him. She needed an additional second to realize she should go after him.

"Memphis, wait. Please," she called as she hurried toward his rapidly retreating back. "We have to talk."

He kept on walking, though his pace might have slowed a bit. Or she could have been imagining that because she wanted so much for it to be true.

"Please, Memphis, I have to talk to you," she pleaded. "I'll tell you whatever you want to know."

He stopped still in his tracks at that, but he didn't turn around. She crossed the distance between them as fast as she could go without breaking into a full run. Max, the door-man at the Water Club, was already paying them more at-tention than she would have liked. When she got to where Memphis was standing, so stiff-backed she could almost see a dense moat of stubbornness around him, she scurried around in front of him to block his path in case he decided to run off again.

His eyes were hooded by the set of his lowering forehead. She could not remember ever having seen a man look so unmistakably belligerent. Even so, the flash in his shadowy eyes blazed straight to the pit of her stomach and made it leap and ache all at the same time. He was not the most handsome man she had ever seen, but he was certainly the most forceful. The naked power of that force was part of what had such a deeply felt effect on her. It occurred to Bennett that his naked thighs had a powerful effect on her, as well. There was no point in trying to pretend they did not.

"You said you had something to tell me," he said, and his tone of voice was just as uncompromising as his facial ex-pression.

"I came over here to get a look at Royce's car," she said.

"How did you know where to find it? I left it on the street waiting to be stolen or towed away."

"I called Royce's answering service and found out. I had his card in my dress pocket from last night."

"You called up and asked the whereabouts of his car? Didn't they think that was kind of strange?"

"Maybe they did. They didn't say."

"You just dropped the St. Simon name and, no ques-tions asked, they spilled their guts about everything you wanted to know."

Bennett sighed at the sneer in his words. They really did seem to have become enemies almost as fast as they had become lovers.

"Something like that," she answered, because it was true. "First, I asked them where Royce was. Then I said I'd heard his car was taken and wondered if he got it back yet. They told me he had it with him and drove it to lunch at the Water Club, which happens to be a favorite place of his."

"Because it's so close to the marina and his buddy Quint's yacht, the *Fiddlehead?*"

There was the sarcastic edge again, heavier than ever.

"The *Fiddlehead* isn't usually docked here. It has a slip at the New York Yacht Club."

"I seem to remember picking up that piece of info this morning."

Bennett ignored the references to her bathroom phone call. She didn't want to get into that right now.

"So, what's your big interest in the Jag?" he asked.

"Come back to the parking lot with me, and I'll show you."

She put her hand on his arm to steer him in that direction, but he shook her off. His action made her undeniably sad. She could have walked away from him then, but she didn't. If he saw her sadness in her eyes, he would probably also see that she felt more for him than was wise. She almost wished he would see that, and how she was hurting because he obviously resented her so much. She had been raised to hide that kind of vulnerability at all costs. She wasn't entirely sure why she was willing to cast aside those years of breeding for him, especially since he was making no secret of the fact that he had none of the same feelings for her.

"Come with me," she repeated. "I think you might find this interesting."

She started walking back toward the parking lot. She was gambling that he would follow her. She wasn't sure she could handle the humiliation of running after him again if he took off in the other direction. Fortunately, she didn't have to find out how much humiliation she was ready to endure at his hands. He came up almost next to her, and they continued back to Royce's car in silence.

Bennett had left the low-slung door ajar when she went after Memphis. She pulled it wider open and slid inside again. She went through the same routine of activating the car phone that she had followed the previous evening when Memphis was driving around Columbus Circle with her as his unwilling passenger. She pushed the top button in the row of preset automatic dialing numbers. She pressed the control that turned on the speaker phone and waited while the dial tone reverberated throughout the compact interior of the small car. The sound of a machine going on to answer made Bennett's heart jump. She was about to find out who she had left her message with last night. She knew that had to be the same person who had sent Nick and Rudy after her and Memphis.

"This is your time and weather line," a mechanical-sounding voice said. "At the tone, it will be 1:27 p.m." The tone buzzed. "The weather for this afternoon is sunny and mild, with—"

Bennett disconnected the call before the voice could say just how mild this afternoon was going to be. The sunny forecast didn't please her as it might have on a usual day. The weather inside her was hardly balmy at the moment. In fact, she felt something like a storm coming on, a storm of frustration that this clue she had counted so much on leading to an important revelation had turned out to be a dead end instead.

"What was that all about?" Memphis asked as she exited the car and shut the door.

"Last night, while you were driving us toward that hotel at Forty-second Street, I managed to send out a message over this car phone. I pressed that same automatic dial button to do it. Did you hear what happened just now when I did it again?"

"I heard."

"Well, I don't understand it. I know it was a machine that answered last night, and it could have been that recording I heard." Bennett began walking slowly away from the car, without thinking much about where she was going. "But, if my message went out to nothing more than a weather and time tape, who was it that told those two hoodlums where we were?"

Memphis grabbed her arm and spun her around. "Let me get this straight," he said. "You're telling me that you got on that car phone and sent out an SOS about where I was taking you?"

"That's right. I did."

Bennett didn't like the way he was gripping her arm. She hated being manhandled. This also reminded her of being dragged through the park by him last night, and of how they had really gotten together in the first place because he just might be a murderer. She liked thinking about that even less than she liked his grip on her arm. She felt suddenly too discouraged to make even the effort to pull away. This situation was too hopeless to be believed, too maddening to be borne.

"You figured out that this message of yours must have been passed on to those two creeps who tried to take us out in that flophouse. Is that right?"

"That's right."

"Tell me something, Bennett. Did you plan on telling me this ever? Or were you going to keep it to yourself along with the other secrets you've been holding on to?"

There wasn't really an answer to that, but Bennett tried anyway. "I was trying to save myself," she said. "I was your hostage, and you seemed very desperate to me. I needed to protect myself in any way I could."

"Did you still feel you had to protect yourself from me after we made love to each other?"

There was no possible answer this time. Bennett didn't even try to come up with one. He waited a moment, then dropped her arm and turned away. She expected him to make another exit then. She didn't think she would have the energy to run after him again. She felt too dispirited right now to imagine she had anything even close to a run left in her.

"I didn't know who to trust so I decided not to trust anybody," she said.

"You could trust me inside your body but not with the stuff inside your head. Is that what you're trying to say?"

"Something like that."

Bennett felt the color mounting in her face. She wasn't really embarrassed, though she could hear the illogic of her thinking about trust stripped bare by his words. Actually it was his mention of being inside her that made her skin temperature rise. She wondered if references in the future would always cause her to think of him and be aroused by the memory of their bodies rocking and plunging together on the Plaza's fine, soft sheets. She guessed she would be plagued that way for quite some time.

"I know you don't care very much for me right now," she said to cover the emptiness his silence made her feel. "We need to stick together for a while longer anyway. Then you can be on your way."

He was looking down at her. She thought she saw an edge of something else, maybe surprise or regret, invade his angry scowl for a moment. He said nothing.

"We need to stay together because I want to find out the truth and you want to clear your name."

"That's true," he said.

"I think we can accomplish both of those things better together than apart."

"That may be true. Then again, it may not."

She had to overcome his skepticism. She felt as if her entire life might depend on that. What did depend on it was whether he would go or stay. That was truly why her entire body was pulled taut with urgency. She cared about Quint and whoever else among her friends might be involved in something damaging here, but what she cared about most was Memphis. Realizing that under such discouraging circumstances made her wish she had a corner to run off into and cry heartbroken tears. Instead she pressed on in her quest to keep him around as long as she possibly could.

"I have a plan," she said, though that was probably an overstatement of what she actually did have.

"What plan is that?" He didn't sound as interested as she would have liked him to.

"There's an event tonight. Most of the same crowd from the Stuyvesant Club reception will be there."

"You folks sure do get around, don't you? A reception last night, an event tonight. I'm impressed."

His voice told her that he wasn't really very impressed at all. He had a point, of course. This round of social gatherings that Bennett and her acquaintances frequented often felt like little more than a way to compensate for having too much idle time. Tonight's gala was another charity affair. That was her excuse for attending. She wondered if that was the real reason. Maybe she was just as much in need of filling the emptiness of her life as the Sonia Jades of their circle had to be. It occurred to Bennett that what she really wanted to fill that emptiness with was somebody to love.

Standing next to Memphis, as she was doing now, gave that thought a poignant sting that threatened to knock her over right there on the edge of the Water Club parking lot.

"If we show up at that event tonight," she said, despite the weight of her discouragement dragging her down, "I believe we might be able to ferret out the killer."

"How would we do that?"

"By letting him think we know a lot more than we actually do. That could bring him out in the open."

"Because he'll think he has to do to us what he did to Pearlanne Fellows?"

Bennett nodded. "That's what I had in mind."

The words actually spoken sounded even flimsier as a plan of action than they had inside her head. She hoped he might come up with something better, but he didn't.

"I take it you want to bring me along to this classy gig," he said.

She nodded again. "Yes, that was my plan."

"I'm not sure I'd fit in." He cast a downward glance at his black leather jacket and well-worn jeans.

"I have a plan for that, too."

"I'll just bet you do."

Bennett could tell that he was agreeing to stick with her for this one last attempt to uncover the truth. She also couldn't help hearing the sneer behind his words, any more than she could help longing for it not to be there. That longing clung to her like a sodden, hopeless veil as she signaled Max to get them a cab.

If BENNETT HAD NOT been so consumed by the effort to keep herself moving forward despite her near despair, and if Memphis hadn't been so preoccupied with wrestling against the jumble of his thoughts and feelings—if they both had been paying more attention to what was happening around them at the moment, they might have looked up toward the second floor of the Water Club. If they had done that, they would have seen Royce Boudreaux watching them with great interest.

Chapter Twenty-Three

When Bennett explained the details of what she had in mind, Memphis couldn't say he liked it very much, especially the part about boosting a tuxedo right out of the tailor shop where it was being made. Memphis had never worn a tux in his life, and he wasn't crazy about ending that tradition now. If he'd been a hundred percent straight with himself, he would also have admitted that he wasn't sure he could carry off wearing a tux and looking like he belonged in it. Even tougher to swallow was the fact that these were Quint Leslie's clothes they were planning to make off with. He was Bennett's fiancé, or whatever. She hadn't been too clear about that.

What did come across clear as glass, at least to Memphis, was that she was still involved in this mess—exposing herself to danger and the whole nine yards—because she thought Quint might be mixed up in it somehow. Memphis didn't doubt that for a minute, and that was truly why he didn't want to wear her fiancé's suit. She'd talked him into it anyway. She just might be able to talk him into anything without half-trying. That didn't happen to him very often. The opposite was more likely. Somebody could rattle off a list of facts and figures a mile long. Memphis wouldn't buy it till he'd seen the proof right in front of his eyes. Till then, he was from Missouri.

He'd learned that in the orphanage. Believing people, counting on what they said could leave a kid with his heart broken more often than not. Memphis didn't ever count on anybody. Now here he was laying it all on the line for her, a woman who had hidden important information from him when he needed it. Why was he doing such a stupid thing? Because she asked him to, that's why. He'd never let any woman twist him around her little finger like this before. But, with Bennett, if he could fit around her finger, that's where he wanted to be.

In the cab on the way uptown, she'd filled him in on how she was going to scam the tuxedo out of the tailor. She'd gone to the shop with Quint when the tux was fitted. She said it would be ready by now, and they wouldn't think there was anything out of line about her going in there to pick it up. Memphis asked if Quint might be picking it up himself to wear to the gig they were all going to tonight, but she said he'd wear his regular tux tonight. The new one was for something coming up in a couple of weeks.

The guy owned not just one tuxedo, but two. Memphis knew how far out of his league he was wandering with all of this. He was in very unfamiliar territory. That made it even more possible that he could slip up and get caught and end up behind bars in the bargain. He was going along with it all the same, and he knew why. Sure, he wanted to find out who really killed poor Pearlanne. He could get himself off the hook for a murder rap that way. Still, what he wanted even more was to stick with Bennett for as long as he could. She would be back in her own life soon enough. He'd be history then. In the meantime, he'd go along even if it was just to be in range of the smell of her perfume. That's why he was hanging out here now, on the corner of Madison Avenue and Sixty-second Street in Manhattan, feeling like the squarest peg in the roundest hole there ever was.

Memphis couldn't help thinking he'd been set down on this particular corner to let him know just how far out of place he was in Bennett's part of the world. Most of the people hurrying past appeared to have gotten dressed that morning with a fashion magazine open in front of them to follow. Memphis had taken his leather jacket off and slung it over his arm. He thought he might be too noticeable, hanging around the corner mailbox the way he was, but nobody gave him a look or a thought. They were all in too much of a hurry for that.

Memphis shook his head. He was definitely a downtown type of guy, and this was so far uptown he could be in danger of getting the bends. The chances of him ever being able to fit in here were slim to none, and he knew it. He imagined that if any of these people passing by slowed down long enough to give him a good look, they would know it, too. Memphis shook his head again, in amazement at himself this time that he could have been fool enough to think even for a minute about him and Bennett making it as a couple.

She had disappeared into a granite-faced building near the corner. "The tailor's up there," she had said, pointing to the second story with its balconies and scrolled ironwork. There were drapes at the windows, no mannequins sporting the tailor's handiwork. Memphis supposed this neighborhood was too discreet for anything that showy. He glanced up there now, hoping he'd catch a glimpse of her, but she was nowhere to be seen. He checked out the street, as he'd been doing regularly ever since she left him here. He hadn't forgotten he was on the run, not for a second. That's when he spotted the sleek, dark sedan up the block a ways, negotiating for a parking place by waiting for the car already in it to pull out. Memphis was surprised anybody would bother with that on streets this crowded when there were parking garages around just about every corner.

He rounded his shoulders to make himself appear shorter, and crossed the street, heading in the direction of the sedan that was on the other side of the avenue. He kept close to the parked cars so he wouldn't be too obvious, though he felt he might as well be dressed in Day-Glo the way he stood out from the style setters around him. He had to try for a look at whoever was in that sedan. He could make out that it was one person not two. If this was the creep hoods' car, one of them had come solo, unless the other one was out prowling the street already. Memphis glanced up and down the avenue but didn't see anybody he recognized.

He was as close as he dared get to the sedan now and he strained to see who was inside. This time a flash of recognition did hit him, but he wasn't sure what direction it came from at first. This guy wasn't one of the thugs, but Memphis had seen him before, and recently, too. He made the connection and turned around to head down the avenue. The guy in this particular pricey, dark sedan was none other than the man whose clothes Bennett was in the process of stealing at this very moment. The guy in the sedan was Quint Leslie.

Memphis forced himself not to run. That would make him too conspicuous. He was making a beeline for the tailor shop all the same. He was also thinking how Bennett wasn't able to second-guess Quint's every move as perfectly as she thought she could. That made Memphis feel good somehow. He hadn't liked that she seemed to be under another man's skin. Memphis hadn't liked that one bit.

He bounded through the doorway of the tailor's building and took the stairs to the second floor two at a time. Memphis wasn't sure how he'd handle this once he was inside the tailor shop. That would be a tricky situation. The last thing they wanted was to attract suspicion, and it would definitely look suspicious for him to grab Bennett and take her out of there. Luckily, that wasn't necessary because she was on the way out of the shop door just as Memphis hit the stair landing.

"We've got to move fast," he said, taking her by the hand and starting back down the stairs with her in tow. "Quint just pulled in up the street. I think he's on his way here right now."

"Oh, no," she gasped.

She was carrying a vinyl, zippered garment bag so she'd already copped Quint's suit. That might be tougher to explain than Memphis was.

"We'll go out the side door," she said. "If we take the front way, we could run right into him."

"Okay."

Memphis almost smiled at the way she could think like somebody on the run and on the edge, even though he was sure she'd never been either of those things in real life. She'd shown how good she could be at it last night, but he had thought that might have been sort of a game to her. Today, she was back to her old self, looking as uptown as anybody can. Still, she knew how to be street savvy when need be. For a part of an instant, he let himself think that maybe they weren't so different after all. The rush of warm air that hit him in the face as she hurried them through the back door and onto the street brought him back to his senses. He reminded himself once more about not believing in fairy tales.

Bennett was crouched down, peeking around the doorway. Memphis peeked around above her. He didn't see Quint. Maybe he'd passed the corner already. Maybe he hadn't. One of them had to go out and try to spot where Quint was.

"I'm going to go take a look," Memphis said.

Bennett grabbed his arm. "I don't know if you should do that."

"One of us has to do it, and that means me. He didn't get that good a look at me last night, but he'd definitely recognize you." Memphis took a pair of dark sunglasses out of his jacket pocket and handed the jacket to her. "Hold this for me," he said as he put on the glasses. "Maybe he won't recognize me with these on."

"I don't know," she said. "You're pretty unforgettable."

Memphis stopped in his tracks and turned to look her full in the face. "Are you sure about that?" he asked.

"I'm sure."

He could hear in the way she said those words that she wasn't talking about Quint. She was telling Memphis she wouldn't forget him. She was talking about after they went their separate ways. Memphis could hear that, too. There were so many things he would have liked to say, but they wouldn't do any good. What is, is. He was clearheaded enough about life to know that. So he didn't say anything to her. He just took off out of the doorway and down the side street toward the corner where he'd been hanging out at the mailbox before.

Quint was coming down the street, on the other side, so that was lucky. Memphis should have hurried back to tell Bennett that straight off. They could duck into the doorway and wait till Quint got past and take off then. Memphis didn't do that just yet because he couldn't resist the chance to get a good look at the man who was going to end up with Bennett. Memphis couldn't hope to deny the pain he felt in his heart from thinking that.

He also couldn't deny that Quint Leslie actually looked like a decent guy. He walked tall and fast, like a man with a purpose. The cut of his features was clean and straightforward. If Memphis had been wanting to see something weak in this man, he was bound to be disappointed. At least on the surface, Quint Leslie looked to be the kind of man Memphis could respect. That was the last thing he cared to be admitting, but he was too honest with himself to do otherwise. Quint turned to cross the avenue toward the tailor shop. He was facing in Memphis's direction now and getting too close for comfort. Memphis headed back toward the doorway where Bennett stood waiting.

"Did he see you?" Bennett asked.

"I don't think so."

"Maybe you shouldn't be too sure about that. Quint is very observant. He doesn't miss much, and you stayed up there near the corner long enough for him to notice you."

"I said he didn't see me," Memphis snapped. He didn't want to hear her talk about how smart her boyfriend was.

"Okay," she said. "You don't have to take my head off."

"Let's get out of here. He's passed by now."

Memphis could have kicked himself for yelling at her like that when what he really wanted to do was wrap his arms around her and hold her so tight she could never escape. Instead, he was acting as if he wanted to push her away from him.

"Which way are we headed?" he asked much more softly.

"Uptown," she said, and moved out of the doorway looking cautiously to the right and left before stepping to the curb and raising her hand to flag down a yellow cab.

"Where are we going, anyway?" he asked, suddenly realizing that he had no idea what came next.

"To my house." She'd spotted a cab and was waving it over to the curb. She looked at Memphis, probably wondering why he made no move to join her there.

"Is this your family's house?" he asked.

"Yes, it is."

"I don't think that's a very good plan, not for me at least."

The cab was at the curb. She opened the back door. ''What other options do you have?'' she asked.

Memphis thought for a moment, but he couldn't come up with a single one. He shrugged and followed Bennett into the cab. Whatever would happen, would happen. He just hoped he'd be ready for it when it came.

Chapter Twenty-Four

Bennett was almost certain her mother would be home and that explaining to her what was going on would not be easy. Dilys St. Simon was, above all things, a practical woman. What Bennett was doing would not seem sensible to her mother. There was too little chance of success in the enterprise. Bennett was too inexperienced in such matters to have any advantage at all. Dilys was a strong proponent of advantage. She knew how to get it, how to use it and how to keep it. Bennett's behavior would appear to her mother to be pure foolishness with no saving grace to recommend it. Even Bennett understood that her mother was at least partially right on that score.

Bennett had not told Memphis that her mother was likely to know he was in the house. Hardly anything ever happened at the St. Simon town house overlooking the east side of Central Park that Dilys didn't know about. Bennett's escape had been a fluke, and even then, Dilys had known within minutes when Bennett had left the house. Dilys kept an overseer's eye on everything from the ordering of the groceries to the most minute details of her husband's health and schedule. She would not be likely to miss the presence of an accused felon and hunted fugitive within the regularly patrolled boundaries of her realm.

Maybe Memphis sensed that when he saw the immense, carved oak door with the St. Simon crest above it worked in brass and surrounded by an impressive curlicue pattern in black metal. Bennett was about to turn the key in the wrought iron front gate, which had been designed by the same craftsman who did the doorway crest, when she felt Memphis back away from her side. "This is not a good idea," he said, just as he had on Madison Avenue and again several times in the cab. "I'm going to take off now."

Bennett's heart leapt to her throat in near terror. She told herself to remain calm. If she let him know how desperately she wanted him to stay, that might spook him even further. Still, she felt she had to play the personal card because it was the only one left in her hand.

"If you leave now, we may never see each other again," she said. "Is that really what you want?"

It was a gamble, and she knew it. She tried to read the expression in his eyes, but he had tucked his emotions away for the moment behind a facade of blankness. Perhaps he had to do that because those emotions were as confused and chaotic as her own. A single flash of response gave her hope. She might have won her gamble.

"No," he said in a voice that was low-pitched but resonating with feelings he apparently couldn't tuck away. "That isn't what I want."

Bennett turned back toward the gate and finished unlocking it. She pushed the heavy metal open and stepped through into the courtyard, willing him to follow. She tried not to make her sigh of relief too audible when he did follow. She closed the gate as gently as possible so there would be no clang of metal against metal. If that happened, he might think she was locking him into something.

Up the stone steps to the massive door, he was still in her wake though not as close behind as she would prefer. She guessed that he was hanging back in case he needed to make a run for it. She wished the place she lived in looked more like an ordinary house. All of this pomp and circumstance was enough to spook anybody who wasn't used to it. In fact, sometimes it even spooked her.

Bennett pushed through the heavy door without letting on that she noticed how far Memphis was lagging behind. He continued to trail her at a distance but still kept following as she hoped he would. The door shut after them, and she knew he wasn't about to make himself look foolish by trying to scramble out of it again. She already understood Memphis well enough to be certain he wasn't the kind of man who cared to appear ridiculous if he could help it.

She was afraid her mother might make him feel that way, just by being what and who she was. There was no way to keep him from Dilys. No way short of sprouting wings or becoming invisible or something equally fantastic. A wild thought struck Bennett with the force of wonderful possibility. What if her mother liked him? The elation of that prospect lasted hardly as long as it took them to cross the parquet foyer. The thought was even more fantastic than sprouting wings. The sight of Dilys emerging from the library confirmed that reality.

She looked cool as January as always. She was dressed in a dove gray outfit, a color that brought out the soft lights of her eyes. Bennett wondered if she had ever seen her mother frazzled. It was a word that sounded foreign as Swahili in Dilys's world, almost as foreign as Memphis looked in his jeans and T-shirt with the leather jacket slung over his arm.

Dilys must have been deep in thought, because she didn't appear to notice Bennett and Memphis. Last chance to make a run for it, Bennett thought, but she held her ground until Dilys looked up from studying the parquet in front of her Italian leather-clad toes as she walked, more slowly than usual, toward the staircase. As she drew closer, Bennett could see the lines of tension etched across her mother's normally smooth brow. Perhaps Dilys St. Simon got frazzled after all.

"Mother, I'm home," Bennett said, feeling for the first time in her life that she should treat her ever-in-control mother gently.

Dilys looked up and her manicured hand shot to her lightly tinted mouth. "Bennett," she gasped. She reached for the banister to steady herself. "Thank God."

Her eyes glistened with a show of emotion Bennett could not remember ever having seen before from her mother. That film of tears prompted an equally strong flood of feeling in Bennett. She dropped the tailor's bag she had been holding and hurried to Dilys's side.

"I'm fine, Mother. Really I am," Bennett answered her mother's searching gaze.

"Are you truly?"

"Truly," Bennett said, and took her mother's trembling hand, which had drifted from her mouth to midair.

Ordinarily the St. Simons didn't do much embracing, but there was nothing ordinary about today. Suddenly Bennett found herself in her mother's arms. The difference in height placed Bennett's chin almost atop her mother's head. Bennett was glad of that because she would be blocking the view of Memphis still standing in the foyer. She dreaded her mother's reaction to him now more than ever.

Dilys's desperate grip on Bennett's body told her these had been terrible hours for her mother. Bennett felt surprisingly guilty about that, much more than after her Mexico escapade when she'd mostly been annoyed for being dragged home. She'd always felt admiring toward her mother but distant from her. At the moment, however, that feeling was very much changed. Bennett returned the embrace while her own tears churned inside her.

Then Dilys pulled abruptly away. At first Bennett thought her mother might have reconsidered this uncharacteristic show of vulnerability and snapped herself back to her trademark cool facade. Actually Dilys must finally have taken note of Memphis's presence. She had pushed herself arm's distance away from Bennett but did not let her go.

"Who is that?" Dilys asked. She didn't sound happy about what she saw. "It's him, isn't it?"

"This is Memphis Modine," Bennett said.

She also maintained her grasp on her mother's arms. She couldn't imagine Dilys tearing after him, but for one wild moment that seemed possible, as she breathed audibly through her narrow, patrician nose and glared at Memphis.

"He is my friend, Mother," Bennett said softly. She would have preferred to shout, but that felt like the wrong tactic here.

"Your friend?" Dilys exclaimed. "Isn't this the man who dragged you off with him last night and stole Royce Boudreaux's car? Isn't this the man who threatened to shoot Quinton Leslie?"

"Mother, Royce was the one with the gun."

Bennett would have attempted to explain, but Memphis stepped forward. He had picked up the tuxedo bag and draped it over the newel post at the foot of the stairs.

"Yes, Mrs. St. Simon," he said. "I did those things. I didn't have a gun, as Bennett says. But I had a knife, and that's just as bad. I'm not proud of what I did, and I'm very sorry to have caused you so much worry. All I can say in my defense is that I would never have harmed Bennett in any way."

"You think that kidnapping a young woman and frightening her out of her wits is not harmful?"

Bennett understood that Memphis wanted to talk for himself, but she spoke up against her mother's anger anyway.

"I am not harmed. You can see that."

"You certainly don't look yourself, either," Dilys said. "Your hair," she exclaimed as if noticing her daughter's shorter, darker locks for the first time.

"I cut it so I wouldn't be recognized," Bennett said.

"Did he force you to do that?"

"Memphis hasn't forced me to do anything. At least, not since shortly after we met. I made myself less recognizable because I didn't want us to be caught."

"I can hardly believe what I am hearing," Dilys said. "This must be one of those hostage syndrome situations. He has brainwashed you into becoming his accomplice. I am going to call your father and the police right now."

Dilys moved to pass Bennett in the direction of the library, but Bennett took a firmer grip on her mother's arms and would not let her leave.

"There is no brainwashing here, Mother. Everything I've done has been of my own free will." Bennett took a deep breath before plunging on. "I care for Memphis very much."

Bennett heard two gasps, one from her mother and one from Memphis. Bennett didn't dare look in his direction for fear of what she might, or might not, see.

"That is absurd," Dilys cried out so loudly that Bennett expected servants to come scurrying forth in response.

"Your mother's very right about that," Memphis said. His voice was deep and quiet and rumbled through Bennett like thunder rolling. "I think I'd best be going now."

He turned toward the door, but Bennett was after him in a flash across the polished parquet.

"Are you sure that's what you want?" she asked, planting herself solidly across the path of his escape. "To walk out of here and never see me again?"

"You are likely to see one another again in court," Dilys interjected.

Bennett heard her mother but didn't respond right away. The answer Bennett sought was in Memphis's eyes. He could not hide his struggle from her—the struggle that told him he should go, while he knew how much he wanted to stay. She didn't wait to find out which powerful force would win.

"There is something crucial you don't know, Mother," Bennett said without taking her eyes off Memphis. "Something that changes everything."

"What could that possibly be?" Dilys asked, sounding as if her patience couldn't stretch much further.

"Memphis didn't kill that young woman last night. Memphis could never kill anyone. I am absolutely certain of it."

"How can you be so certain? Did you see what happened?"

Bennett still didn't face her mother to answer, because Bennett was actually answering the questions Memphis must be thinking but hadn't yet asked.

"I can be certain because I have seen into his heart," she said softly and with a tremor in her voice she didn't try to hide. "There is no murder there."

Dilys opened her mouth to speak, but Bennett cut her off. She did look Dilys in the face this time.

"This not Mexico, Mother. This is very different from back then. I am a grown woman, and I know my own mind. I need you to trust me now, and I need your help."

No one spoke for a moment, as if they were all waiting in suspense for the reply, including the woman called upon to make it.

At last, Dilys heaved a sigh. The indignation that had lifted her practically onto her toes seemed to deflate as she took a moment to compose herself into the unflappable woman Bennett had always known her to be.

"What is it you need from me?" Dilys asked.

Bennett restrained the impulse to grab her mother and hug her hard, though Bennett vowed she would do exactly that later when there was time. She no longer cared how lacking in St. Simon decorum such a hug might be.

"I need you to help us get ready for the reception at the Modern tonight," Bennett said.

Dilys's facade appeared about to become ruffled once more. "You intend to put in an appearance at the Museum of Modern Art with the police, your father's private detectives and who knows who else after you? Whatever for?"

"I told you that Memphis didn't murder Pearlanne Fellows, but someone else did, most likely someone we know."

"That could not possibly be true," Dilys protested.

Memphis came forward. He had stepped aside previously, as if hesitant to interfere between mother and daughter even when he was the subject of their conflict.

"I don't like to contradict you, ma'am," he said, "but it appears that Bennett could be right."

"The only way we can prove Memphis isn't guilty is to find out who is," Bennett said. "Mother, please help us to do that. I have never in my life needed anything from you as I need this."

It was her final plea, and she knew it. If her mother refused this, there would be no point in begging her further. Memphis and Bennett would be on their own. She no longer had any doubt to whom her loyalty belonged. She would not desert him, not now, not ever.

"We had best get busy then," Dilys said, glancing at Memphis's attire. "We have some making over to do if this young man is to be ready for the Sculpture Garden by this evening."

Bennett glanced nervously toward Memphis, expecting him to react. He wouldn't care to be anyone other than himself.

Bennett took his hand. "I did it for you last night," she said. "Tonight you have to do it for us."

He hesitated only a moment longer before scooping up the tuxedo bag from the newel post. Dilys swept around them to lead the way up the broad staircase.

"We will begin with your name," she said, for the first time speaking directly to Memphis without either anger or disdain in her voice. "Do you have any other besides Memphis?"

"Yes, ma'am. As a matter of fact, I do," he said. "My given name is Montgomery. Montgomery Modine."

"Much better. Much, much better."

Dilys nodded her approval as they followed her upward. Bennett, meanwhile, marveled at this and all the other surprising discoveries she sensed she would be making about the man whose hand she still clasped tightly in her own.

Chapter Twenty-Five

Memphis was surprised at how comfortable he felt in a tuxedo. The black tie was a lot to ask of any man, but he could wear it for a good cause. Nailing whoever killed that girl was good cause enough, especially since he'd tried to kill Bennett, too. That was one thing Memphis would not forgive. When he thought about somebody hurting her, he had to grind his fingernails into his palms to keep from cursing out loud.

This definitely wasn't a spot where cursing would be okay. He and Dilys St. Simon had come in from the street through revolving doors onto an open space that fronted nearly the width of the museum. Memphis could tell that there hadn't been much misbehaving here ever. In every direction, there were men in penguin suits and women with rounded hair that wouldn't have moved a wisp in a windstorm.

After developing their strategy, the three of them had decided that Dilys should bring Memphis in here on her own. His cover wasn't so likely to get blown that way. Not many people knew Bennett had been snatched, but maybe the wrong ones did. If she showed up now, that might tip their hand too soon. This way, Memphis would be a stranger to everybody, except the guilty parties, at least till he could check out the lay of the land.

Dilys had no trouble getting him past the squad of security people at the door. This was a very top drawer affair, and they weren't supposed to let anybody in who didn't have an engraved invitation. Even so, Dilys slipped him in like oil through water. He could see how Bennett came by her talent for getting what she wanted when she wanted it. She had her mother's smile, too. He recognized that when Dilys beamed up at him as if he were the man of the moment out of all the first-class gents in this crowd.

They stepped into the Sculpture Garden from the foyer. Memphis had to admit this was a great place for a party. They'd set up four musicians playing classical music at one end and food and drinks at the other. In between, pieces of sculpture blended with trees and ivy and stone steps and pathways. Even the wrought-iron chairs and tables suited the simple beauty of the setting to a T.

Bennett had told him how she liked to come here sometimes on a sunny afternoon just because it was so lovely and peaceful. Memphis could understand why she would feel that way. Even with clusters of people all around, there was a feeling of quiet here. For an instant, he wished everyone else would disappear. He and Bennett could sit together under those two gnarly trees with nobody trying to chase them down for anything.

"May I present Mr. Montgomery Modine."

Dilys's words pierced the bubble of Memphis's fantasy like a knife blade. In the next moment, he found himself bowing slightly and smiling in a genteel way he'd never done before. The suit and the surroundings were having their effect on him.

"Of the Atlanta Modines?" a bejeweled matron was asking. "I do believe I recall a line of Montgomerys in that family. And, if I'm not mistaken, young man, I detect a strong resemblance to you."

Memphis had no idea what to say to that. He was relieved when Dilys stepped in.

"Mr. Modine hails from a branch of that family, to be exact."

The matron nodded her head approvingly. "Pillars of the Atlanta arts community," she said.

"That is why Mr. Modine is here tonight," Dilys said, "to observe our cultural and charitable efforts in person. He has an avid interest in this type of event in particular. Isn't that true, Monty?"

She beamed up at him again, as if to will the right answer out of him.

"Definitely," he said, and did some dazzling of his own that made the matron's head bob and set her jewelry sparkling.

Luckily Dilys guided them away then. He wasn't sure he was ready for much more than one-word responses just yet.

"Wasn't that a chance to take?" he asked. "Setting me up with a real family could backfire."

"If I say you're one of the Atlanta Modines, no one will question that. In fact, very shortly now this entire gathering will have been apprised of your identity."

"That's what I'm worried about. What if they ask me things I can't answer?"

"In that case, all you need to do is flash your most winsome smile and be evasive. That will put them roundly in their place for being more inquisitive than is acceptable in the reserved Southern society where you were raised."

"Do you really think I can bring that off?"

Dilys studied him for a moment. "Actually, I believe you can," she said. She took a commanding grip on his arm and steered them into the gauntlet.

BENNETT MADE HER ENTRANCE, as previously orchestrated, into the museum shop adjacent to the museum foyer and waited there. She wandered among the stacks of art books, occasionally flipping a cover to read the copy on the dust jacket flap. She could hear the faint strains of a string quartet playing Mozart in the Sculpture Garden. She longed to know how Memphis was doing among the crème de la crème of New York society. She wished she could sneak out and have a look, but she had agreed to wait awhile before doing that.

The idea was for Memphis and Dilys to make their entrance and introductions, then blend into the crowd where they could watch the reaction to Bennett's arrival. That was the first phase of their plan. The second was for Bennett to talk about last night's murder at the Stuyvesant Club, intimating that she knew who did it and why. They would see what kind of reaction that got and from whom. She had to admit that this was a fairly vague strategy with no guarantee of results. It was, nonetheless, the only strategy they had.

That thought made her all the more restless with waiting, but she had another reason for staying here, as well. At the house, she had stolen a moment to call her brother's message service. She hoped he would get that message in time to meet her here. Dilys said Forth was very upset when he heard what had happened to Bennett. He made some wild threats about what he would do to Memphis. She wanted to make sure Forth knew the truth before anything unfortunate could happen. Thus, she was both pleased and relieved to see her brother's blond head hurrying through the revolving door that led into the museum shop from the street.

"Sis," he called even before he saw her.

He hadn't called her that since they were children together in day school. That lapse into boyhood sentiment was the only sign he gave of agitation. Otherwise, he looked as perfectly sophisticated and in control as ever. He quickened his step only a little when he saw Bennett waiting for him near a display of art posters. Maybe that was why she didn't experience the compulsion to lock him in an embrace, as she had earlier with her mother.

"Are you absolutely certain you are all right?" he persisted in response to her assurances. "Where is that monster who absconded with you? I shall tear him limb from limb, I swear."

Bennett was only mildly surprised that he could say such things and still sound so cool and distant. This was Forth, after all.

"I'm perfectly fine," she repeated. "Memphis is here at the museum. Mother is introducing him around."

That did crack the Forth facade some. Bennett had said it so straightforwardly to see if she could get a rise out of her imperturbable brother.

"You must be joking," he said. "Why would Mother be introducing that man to anybody but the police?"

"I am not joking, and neither is Mother. Memphis didn't kill that woman last night. As for the kidnapping, he was forced into it when I barged in on him. He never intended to do me any harm, nor would he have."

"I cannot be hearing this. Do you actually believe these rantings?"

"Yes, I do, and so does Mother." Bennett added her comment about Dilys even though it might not be entirely true. "We've come here tonight to prove we are right."

"How do you plan to do that?"

"We're going to spread the rumor that we have information about the murder and see what happens."

"You suspect someone who might be here tonight? Someone from our crowd?"

"We're quite certain that is precisely who is involved."

"And, is there any truth in these rumors you intend to spread of having information about the murderer and his or her motives?"

"Quite a lot of truth actually." Bennett hoped he didn't ask her to be more specific than that. The thin limb she was out on might snap if he did.

"Absolute insanity," Forth exclaimed. "I am going to put a stop to this absurd amateur sleuthing right now. You are coming with me."

He gripped her arm firmly above the elbow and started toward the revolving door onto the street. Bennett was so surprised by his sudden action and its vehemence that she scurried along with him for several steps before mounting a protest.

"Forth, let go of me," she said, and planted her feet against being compelled to follow any further. He pulled her along anyway.

"I am not about to let you go anywhere," he said without slackening his pace.

Bennett was suddenly reminded of last night and being dragged through Central Park against her will. She'd had enough of that then. She wasn't going to put up with any more of it now. She reached out with her free hand and grabbed on to the corner of a display counter. That halted their forward progress for a moment and turned Forth back toward her.

"What are you doing?" he said.

"I'm not going with you," Bennett insisted, straining against his grip with all her might.

"Yes, you are. This is for your own good."

Forth pulled hard on her arm.

"You're hurting me," she said, but he didn't stop.

Bennett knew she couldn't maintain her clutch on the counter's edge much longer. She had to do something more aggressive than that or Forth was going to drag her out of here. She let go of the counter and latched onto one of the heavy art volumes on top of it.

"Let me go right now or I'll crack your wrist with this," she said, brandishing the ponderous book.

Forth stopped still for a moment to stare at her. Bennett stared back. They had played this stare-down game when they were children, and she had always won. She wouldn't have looked away now if it hadn't been for a flash of movement at the edge of her vision. That flash was moving toward them from the revolving door and had unmistakably red hair.

"I'll get her, Stitch," the redhead named Nick cried out.

It took a moment for Bennett to realize he was speaking to Forth and another moment for Forth to know she had made the connection. In that second moment, his hold on her loosened just enough for her to yank herself out of it and begin to run. She headed toward the side exit from the shop and into the museum foyer as fast as she could go.

Chapter Twenty-Six

Memphis didn't actually see Bennett first, he saw the reaction to her. He happened to glance in the direction of the wall that separated the Sculpture Garden from the museum and noticed heads pivoting sharply beyond that glass. They were turning to stare at Bennett running along the wide corridor from the foyer to the museum café. Memphis started running himself then, parallel to her along the garden side of the glass toward the door into the café. He waved and called out to her, but she wasn't looking in his direction.

He glanced back to find out what she was running from. A blond man Memphis had never seen before had entered the corridor, also at a run. Behind him, still in the foyer, a red-haired man was struggling with two security guards while a third approached to help. Nick was being taken care of as he deserved. Memphis was relieved to see that, until he heard screams loud enough to penetrate the glass wall.

The screams were coming from the corridor where the blond man was still running. People were shrinking out of his path and fleeing from him back toward the foyer. Their movement blocked Memphis's view of the man until he was near the end of the corridor. Then Memphis saw what had sent the crowd into panic. The man was brandishing a gun. He was pointing it straight at Bennett and shouting. Memphis sprinted the few remaining feet to the café door. He barely noticed the havoc of spilled drinks and startled society types he left in his wake. He only cared about getting to Bennett and keeping her from being hurt, whatever the cost.

By the time Memphis made it through the empty café, the blond man was chasing Bennett up a flight of stairs at the end of the glass-walled corridor. A sign near the entryway to those stairs read Sette Moma. A menu stand next to the doorway told Memphis this was a restaurant also closed, like the café, during tonight's exclusive event in the Sculpture Garden. A member of the museum's serving staff emerged from the café kitchen and tried to divert him from his mad dash but was swept aside. Nothing was going to keep Memphis from getting to Bennett.

"Hey, buddy," Memphis shouted when he got to the bottom of the stairs. "I'm the one you should be after, not her."

He had already figured who this blond guy had to be, and when Memphis heard him shout to get the hell out of here, he was sure. He'd heard that voice enough times on the phone to peg it for Stitch Falcone without a doubt.

"Hey, Falcone," Memphis called out. "Who are you really, anyway?"

Falcone was halfway up the stairs. Bennett had made it to the top and was about to disappear through the doorway there. Memphis hoped to distract Falcone long enough for her to do just that. Instead, she stopped running and turned back toward the two men below her.

"He's my brother," she said.

Memphis heard the heartbreak in her voice and saw it in her eyes. He longed to run to her and take her in his arms and whisper what comfort he could give against the pain she had to be feeling, but he would have to climb over her no-good brother to get to her. Memphis mounted the first step at the bottom of the stairs on his way to doing exactly that.

"I'm her brother, all right," the man also known as Stitch Falcone said. "Raeburn St. Simon the Fourth. Forth to my friends and family. You should know that name, Modine. One should always know the name of one's executioner."

Forth raised the gun and pointed it at Memphis, who was bracing to make a charge, into a hail of bullets if need be.

"Stop, Forth. Please, don't shoot," Bennett called out. She had abandoned the doorway and was headed back down the stairs. "You mustn't hurt him."

"Why ever not?" Forth scoffed. The gun was still leveled at Memphis, who had stopped in his tracks when he saw Bennett approaching. "Why should this sea trash merit such concern?"

"Because I love him," she said.

Memphis had been planning his next move. Her words chased those plans straight out of his head. He looked up at her. His heart told him the tears glistening on her cheeks weren't for her brother. An answering emotion surged from Memphis's chest to his throat. He had to swallow to keep it from rising farther. He needed his head clear for action now. The first thing he had to do was turn Forth's attention away from Bennett again.

"And I love her," Memphis said.

Forth spun back toward Memphis. "All the more reason for me to shoot you down where you stand," Forth said, aiming the gun even more deliberately at Memphis. "The thought of my sister with the likes of you is preposterous."

"Think about what you're saying, Forth," Bennett said. "Don't get yourself in any deeper. Father's lawyers can help with what has happened so far, but you mustn't make it any worse."

"Father's lawyers." Forth gave a short, scoffing laugh. "A fat lot our father would ever do for me. You're the golden child, my dear, not me. Father lets me know regularly what a disappointment I am to him, whether I care to hear it or not."

The resentment in those words put Memphis even more on guard. He didn't dare make a dash for the gun just yet. There was too much chance Forth would turn it on Bennett. Memphis had to get Forth's mind moving in another direction.

"I've got a feeling your father would be pretty impressed with this operation you set up on the *Fiddlehead,*" Memphis said. "Seems to be a very tricky scheme to me."

"Very tricky indeed," Forth said, sounding proud of himself.

"How does it work exactly?" Memphis asked. "You have the *Fiddlehead* transport goods past customs. I understand that part. What kind of goods would that be?"

Forth studied Memphis for a moment, then shrugged. "What harm can it do to tell you now? I am apparently being put out of business, so to speak."

Memphis didn't want Forth to think about how desperate his situation was. He might do something just as desperate then.

"So tell me what exactly you've been bootlegging," Memphis said.

"Whatever the market would bear. Lately, the real money is in black market computer chips. An associate of mine gets them from the Orient to the Caribbean, all via the rag trade, garments knocked off in Asia. I bring them from the Islands to the States."

"I didn't notice any extra clothing aboard the *Fiddlehead.*"

"Nothing that obvious is necessary. Computer chips are very small. Enough of them can be sewn into the linings of my own personal wardrobe to make quite a haul. A small fortune's worth, in fact."

One of the owners did have a closet on board, and there was a lock on it. Memphis had never paid that any special attention till now.

"Why did you need so much money, Forth?" The anguish in Bennett's voice made Memphis want to run to her again. He had to hold himself back from doing that.

"I happen to have a few obsessions the trust fund doesn't cover," Forth was saying. "Gambling for one. Women for another."

"Was Pearlanne Fellows one of those women?"

Memphis wished she hadn't asked that. He steeled himself in preparation for another shift in Forth's mood, a return to belligerence. Luckily that didn't happen.

"Pearlanne was an obsession indeed," Forth said. "Unfortunately, the obsession was mutual. She was far too avid for her own good and far too candid, as well. She found out more about my business than was healthy for her to know. Then she wasn't smart enough to keep it to herself, or such was my suspicion."

"You killed her for that, didn't you?" Bennett sounded more stricken than ever.

"Yes, Sis. I fear that I did. I had to do so to protect my business. I truly had no choice in the matter."

"Was Quint in that business with you?" Bennett asked.

"Mr. Straight Arrow?" Forth laughed. "You must be joking. Good old Royce, however, was involved up to his ears."

"Was it your number I called from his car phone last night?"

"Exactly, my dear."

"Then you sent those two hoodlums to kill Memphis and me."

Forth shifted uneasily up one step then down again. She had taken him into touchy territory once more. Time for Memphis to create another diversion.

"Where is good old Royce anyway?" he asked. "We thought he would be here tonight."

"Taken off for parts unknown, I would suspect," Forth said. "You spooked him this afternoon when he saw you at the Water Club. I didn't expect to be seeing him again after that. Royce was in this strictly for the thrills. He was looking for some excitement to put a stir in that blue blood of his, but only till the going got truly dicey. I always knew he would make a run for it then. I imagine the police will be overtaking him soon. Royce really hasn't much talent for the outlaw life."

Memphis was amazed at the way Forth could stay so cool in the middle of what had to be the final act of his life as a free man. There was no place for him to run.

"Apparently, I haven't enough of that talent myself, either," Forth said, sounding like the air had suddenly gone out of his balloon. "Otherwise, I might have made less a scramble of this. I didn't even have the nerve to do in old Pearlanne myself, had to have Nick take care of it. Of course, I meant you to take the blame, old man." He looked at Memphis. "Invited you to the Stuyvesant so that would happen. Thought it was damned clever of me, too. Even planned to have my colleagues make you disappear for good so there'd be no worry about what you might reveal when the police gave you the third degree. But we can see how that turned out, can't we."

"What about me, Forth?" Bennett asked. "Did you plan to have me disappear, too?"

Forth sighed and smiled sadly. "Alas, Sis, you're too like our dear mother. You think me much more of a decent sort than I am. I've always been willing to do whatever was needed to keep my life running smoothly, just as long as I could pay someone else for the dirty work and cover up nicely afterward.''

"But why would you need to kill her?" Memphis couldn't help but ask. "She didn't know anything."

"She'd come to know you, old chap, apparently quite well, or so it seems now. I couldn't be certain what you would tell her or whether you might win her to your cause. She was a loose end I simply couldn't afford to leave un-snipped.''

Memphis was almost too focused on Bennett and the way she was biting down hard on her lip to hear the movement behind him. Then he saw that Forth must have heard it, too. Suddenly his quietly resigned manner was gone. He stared at the doorway behind Memphis for a moment then turned and hurried up the stairs toward Bennett. Memphis looked back to see what Forth had been staring at. The corridor was unnaturally still beyond the doorway. While the three of them had been talking, someone had cleared out all of the people. Memphis could almost smell the police poised just out of sight with firearms at the ready.

Bennett! They could shoot Bennett by mistake!

Memphis looked up the stairs. Bennett and Forth had already disappeared into the restaurant.

THERE WAS REALLY NOWHERE to run. Bennett knew that, and she was certain Forth did, too. He was only going through the futile motions now, playing the scene out to the end. He had a gun, of course, but she no longer feared he might use it on her. She sensed that he was even past using it on Memphis. The strongest likelihood was that Forth would turn the gun upon himself. Bennett had accompanied him without resistance in the hope of preventing his self-destruction. Unfortunately, she didn't truly believe she had that kind of influence over him. Only one person did. Perhaps Forth was thinking this, too. Perhaps those thoughts were what drew him through the restaurant and out onto the terrace overlooking the Sculpture Garden, and Dilys St. Simon standing below.

"Is your sister all right?" Dilys asked him. "You haven't harmed her, have you?"

"No, Mother, I have not harmed her." He sounded very calm.

"And, Mr. Modine. Have you harmed him?"

"No, Mother, I haven't harmed anyone. At least, not today."

Dilys nodded gravely, still looking up at him from the deserted patio where only a scattering of abandoned glassware and a few overturned chairs attested to there having been a party tonight at all. Even the corridor beyond the glass wall to the museum was empty—except for several policemen crouched low on either side of the doors to the garden area.

"It is finished then," Dilys said, also speaking calmly.

"Yes, Mother, it is," he answered.

"Then, my son, you must do the gracious thing and cause no one any more difficulty than has already been done."

Forth hesitated a moment. "You are exactly right, as always. I must do the gracious thing. Besides, even I am wise enough to know when all is lost."

"And to remember who you are and what you represent."

"Yes, Mother, that, too."

Bennett tensed in fear of what he might do next. Then he lifted the gun and tossed it over the railing. It clattered against the stones below.

In what seemed like less than an instant several officers swept out onto the terrace from the restaurant and Forth was in their custody. Memphis appeared just behind them and took Bennett into his arms. She clung to him but could not move her gaze from her mother's tear-streaked face below.

Epilogue

Even a year later, the sadness hadn't totally deserted Dilys St. Simon's heart. No one was more aware of this than her daughter. Dilys took responsibility for allowing Forth to grow up as weak and corrupt as he turned out to be. Fortunately, she could also take joy in the prospect of a first grandchild soon to arrive. Dilys raised a finely arched brow when Bennett joked about calling the baby Eloise after the little girl in the children's story who lived at the Plaza Hotel. Dilys may have understood that this was a private joke between her daughter and new son-in-law, but she was too discreet to say so.

Bennett and her beloved husband still saw Dilys regularly despite how involved they were in their project for homeless children. Memphis taught them to sail while Bennett introduced them to books and drawing and playing music. He emphasized responsibility and hard work, while she allowed their spirits to express themselves. Dilys told every philanthropist she knew that this was without doubt only the first of many works these two loving people would perform to make the world a better place.

Meanwhile, Dilys had offered to research the Atlanta Modines regarding Memphis's supposed family resemblance.

"I don't think so," he replied.

"That's right, Mother," Bennett said, staring up at the man with whom she had so incredibly and miraculously found true love. "We have each other and a life ahead together. That's all we could possibly need."

"Amen to that," said Dilys St. Simon, and heaven help anyone who might dare to disagree.

COMING NEXT MONTH

THE CHARMER   Leona Karr

Avenging Angels

Ever since an 'accident' temporarily took single mother Shanna
Ryan's eyesight, both a little guardian angel and sexy Jay
Harrison have been operating as her eyes. And Shanna needed
more protection than she knew—because she and her daughter
had been targeted by a killer!

LOVE VS. ILLUSION   M.J. Rodgers

Justice Inc.

When her brother is betrayed by his own client, it's up to Ariana,
Justice Inc.'s ace investigator, to prove his innocence. But to do that,
Ariana will have to live out another woman's fantasies...with Zane
Coltrane, her sinfully sexy competitor, coming along for the ride.

BELLADONNA   Jenna Ryan

Her Protector

Bella Conlan was a woman with a past...one she couldn't remember.
The first nine years of her life were shrouded in a mist as thick as the
fog of her native San Francisco—and now those lost years were
coming back to haunt her. Then, out of the darkness, came a man
named Malone. Was he there to protect or betray her?

MYSTERY BABY   Dani Sinclair

Lost & Found

Steve Gregory didn't have a clue about the baby on his doorstep.
But what he *did* have was an excuse to cozy up to Lynn Rothmore,
the neighbour whose touch-me-not air had taunted him for weeks.
He was certain the uptight woman had a softer side—*and* that she
knew more than she was letting on about the mystery baby.

COMING NEXT MONTH FROM

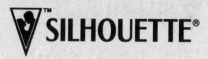 **SILHOUETTE®**

Sensation

A thrilling mix of passion, adventure and drama

DRIVEN TO DISTRACTION Judith Duncan
MACKENZIE'S PLEASURE Linda Howard
MICHAEL'S HOUSE Pat Warren
UNBROKEN VOWS Frances Williams

Special Edition

Satisfying romances packed with emotion

ON MOTHER'S DAY Andrea Edwards
A COWBOY IS FOREVER Shirley Lawson
THE CASE OF THE BORROWED BRIDE
Victoria Pade
THE FATHER OF HER CHILD Joan Elliott Pickart
THE WOLF AND THE WOMAN'S TOUCH
Ingrid Weaver
**THE RANCHER AND HIS UNEXPECTED
DAUGHTER** Sherryl Woods

Desire

Provocative, sensual love stories for the woman of today

YOU'RE WHAT?! Anne Eames
SURRENDER Metsy Hingle
THE TEMPORARY GROOM Joan Johnston
MICHAEL'S BABY Cathie Linz
THE BRIDE'S CHOICE Sara Orwig
REGAN'S PRIDE Diana Palmer

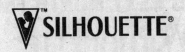
™ SILHOUETTE®

Treat yourself to...

Wanted: Mother

*Silhouette's annual tribute to motherhood takes
a new twist in '97 as three sexy single men
prepare for fatherhood and saying "I Do!"*

Written by three captivating authors:

*Annette Broadrick
Ginna Gray
Raye Morgan*

Available: February 1997   Price: £4.99

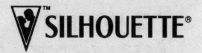

SILHOUETTE®

Spring is in the air with our sparkling collection
from Silhouette...

SPRING
fever

Three sexy, single men are about to find the love
of a lifetime!

Grace And The Law by Dixie Browning
Lighfoot And Loving by Cait London
Out Of The Dark by Pepper Adams

Three delightful stories...one romantic season!

Available: March 1997   Price: £4.99

FOUR FREE
specially selected
Intrigue™ novels
PLUS a Mystery Gift
when you return this card...

Return this coupon and we'll send you 4 Silhouette® Intrigue™ novels and a mystery gift absolutely FREE! We'll even pay the postage and packing for you.

We're making you this offer to introduce you to the benefits of the Reader Service™– FREE home delivery of brand-new Silhouette novels, at least a month before they are available in the shops, FREE gifts and a monthly Newsletter packed with information.

Accepting these FREE books and gift places you under no obligation to buy—you may cancel at any time, even after receiving just your free shipment. Simply complete the coupon below and send it to:

THE READER SERVICE, FREEPOST, CROYDON, SURREY, CR9 3WZ.

EIRE READERS PLEASE SEND COUPON TO: P.O. BOX 4546, DUBLIN 24.

NO STAMP NEEDED

Yes, please send me 4 free Silhouette Intrigue novels and a mystery gift. I understand that unless you hear from me, I will receive 4 superb new titles every month for just £2.30* each, postage and packing free. I am under no obligation to purchase any books and I may cancel or suspend my subscription at any time, but the free books and gift will be mine to keep in any case. (I am over 18 years of age)

I6XE

Ms/Mrs/Miss/Mr _____
BLOCK CAPS PLEASE

Address _____

_____

_____

_____Postcode _____

"Mortimer has a special magic."
—Romantic Times

CAROLE MORTIMER

*Their tempestuous night held a
magic all its own...and only she
could mend his shattered dreams*

Merlyn's Magic

MIRA®

AVAILABLE IN PAPERBACK
FROM FEBRUARY 1997